I0599124

Passengers

ELIZABETH COLLUMS

RopeSwing Press
an imprint of
Rope Swing Publishing

Paperback ISBN: 978-1-954058-07-1

PASSENGERS

2nd Edtion
previously released December 2018

RopeSwing Press

an imprint of
Rope Swing Publishing

www.ropeswingpublishing.com

TO MY MATERNAL GRANDPARENTS,

ROBERT LEE AND WILLIE JOY EWING CULIPHER

PART ONE

CHAPTER 1

The Letter

MEMORIES ARE MOMENTS etched together forever. They can either make us lean forward with an exuberant thrill or live a kind of end-of-the-line life. My mama was the latter. Her unwillingness to live each day as a new day with bright promise was always overshadowed by some kind of deep, unhinged darkness.

I'm sitting in the back with Lily just like Mama said to. "Annie, I don't want you girls missing church because you know how people will talk."

I don't understand why all of a sudden our presence

here matters to her because it was never something that she cared about or even wanted to bother with when we all lived together on the farm. On the contrary, I remember the quiet disagreements that Mama and Daddy would have when he would on occasion take Lily and me to church. Being raised in the church with Pastor Wynne and his parents by his side was something that my daddy longed to experience with his own family and for reasons unknown to me she never wanted to be a part of that. And now that he has been gone she's insisting we attend. Nothing she says or does makes any sense. The best I can figure is that she probably just wanted us out of the way and out of her sight and this was as good an excuse as any to be rid of the two of us for a while. Mama hasn't made many trips into the village in the last few years that I can recall either, until the life we all knew became completely unraveled. Daddy said the stares from people made Mama feel uncomfortable and he didn't want to push her. However, it's my opinion that he didn't push her enough. It seemed to me that he was always trying to protect her from some unknown person or thing that I've never been able to understand. We were all tenants of some kind of the estate, either on the farms or shopkeepers of one sort or another. I have to admit I've always been a bit annoyed with Mama's intentional isolation from the village and my daddy's willingness to go along with it. And I finally just made up my mind not to care what people said or thought about our comings and goings now that Daddy left weeks ago to find work. I just know that any day he will be returning for us and we will start our new lives somewhere else.

Now this doesn't mean that I disagreed with everything that was said by our neighbors or the villagers. Because when I was with my daddy and people would remark how much we were alike even commenting that we had the same bones, that always made me feel like I was more a part of the good side of the family. I just loved to hear "you look just like your daddy, same dark brown eyes and thick, dark, straight hair" and was quite proud to agree except I knew that our eyes were different. He was always able to look at life with hope and I looked in his eyes for my hope.

Jonathan Ewing was, in my mind, the noblest man in the entire village. Every day he lived his life with such a serene dignity and tall straight walk. I can't remember a single day that my daddy didn't live with his head held high. It wasn't that he thought he was always right it's just that he wasn't afraid to be wrong. And spending time with him was the thing that meant the most to me. It didn't matter whether it was a chore that I needed to do, lessons to be learned on how to carefully plant or dig potatoes, the long lazy afternoons we spent together fishing, reading or just talking about what dreams we shared, I knew his words were true and finished. I was certain that I could always count on his wisdom.

Lily, on the other hand, is my mama through and through. She is so beautiful, fair and yet so fragile, much like the flower she was named for. She had already laid her head in my lap as I stroked her long auburn curls. I truly felt sorry for her and what appeared was to be her lot in life. Daddy said she was born too soon in that she should have stayed inside Mama a few weeks longer. Mrs. Beaker, who was our closest neighbor and practicing midwife, nearly rubbed her skin off trying to warm her cold and lifeless body that day when she finally let out a tiny wail. When I finally got a chance to hold her and pulled back the blanket, I still remember how shocked and frightened I was to see just how unusually small she was. Mrs. Beaker just shook her head and said that it was Mama's fault for not holding on longer because God wasn't finished with Lily yet. And in some strange way I believe that she has been clinging to Mama ever since waiting for her finish outside of the womb. That was over six years ago and still she barely stands as tall as most of the neighboring three and four year olds. And now that all our lives have become so dreadfully bleak and meager, I'm afraid she's never going to be finished, as her eyes are starting to hollow out more.

Even before, when things were good and plenty with a whole world of fresh air outside, Lily would linger indoors just wanting, always wanting, just like Mama. It didn't help much that Mama fell into such a deep depression in the days, months and now years that have passed. Lily has never known the loving warm embrace or words of encouragement from the woman that God assigned to be our earthly mother. And even though I'm doing the best I can as her big sister and I think I'm as responsible as any fourteen year old can be, I'm finding it harder and harder to fill in for both Mama and Daddy now. It's been years since I've known or felt those things from Mama and I sometimes wonder if they were ever really there and I've just imagined her being different. But I've learned how to give what I need. My daddy taught me that.

"Always try to give what you know you need and it will somehow come back to you," Daddy would often say. All I can do is hope and pray that Daddy will someday get back all of what he has given or even just half of it. For he has always been the first to help one of our neighbors and the last one to leave and never complained about Mama's emptiness toward him or us but did what he could to fill that void. He was also a constant advocate for justice for those that had been treated unjustly. There had been a lot of that in the weeks and months before he left. We all knew there was food to be had for the people that were starving here but the government turned a blind eye as though we were as disposable as some of the animals that had wasted away. He pleaded before this board and that committee and still no real help came for the farmers and their families. Most of the other estate owners lived in England and had hired managers that had very little personal connection to the people that were born, worked and died here. However, our landlord lived on the land and according to Daddy had tried to keep things going making them the last holdouts trying to make ends meet.

The organ music echoed to an end and Pastor Feil has taken his place in front of the Highland Way Presbyterian Church. The outside is a modest building of white washed boards with a steeple that makes it the tallest point in the village. But inside, it's certainly the most beautiful place I've ever been in, not that I've been in many. The stained glass panes of red, white, blue, green and yellow form a large arch in the front of the church and within the panes someone's wonderful skilled hands created the formation of Christ with his arms outstretched with tiny pieces of the same glass. The bands of sunlight stream through with swirling tiny dust dots filling every ray of light. The large wooden cross stands just below the body of Christ breaking apart the pattern of light through the window as it splits it in different directions. The walls from floor to ceiling look like they must have been transported aboard a ship from some far away exotic country. The one foot wide boards nailed side by side are a deep dark brown and as I look around I can just imagine that it must be the same wood as was described in the building of Noah's Ark. This dark wood also forms the small cathedral ceiling from the top of the wall to the center part of the ceiling with thick cut beams holding it all together. There are four large silver candelabras holding six lit candles, each flickering at a different rhythm, two in the front and one on each side of the church on stands built just for their use. These were given to the church over a hundred years ago by the ancestors of the current North Highland Estate. The pulpit that Pastor Feil just stepped into makes him just barely taller than his five-and-a-half-foot frame and the still breaths from the two dozen rows of parishioners gives off the kind of reverence deserving of a man of God, but not this man. I don't like him for a minute because he can't begin to fill the shoes of our previous beloved and devoted pastor.

He's nothing like Pastor Wynne. He was like a grandpa to me and a father figure to my daddy. My grandparents died before I was born and although he has often talked of happy times with Grandpa and Grandma Ewing, Mama has never uttered a word or shared a single memory of her parents. It's almost like that part of her life is a blank page. I just can't imagine not wanting to tell my children, who and where I came from. This was yet another occasion that Daddy would cover Mama when I would question her about my other side of the family.

"Just leave it be, Annie. Some things are better left unsaid. Give your mama some peace," he would plead and then look away as though he felt a heavy burden on him for something he had no fault in. This was one of the only times that I could ever remember Daddy not looking me square in the eyes. Maybe this was the reason for the emptiness in her eyes, almost like she has no past. But still I struggle with why Mama can't be happy and satisfied with her now with us?

Pastor Wynne wasn't much taller than Pastor Feil but he was such a bigger man in so many ways. I'm sure that was why he and Daddy had become such good friends. He would often stop us when we were in the village and made the four mile walk back home along with us. In that hour or so he would talk about things that always seemed to be within my mind's reach. And since I've really had no proper schooling, he would patiently take the time to bring me around when I didn't or couldn't grasp new information. Then he would wink, pat my head, tease me about being Daddy's shadow and head on to visit yet another tenant. It didn't matter to Pastor Wynne if you attended his church on Sunday or not, or whether you were Catholic or Presbyterian. He was truly a devoted man of God that loved, visited and prayed with and for everyone.

Pastor Feil has big bushy white eyebrows and big wild eyes that bulge behind his wire rim spectacles and at times pieces of spit spray out when he talks. He screams out such hellfire and damnation, that I'm certain that I don't want to know this God that he speaks of. Pastor Feil arrived shortly after Pastor Wynne died. His passing was to me one of the worst casualties in all this sudden strife and tribulation, because as the potato crop began to wither away so did Pastor Wynne. Daddy told me it was his heart that finally gave out but I'm convinced that he was just worn out all over. He would spend hours and hours praying for us, our neighbors, the land, the village and probably the whole of Ireland. That day was the beginning of so many losses we would all endure.

Lily sat up with the sound of his thunderous fist bumps and again I've pressed her back down while rubbing her back for a few more minutes. My worn out leather Bible sits on the other side of me and rather than listen to Pastor Feil, I feel better reading the last verse that Daddy read aloud to me on the night before he left. "But they that wait upon the Lord shall renew their strength; they should mount up with wings as Eagles; they shall run, and not be weary; and they shall walk and not faint." Isaiah 40:31.

I'm still trying to figure out what this one means. Usually, Daddy would spend the time I needed afterwards breaking the verses down bit by bit because the meanings were sometimes hidden to me and it was his wisdom that would open my eyes. But he is gone as was Pastor Wynne and I have no one to explain to me how the words apply, not only to my life but to all our uncertain lives now.

Pastor Feil slams his fist down again and spit-shouts "The sins of our fathers shall be visited on the children and the children's children to the third and the fourth generation." I'm not sure whose father he is talking about, but I know my daddy is a good, kind and gentle man. This has to be someone else's father that has brought all this pain on us. Pastor Feil has continued to blame the famine on all of our sinful and unruly lives which I refuse to believe. Why would a loving God bring such misery and damnation on children who have only begun to live and have no idea what sins they've committed?

We had a couple of cows, a few chickens and pigs, but the rows upon rows of potatoes were our main source of income. They were so hardy and beautiful at the same time. It's funny how Daddy and I created our own little game where we would look for the different shapes and faces in each one. The pits and bumps would sometimes look like some old man or maybe an owl's face or that of a clown that I once saw at the traveling circus.

It was as though there were sachets of fragrance hanging from every tree and it was better than any sweet water scent on the ladies in the village. On many mornings Daddy would holler "come out and smell God's sweet Garden of Eden!" Mama would just give him one of her empty gazes out the window, Lily would tug on the skirt of her dress but I would quickly finish whatever chore I had in my hands and follow his voice. There were huge puffs of deep green clover, fields of wild flowers, the new misty rain, the rainbows that would follow and the fresh tilled dirt in the spring. Daddy's Great Grandma Ewing planted dwarf yellow verbascum and Irish yew that had miraculously lingered for five generations. And Daddy and I planted snapdragons and forget-me-knots last year on one of our morning celebrations outdoors.

We had a small three room cottage with worn red, yellow and purple flowered curtains in every room that Grandma Ewing had made. Our thatched roof cottage had laid stone floors and not dirt like so many others with a large fireplace that spit and crackled all year long. I said many times and Daddy agreed that we had one of the better cottages inside and out because Grandpa Ewing was also a skilled carpenter and had built most of the furniture as well as the extra shelves, cabinets, window boxes and the picket fence that framed our perfect flower garden yard. We had a spread, as Daddy liked to call it, of over thirty acres that was one of one hundred twenty other tenant farms under the ownership of Lord Byron McLaughton. And he would often tell me just how blessed we were to be able to work and live under an Irish born estate holder. His estate and all the small tenant farms sectioned off and the nearby village of Highland Way was essentially all his. The Ewing family had worked this small farm for over two hundred years. And right before our eyes, in a matter of weeks, it was all gone.

Our wanting, all our misery was the result of hunger, the famine no one saw coming. I can still remember just like yesterday when Daddy cried fitfully as all the other tenant farmers when the reality hit that it was something called potato blight and there was no fix for it. This infectious disease would spoil for so many our main source of income that would be the cause of hundreds of thousands of Irish folks that would either leave for some place far away or eventually die. So, we finally left the countryside as so many others and came to Highland Way looking for hope, or rather hoping for hope.

It was though everything bothered Mama but then at the same time nothing would. She always seemed to have that same far away stoic look on her face. The crop failure, the move, Lily's constant neediness, the loss of our home, this new unsteady way of life and now Daddy is gone, and Mama just seems to just walk a kind of closed off walk. It seems as though she's always reaching out for someone to take care of her, like she has no bones to hold herself up. She often reminds me of the rich ladies that have to have someone dress and undress them. She has quite a snobbish air about her, too. It's as though she doesn't belong here or there or anywhere for that matter.

Mama hated life on the farm and complained about it constantly, as if somehow, she thought she deserved better. She grew up on the North Highlands Estate, the daughter of Lord McLaughton's horse trainer, Jeremiah Fletcher. I remember how Daddy's face beamed when he told me about the day they first met when he was a young man. "Annie you should have seen her back then. I'd look up and there would be this auburn, braided hair beauty, riding from a distance like she owned the whole place. And then one day it happened, like it was meant to be. I have no other way to explain it. God just put me in the right place at the right time... because, out of nowhere, a rabbit ran right in front of her, the horse reared up and off she tumbled and she was only a few feet away this time." He knew word-for-word along with every movement they made.

***

"Are you OK?" Jonathan reached out to her with his calloused hand.

"I'm fine, thank you very much and where did you come from?" Katy brushed her faded and worn riding pants off.

With a smile he said, "Nice to meet you, my name is Jonathan Ewing and my family works this farm."

She held her gloved hand out with some disregard and introduced herself. "Katy Fletcher and my father is the stable manager at the estate. Now I'll expect that you won't mention this. I'll be on my way, thank you."

Jonathan said he knew from that moment that one day she would be his wife but Katy knew that she deserved better.

She had her eye on Lord McLaughton's son, Samuel. She just knew that when he brushed her hand when she handed the bridle of her favorite horse, Gallo, to him that somehow meant something. She would tell herself that he was different. He would look into her eyes with meaning when he talked to her. Like he knew, or he somehow needed to know her. She knew these things could happen and for her to live the life she felt she deserved, that it must happen. She would spend hours dreaming of the day she would share his bed, sit by the roaring fireplace and eat the many fine meals served at the long exquisite dining table with the countless plates, silverware and glasses. She also knew there were no other women living in the house, other than the servants. Samuel was an only child and Jeremiah told her Samuel's mother died of the fever. She would one day be Samuel's loving wife and dutifully help run the fine North Highlands Estate.

Katy would often gaze out her tiny window with this wanting look that made her father nervous and agitated at the same time. To her his words were always bitter and harsh as he would shake his head as though it was his duty to remove any thought of seduction. "Katy don't let your dreams drown your reality child, you should be so lucky to one day become the stable manager on this estate." She knew this sort of thing would never happen since women were not allowed to run anything. If she wanted to stay on at the estate to be near Samuel and the horses she would have to settle for and marry one of the young men that worked around the stable and the thought of that turned her stomach.

They lived in their own small thatched roof cottage behind the stables, and it was Jeremiah's responsibility to make sure the horses were properly trained, fed, groomed and cared for. They had at times at least a dozen or so of Irish Draught that came from a long blood line of Spanish horses and English warm bloods that were perfect riding and hunting horses. Katy filled her days cleaning out the stalls, replacing straw, making sure their feeding troughs were clean and full and shaking out the rugs and blankets used to cover the horses. She loved the sweet smell of the horses but hated the noxious odor of manure and urine that lingered in her hair and clothes and how all the work made her hands rough and calloused. However, she felt exhilarated and entitled when she could put on her gloves and the riding outfit she had and at least for a bit pretend she was someone else.

She just knew something was very familiar there. Although she had only been able to glance through the large glass window panes in the library and sitting room, she somehow felt she knew the inside of that great estate. She imagined the bouquets of pink flowers on the wallpaper in the dining room, and the large staircase that led to the bedrooms upstairs with soft pink, blue and yellow hues on the walls. There was a long open kitchen with shelves full of pots, dishes and glassware along with several women in gray dresses, wrapped in long white aprons and head scarves, busy making delicious meals of fresh potato bread, roasts and cobblers of every kind. There were times when she thought she could smell the wonderful aromas. And what was even stranger to her was a reoccurring dream of a young woman that had the features of herself when she looked in the mirror and this same woman would try to cover her head and she couldn't breathe. Then she would awake and through her open bedroom window smell the straw and the flesh of the horses that she was bound to care for the rest of her life.

Pastor Wynne would visit the estate often. But this day he would for some reason make his way over to the stables as if to finish his business for the day.

"How are you today my little Katy mate!" said Pastor Wynne.

"I'm not little and I'm not your mate, I'm a girl, so please sir, I beg you to call me Katy Fletcher. My father as you know is Jeremiah Fletcher and he is the stable manager here," replied Katy with a stifled tone of smugness.

"Yes, indeed, I know who both you and your father

are as I've known you since you were born and I will be kindly obliged to speak to him for a few minutes," replied the Pastor.

She was struck by this seemingly framed announcement that he knew her since she was born. They didn't attend church in the village, matter of fact she had never seen the inside of a church. Her father rarely traveled into Highland Way because most things needed were delivered and it was only an occasion or two he had taken her. He said he had no use for the busy body biddies and the air down that way smelled rotten. She knew her father had told her that she was born over the meadow in Preston and they supposedly moved here when she was only three.

"Why are you here? Is his Lordship unhappy with us?" asked Katie.

"Nonsense dear, just a word or two with your father," answered the Pastor.

She wondered why Pastor Wynne would suddenly make time for her father. Was he ill, were their days numbered here, it can't happen. Jeremiah was her only family. Her mother died when she was too young to remember and as far as she knew she had no other family. She couldn't imagine the day she would be all alone. She had just turned fifteen, too young to marry and too old for the church orphanage. Katy wasn't very close to her father although she wanted to be. She somehow felt being a girl had been an inconvenient and uncomfortable burden on him, being without a wife for so many years now. She didn't know the first thing about fixing herself up not like she had any occasion or cause to. All her clothes were work clothes and her hair had to be weaved every day in braids so as not to get tangled on anything. He rarely spoke much of her mother and there were no photographs or remaining tangible pieces of her life in or around their cottage. However, he would occasionally tell Katy how much she looked like her and he was sure she would be proud of her if she were still here.

When Pastor Wynne left that afternoon Katy asked Jeremiah. "What did he need to see you about today? Are you well? Do we have to move? Where will we go? Is his Lordship troubled with us here?"

And Jeremiah quietly assured her that she had a right to be here just as much as anyone else and she would always have a place here.

"How is that possible?" Katy said out loud. But Jeremiah didn't answer.

***

Meanwhile on the other side of the estate, Jonathan also had his own dream. He would one day follow his father's hand and become the next generation tenant in line to work the land he loved and grew up on, as his grandfather and his great grandfather had done. Katy would be his bride and they would have a family. What a magnificent place to live. Jonathan loved life. His heart was one of such gratitude and faith. He had faith that there was and had always been a loving and merciful God. He was taught this faith by his grandparents, parents and Pastor Wynne.

"Be grateful, my son, for Ireland is the land of plenty and our heavenly Father trusted us to use it well," were the final words of Jonathan's beloved father and these words of wisdom had been passed down to Annie.

Annie sat there wondering if that was what happened? Did they not use it well? The land of plenty was now just dust and death everywhere. There was no way. She refused to believe that all hope was gone, because her daddy had always been able to fix everything.

***

It was Jonathan that saved Katy the night the stable and all she knew were destroyed in a fire because Jonathan gazed out his window, too. On the nights he couldn't sleep or before he went to bed, he would always tell his bride to be, "good night." And that fateful night when he saw the heavy gray smoke billowing from the direction of the stables, it was as though within minutes he was there pulling Katy from the raging inferno. Some of the other servants from the estate as well as Samuel arrived to help but it was too late. The dozen or so horses were dead and so was Jeremiah. Everything was just a pile of black burnt rubble and the only sign that there was once life there were bones. Distraught, confused and badly burned and with no place to go, Jonathan and his parents took Katy home. The left side of her face was badly burned and her lungs had suffered from the smoke and for the next several weeks Grandma Ewing nursed her back to health. As her body began to heal her face did not. She would be scarred for life and she knew her dream of living in the estate house was gone.

There would be no way Samuel would want to marry someone that now looked so ugly and deformed. When there was no more that Grandma Ewing could do for Katy, Pastor Wynne took her in. Over the next two years Jonathan would make regular trips into town to visit her. And then on Good Friday, April 17th, 1835 with two gold bands that he had been carrying in his pocket for months he took a chance and asked her to marry him. By this time Grandpa and Grandma Ewing had died and he was now ready to start his own family. Katy was scarred inside and out and with no other possible prospects she accepted, and Pastor Wynne performed the ceremony with two witnesses borrowed from the church.

***

And once again it was her daddy's faith that brought them to Highland Way. Jonathan and their neighbor, Mr. Beaker, settled his wife and three children with Katy, Annie and Lily into a dirty run down small flat. There were seven of them, five children with their mamas and they had to share two bedrooms and a small living area. The men pooled together enough money for rent and food for three months and took very little with them. The hope would be they would find work at the harbor sixty miles away in Dublin and they would return for them when they had enough money to relocate both families.

She desperately needed her daddy's hope now as they only had one week left before the next rent and hunger visited them more each day. Annie needed to look in his eyes and hear him tell her that things would all work out. Right now, they were lucky if they had a few pieces of potato bread each day. Mrs. Beaker worked and earned a little money by taking in as much sewing and ironing as she could handle with her three children. But Katy did nothing but sit and stare and tell her daughters to leave her be.

Annie looked around at all the sad eyes and many were as hollowed out as Lily's. The other children were not much better off than they were. Many of them had become orphans and were huddled together on the front two rows as they had essentially become wards of the church. Annie heard that some people of plenty in Dublin would occasionally send money to help care for and feed these children. Today, however, she did feel lucky that Lily wasn't one of them. She would take care of her, but wasn't sure how. At least for now they were both a little bit warmer. That's really the only reason why Annie came to church now was to be a little warmer and pray. She would just pray that her daddy would come home soon.

Pastor Feil slammed his fist down for the last time and shouted, "Go all you sinners and repent!"

This last fit wakened Lily with such force it almost threw her to the floor. "Annie, I'm hungry."

They filed out slowly as Annie held Lily's little withering hand in hers and then finally picked her up. It's become quicker that way. After four blocks and three over they walked in to find everyone there but their mama.

"Mrs. Beaker, where's Mama?" asked Annie.

"Why, she left here this morning right after you two left for church," answered Mrs. Beaker with her brows raised high.

"She never goes anywhere. As a matter of fact, she hasn't left this place since we got here almost three months ago. Where'd she go off to?" asked Annie.

"Well, she said she was finally going home," Mrs. Beaker declared with a strange grin.

"What home? Lord McLaughton closed up the entire estate last month when he and Samuel left for America." Annie asked, stunned with this news. "There's not a soul there. What is she doing? What's going to happen to me and Lily? What is she looking for? I can't believe this is happening! Don't we matter at all to her?" Tears began to swell up in Annie's eyes, but she refused to let them go. She couldn't let Lily see her weak, or falling apart, even for a moment. Their survival over the last few weeks has been because she had been the strong one. She couldn't afford to lose it now.

"Dear child, don't you know, I mean, didn't your mama and daddy ever tell you?" replied Mrs. Beaker.

"Tell me what?" Annie answered frustrated. She didn't have time for this game.

"Your mama was born in that house," threw back Mrs. Beaker, now with her head cocked to the side.

"What house?" Annie again fired back.

"North Highlands, the big house. People in the village gossiped about it for years" answered Mrs. Beaker.

"Stop! I've heard enough!" Annie screamed, her sense of confusion deepening, but Mrs. Beaker continued, as though she was enjoying this new revelation. "Well I'm not finished. A lot of people that knew for sure have either died or moved away. And some of us were too young to know firsthand whether it was true...that she's the daughter of Lord McLaughton. The story was that one night his wife went insane and he sent her off somewhere and nobody has seen or heard from her since. And God only knows why but for some reason that crazy man sent your mama to live with Jeremiah Fletcher. If you ask me, it was old Lord McLaughton that must have gone insane. I mean, who in their right mind would have sent their little girl off to live with a stranger, a stable hand for all that. And he kept the boy. Anyway, most people around here have heard bits and pieces over the years. I think that's what has been bothering your mama all these years. And I'm sure your daddy somehow should have known. But, there's no doubt now. This letter from Samuel was delivered this morning after you left."

Dearest Katy,

I hope with God's hand that this letter somehow finds you. I'm writing to tell you that our mother, yes, our mother, was a wonderful, kind and gentle soul. Her name was Elizabeth, but Father used to call her Lizzie.

You were only three when Father told me he found her trying to suffocate you with your blanket. He said that he was fearful of the madness that was creeping in her head. The doctors told him the same madness could and would possibly follow you as well. He said that the shame of it all was just too much for him to bear and it was the only way to protect you and me.

He thought you would be better off if you were raised where there were no memories of that night. And as a boy I believed it was his way of trying to at least keep you close by. That was all I really knew and few details I remembered because I was only five and never heard or saw any real proof of this.

I wanted to tell you, talk to you so many times. I wanted to bring you in our house and show you Mother's things and your things and our things.

I'm so very sorry to have not been a part of your life but somehow, I feel our souls have always been connected and you were so much better off where you were with Jeremiah and then as Jonathan's wife.

I was never certain where Mother was sent to or even if she was still alive. Then as we were hastily preparing for the move I found the commitment papers that Father prepared to send Mother to The Weatherly House for The Insane which I believe is located somewhere on the outskirts of Dublin. I've written to them as well but have yet to receive any reply.

Please forgive me for not being forthcoming with this sooner. I was so afraid what Father would do to you or me if the truth came out.

His health is failing and his mind is in and out. If his health improves or fails completely, I promise to return and make things right.

I will be your loving brother forever, Samuel

"Oh my God, my mama is the daughter of a Lord and a mad woman? The sins of our fathers will be visited upon us to the third and fourth generations...could it be our mothers as well, my grandma, my mama and now Lily? Would my sweet little Lily succumb to the madness of the women before us? What do I do? If I stay who will take care of us? I can't do this alone. And if I go who will show me the way? Dear God, if you're listening, Daddy, if you're out there somewhere, please help me. I have to find Mama."

CHAPTER 2

North Highlands

NOT KNOWING WHAT TO make of it, whether it was real or some sick joke, Annie read the letter over and over again. Why would anyone write something like that if it wasn't true? And what kind of brother or uncle for that matter would this Samuel turn out to be? Why couldn't he just leave well enough alone? That's what her daddy meant that day when she asked about her mama's side of the family. He told her outright just to "leave it be" and now she knows why. Annie didn't want or need another emotional cripple in the family and that's exactly what her mama's long lost brother sounded like.

Annie again put Lily on her hip and carried their few belongings along with the letter that she hastily threw in an old potato sack. She had a good strong back from working with her daddy but even this was going to be a physical feat. With Lily on one side she tied the sack to her waist, so it would hang on her other side. Annie thought she now looked and felt like one of the packing mules some of the traveling vendors used coming through the village.

She knew the estate was a good hour or so from Highland Way as she had skipped and walked it many times with her daddy and Pastor Wynne. But, there was no skip in her step today with the extra pounds of Lily along with the weight of their personal possessions and she didn't want to do this alone. She felt like every single clear minded responsible adult had either left or died over the last few months. Since the day her daddy left she felt all alone with her mama, Mrs. Beaker and her children. They had their mama but she and Lily had been tossed into a greater sea of uncertainty. Her heart had ached for years for some glimmer of hope that her mama's maternal instincts would awaken and now she was chasing after her like she was some kind of runaway child. Why couldn't she just wait? The pain wracked her back and she felt her right leg going numb, but she had to make it before dark. She wasn't afraid of the dark but knew it would be at least twenty degrees colder once the sun started to set and their thin, ragged out coats would be of little use. With each step she recounted all the wonderful memories with her daddy and Pastor Wynne along what used to be the road home. Now she had no idea where this dusty, barren road was going to take her and Lily or what fate would be waiting for them at the other end.

Lily had fallen asleep with her bobbing head on Annie's shoulder and within her measured sense of distance and time she began to see a flicker of light from the second floor of the place she just discovered her mama was born. When she decided to stop for the last time to catch her breath and rest her body, she looked up in the full moon night and wondered what her daddy would think of all this.

As she got closer she could see that all the first floor windows were shuttered from the inside like they use to do when they would go away on their vacations abroad. On many occasions, Annie and her daddy had witnessed large wooden crates and suitcases strapped on the back of their carriage as Lord McLaughton and Samuel would pass them by. It seemed as though they had packed up their entire house for what would be several weeks abroad. And when they passed neither of them would ever return their wave or smile which would make Annie glad not to be one of them.

Then when they returned with their picture images from all over the world, The Highland Way News would print a special event section in the paper reprinting some of those along with stories about all the places they visited and the people they met. Annie thought both men looked puny and ridiculous posing in some of the foreign looking outfits they had on. However, Pastor Wynne had politely educated her that those were garments worn by men from other countries and cultures. She was just glad that the men here didn't have to wear those silly looking robe things.

Samuel was almost the same age as Jonathan born only a few months apart. Jonathan had, in fact, grown up knowing exactly who his parents' landlord's son was but had little or no contact until he inherited the tenant rights from his father. Grandpa Ewing had warned him that strange things went on in that house and it would be best that he not wander too close. So, it was no surprise to Jonathan or anyone else that Samuel had never married and thus far had spent his whole life caring for Lord McLaughton. Maybe it was the horror of losing both his mother and sister that kept him there or maybe he was just too weak to leave.

Annie was getting anxious and worried about what if her mama had come up here to kill herself? Then what would she do? What did her daddy ever see in her? And if he knew about all this, why would he keep it from her?

As she got closer, Annie could see that the once great façade already looked sad, empty and even broken. It was never a place she had ever wanted or needed to see inside of. To Annie, there was never any sign of a real abundant life there. They had all the appearance of plenty but not the real kind of plentiful life like she had on the farm with her daddy.

The pale gray stones stacked two stories high had fractures scattered throughout. There were three arched windows on either side of the solid brown weathered doors and across the top were the same sized stones that jutted in and out. The front was just flat and plain and there was no color anywhere. And in the weeks since it's been empty its already being overtaken by some kind of creepy crawling vine overrunning the trellises that made it look even more abandoned and gloomy.

Annie thought about their once thriving farm off in the distance and her heart ached to see it again, only not tonight. And then she became more downhearted over the whereabouts of all the people she once knew that had worked on and around the estate. She had no idea where most of them have now vanished to. It just seemed like every day for months, families were packing up and heading to only God knows where. She only knew for sure of the fate of Mrs. Beaker and her children as they had been sharing that terrible place in town and now, of course, Lord McLaughton and Samuel. She didn't feel bad for them at all when they left for America even though it meant life as they knew it was over. All Annie wanted was to be in the same house, she didn't care where, with her only remaining source of comfort and support, her daddy.

"Lily get down and stand here for a minute" Annie said. She had finally reached the front of the house and needed to free herself from both Lily and their belongings.

"No, I'm cold and tired," Lily said as she stomped her feet.

"For Christ's sake Lily, just let me see if this stupid door is open," Annie said in an agitated tone.

Annie grabbed and turned the round gold door knob and pushed her weight forward only to have her shoulder and face planted in the wood.

"Mama, Mama, open the door! Open the door right now!" Annie screamed and banged. She paced and banged and screamed while Lily just squatted and cried more.

She pulled Lily up and with her in tow followed a gravel walkway to the left alongside the enormous house and found a back entryway. Annie realized that she had never been this close to the estate and had no idea just how wide and deep it was.

"Please God let us in for the night," Annie prayed out loud. Lily was more of a burden than she could bear any longer, her feet hurt, they were both cold to the bone and hungry. Annie pulled the latch and it creaked open.

Annie whispered to Lily "Don't be afraid, this is just a game of hide and seek. Mama's hiding and we just have to find her," as she held Lily with one hand while holding the other out front trying to be prepared for the unexpected through the pitch dark. Lily giggled a bit then started to whine and planted her feet and stopped moving. All thirty pounds or so of Lily's dead weight had a tight hold now on Annie's coat and she suddenly heard the hand sewed seam in the back tear.

"Let go, let me go! You just stay put. You'll be fine. Just give me a minute," Annie was now completely exasperated. The only coat she owned was now ripped in the back on top of everything else. She reached one last time and felt what she was sure was the heavy fabric of curtains. And with one hard pull back she could see the faint light of a full moon peering through a small sliver between the massive indoor shutters that had to be at least ten to twelve feet high. She pulled one open on one side then the other. Finally, not only had she made the long painstaking walk from the village to the estate and then inside, she had managed to navigate the maze of rooms and now she could at least see the inside of the house they had just invaded. Lily's whining had finally stopped as she seemed to be spellbound by the enormity of it all. The room looked like it had to be a library, with shelves and shelves of leather bound books stacked side by side. Annie turned from the window and she too became overwhelmed with the treasures in front of her. She had never seen so many books in her life nor had she dreamed she ever would. At home, the Ewing family only had two Bibles, Annie's and Jonathan's, Gulliver's Travels, and a World Atlas. Jonathan taught Annie how to read, hope, forgive and dream from those books. What, when and how could one person or two people, do with so many? If knowledge was the source of wisdom and strength like her daddy said, the two men that lived in this house must have never opened a single one.

The room was also filled with small and large monuments of white sheets that seemed to beacon their usefulness again. Annie pulled slowly on one and to her relief underneath was an oversized button backed dark brown leather chair. Then underneath another was a gold velvet upholstered sofa with brass tacks rimmed around the waist high curved arms. It was longer than the bed she once slept in, giving room for at least four people to sit on comfortably at one time. And over in the corner, Lily discovered a small honey color piano with three hand carved spindle legs. Exhausted and weary and not knowing or caring for now, who or what was in the house the sisters curled up together on the long soft and warm sofa, covered up with the white sheet and passed out.

Sunshine was pouring through the dozens of panes of the windows when Annie's eyes finally popped open.

Dazed for a moment she wondered if she had dreamed it all. Had they really broken into the North Highlands Estate? Did any or part of all this now belong to her mama? And what use would it be to her now with everyone gone? What was the point of her coming up here and, if she did, where is she now? This house had always been a dreary looking place on the outside and she never once coveted the life they had here. But, now she couldn't stop her eyes from darting in every direction, from the deep brown wood paneled walls to the chandelier hanging from the ceiling and back down to the oriental wool speckled colored rugs on the floor. Even the deer head hanging on the wall over the large boulder fireplace intrigued her. It was such a beautiful creature with its ten point antlers, light brown fur and the brown eyes seemed to be staring right at her. As Annie was trying her best to capture and absorb all these extraordinary surroundings so she could accurately relay every detail to her daddy one day her ears picked up the sound of humming. Annie had never heard her mama sing much less hum but she knew it was a woman's voice. Her visual recording would have to wait as she slowly pulled her arm out from underneath Lily's head, got to her feet and followed the sound out of the big room they had spent the night in and down the long hallway. The woman's voice was now on the other side of last door on the end. All her muscles tightened as her feet froze to the floor. She had dreams like this before. When she needed to run, when she was being chased and couldn't see who was chasing her, but she still knew she needed to move. Her breathes became shallow and she could feel her heart pounding like her senses were telling her there was danger on the other side. "Oh God, please help me, I'm so tired, I'm scared, and this can't be my fault. Lily and I need somebody. We need our mama,"....then suddenly some invisible strength, not of her own making, lifted her hand as she pushed the hinged door open. There in the middle of this huge stark white kitchen was her mama swirling around. Katy had a long white apron tied to her waist with the bottom lifted like it was a ball gown and she was making her own music while dancing to a waltz. Annie saw her mama's burn scarred face like she had never seen it before. She was smiling and having a whispered conversation with her imaginary dance partner. She had the most peaceful and contented expression that Annie had ever seen before. Annie was certain that this was somehow a miracle in the making. God had finally heard her prayers and her mama had been transformed. If there was a way to stop time, she certainly would have. Annie hadn't heard any movement from where she left Lily asleep and Katy had not yet seen her oldest daughter. As Annie's eyes slowly tried to inventory this new room along with her mama's movements, it appeared that someone had laid out dozens of open jars of plums, pears and apricots on the long counter. Even though her mama appeared to be in her own make believe world as she continued her dance, Annie couldn't believe the people that lived here had really gone off and left all the food that was just within a few steps from her. They had eaten all their preserves months ago and people were starving everywhere. There was a bounty of food right in front of her that made her realize how hungry she was but as she stood there and watched, it seemed like her world was beginning to take another strange and unimaginable twist.

Finally, Annie drew the courage to question her, "Mama, what are you doing and who are you talking to?"

Katy replied in the most warm-hearted voice she had ever heard, "Why Annie, tell Daddy we need flour right away. I can't make biscuits without flour, now can I." She then laughed and rambled on while twirling around again and again.

Annie still wasn't sure if she wanted both feet in the room as she was still standing halfway in the door or take off running. She didn't know if she should be concerned for the safety of her and her little sister or maybe her mama was just playing some pretend like, out loud crazy game. Could she perhaps be witnessing her mama on the brink of the same kind of madness that sent her own mother away? Should she back out of the kitchen now and hope that she and Lily could out run her? And what does a mad mind do when it finally looks and sounds happy? Her daddy used to say that it hurt her mama to smile because of the burn scars but she didn't seem to be in any pain right now. Annie lowered her voice to a whisper and asked, "Who are you calling Daddy, mine or yours?" Her mama did, after all, come all the way up here looking for something or someone. When Katy didn't respond, Annie spoke with her best soft assurance, "Mama, Daddy's gone. Don't you remember? I bet he's probably working on some big fine boat right now. We'll all be together again real soon, me, you, Lily and Daddy."

Then the pain from the burn must have come back,

because her face became familiarly anguished looking as she yanked her apron off and began peeling away at her blouse and screaming like she was on fire.

"What do you mean, Daddy's gone. Shut up you skinny girl! Daddy, Daddy, please help me, please!!"

And then just as quickly as her mind seemed to darken her new reality came pouring out in hysterical sobs as she collapsed on the floor babbling about Samuel. "Why didn't you tell me? I have always loved you!" Then she started to rail about Lord McLaughton. "I hate you, you're a wicked man, I hope you die! Why did you send me away? Why? Why? Oh why wasn't I ever good enough? This just isn't fair, it's not fair. Why didn't he want me, what did I do to make him hate me so much? I was just a little girl. Why make me live with Jeremiah? I don't understand, I just don't understand? And where is my mother? Why didn't she come back for me? Now, I remember running up and down the halls with Samuel and hiding inside the bureaus from Nanny Mae. And mother use to sing and play the piano and we would laugh and dance and sing. And I use to sit right here on top of this table and lick the spoon and bowl when they were making cakes and pies. I remember the smells of this kitchen and the servants running in and out."

Annie had by this time moved every part of her inside the kitchen and with the last bit of reason she had left said, "Mama, I know, I know. Please get up. I can't do this. You've got to pull yourself together. Lily's real weak now and she needs something to eat, remember she's not as strong as you and I are."

With that Katy's mind seemed to swing open to another forgotten and suppressed memory as she rose to her feet, grabbed Annie by the hand and said, "We'll eat later, let me show you around." They headed upstairs first where Katy pulled Annie along from room to room with her faint memories of colors and pictures, this piece of furniture and what was behind this door and that door, however, two of the doors on this long hallway were locked when they twisted the knobs. More than locked, it was as though they had been nailed shut from inside. Unfazed, Katy continued the showing until her and Annie discovered the room that must have undoubtedly been Samuel's playroom when he was a small boy. They both just stood there as though they were two deprived wide eyed children seeing for the first time a room full of endless make believe and amusement. There were dozens of wooden toys scattered about as though the spoiled child who owned them failed to put them away. A dark brown wooden rocking horse was over in one corner along with jigsaw puzzles and dozens of children's books placed haphazardly in a bookcase right beside it. And there was even a red and black checker board game still laid out in the middle of the floor, as if waiting on someone to make the next move.

Katy felt so lost and betrayed. He was her big brother. Why didn't he ever come for her? That familiar touch and glance had all along been about their kinship and not the touch of a lover to be. Her old longings made her feelings even more raw and exposed. She was now and had always been one of them. How could the men in her life that were supposed to be there to protect and take care of her just abandon her? Her father, her brother and now her husband were all gone and she had the most foreboding feeling that she had ever had.

For in that very moment Katy was certain that she would never get what she needed from any of them.

Annie's thoughts were entirely somewhere else on this guided tour. She had never been impressed with the men of this house for who they were. Because it had been clear to her that they had accomplished little in their lives but travel or stay shut away in their big gray stone house. But, looking around she was certainly impressed with the men who built it. It definitely overshadowed the splendor of the inside of the church that she had just sat in hours earlier.

There was the same dark wood used all throughout the house for the doors and elaborate trim work as she counted eight ivory door knobs just in this hall alone. The staircase had a fine carved spindled handrail and every ceiling had a smooth plaster finish. There were thick hand woven green and gold fringed rugs thrown about in every room over the solid dark wood floors. And it was obvious to her that a woman's touch had added all the color and decorations. The walls were draped with hanging tapestries of flowers of every kind and color that must have taken years to hand weave. There were silver candelabras placed on the tops of the hall tables as well as the gold sconce oil wall and ceiling light fixtures. The beds were covered in bright colored satin stitched bedspreads with matching drapes and each bedroom had either a tall or short chest with mirrors hanging just above. She could only assume that the height of the chest coincided with the occupant or guest that stayed there. And then Annie stopped cold when she saw her awful reflection at the end of the hall. Someone had hung a large gold frame mirror just before the turn onto the stairway for what she could only guess was a last look and see and she hated what she saw. The blue and green checkered overcoat was missing all the buttons and only one pocket on the bottom right remained and the collar of the same material had little evidence of the lace that was once sewed around the edges. She was rail thin with stringy long straight black hair, too many freckles on her face to count and a small breasted chest. She had been waiting for something to happen to her body, but so far, she still looked like a gangly boy. The other girls, even the younger, orphaned ones sitting on the front row in church had at least one remarkable feature. They either had bright blue or green eyes, cute turned up noses, auburn hair, locks of curls, flawless fair skin or perfectly proportioned bodies. She knew she had long played the role of the boy that her daddy always wanted, but she had no idea just how much she looked like one. Something awakened in Annie that she had not felt until now. She wanted to be pretty. She wanted her future husband to describe her in the same way her daddy talked of her mama years ago. All of a sudden she wasn't so thrilled to look like her daddy. Even with the burn scar on her mama's face, she still thought she was beautiful. Katy had auburn hair just like Lily with loops of curls and her teeth were perfectly straight with a tiny little nose. She was maybe a few inches shorter than her husband's nearly six foot frame with a slender but shapely build. Annie could definitely see the aristocratic blood in her mama now. She knew she had gotten her looks from her daddy's side of the family while Lily had been blessed with their mama's. However, Annie did have the consolation that her mind was from good stock. This was the first time Annie had seen her mama's hair down and brushed out. Her skin was fair with not a single blemish except for her scarred left side. At this moment Annie wanted so much to look like her mama.

They made their way back downstairs just as Lily woke up and her little body jolted across the room and she began to cry, "Mama, Mama, don't run away again, I missed you last night, can we eat now?"

Katy walked her daughters to the kitchen with one hand in Lily's and the other around Annie's waist and for the first time found her way to be both Annie and Lily's mama. She foraged around the pantry and found some hard biscuits that were left in tins, snap beans in jars and some apple cider. She concocted a feast unlike they had ever known from their mama's making. Katy then placed all the different preserves, beans and biscuits on the long dining room table and they ate using the silverware and china and drank apple cider from the long stemmed glasses. They had no idea which fork or spoon to use or which glass was proper but they didn't care because they were eating at the finest table in the land. They were sitting at the table in the dining room of the grand North Highlands Estate. Who would ever have thought? Finally after over an hour of giggles and spills they got up and went back into the library.

They had spent hours touring the house and filling their bellies. Annie plopped on the big oversized brown chair that she first spotted the night before while Katy and Lily curled up on the sofa.

This was the first time in Annie's memory that the three of them had ever shared anything together. Lily looked so peaceful and content in the arms of her mama and Annie was, for the moment, happy that she made this journey.

When Annie woke up, the afternoon was gone as were Lily and her mama. She pulled herself off the chair and this time mingled around the downstairs rooms almost like she had a place there. She wondered what it would have been like to have been a part of all of this. But, then perhaps she wouldn't have shared all the moments with her daddy that she held so dear. She ran her hands along the dark wooden chair rails and papered walls. After seeing the upstairs earlier in the morning her tour of the downstairs seemed to reveal more impressive furnishings and works of art. There were oversized wall mirrors that she skipped quickly by while stopping and staring at the life sized paintings of people who were either posing from their left side or their right while others were either standing or sitting with their hands clasped. Some of the men were dressed in military outfits and the women had crowns crusted in diamonds on their heads. But not a single one of them looked happy or real or like anybody she had ever seen before. Were these paintings the remnants of all who had one time lived at North Highlands? She finally decided to make her way back upstairs when she heard her mama and Lily giggling. The laughter was coming from the toy room that they had run through quickly that morning. It was as though the flower she had been named after finally started to bloom. Lily was in the middle of the floor playing with one of Samuel's windup toys and

Katy was putting together a jigsaw puzzle of farm animals. Poor Lily had only one worn out baby doll at home that was a hand me down and a couple of wooden pull toys that her daddy made. Annie sat down crossing her feet in front of her and played for a few minutes taking it all in, as the darkness that once covered her little sister and mama seemed to be slowly fading away.

"Mama, do you think Daddy is coming back soon? Should we try to go to Dublin and see if he is OK?" asked Annie.

Her mama suddenly stopped laughing and stared off across the room with the look that Annie had grown so accustom to and snapped, "He doesn't care about us and if he did he'd been back by now."

Tears swelled up in Annie's eyes as she got on her feet and argued back, "That's not true and you know it. He would never have left us this long on purpose, not for a minute, and anyway maybe he got sick or hurt or maybe something bad happened to him. This may be your dream house but it's not mine. This is just a bunch of stuff that's a hundred years old. Please, Mama why don't we try to figure out how to get to Dublin and while we're there we can look for your mama, too. Maybe she's fine now. Maybe the doctors figured out what was wrong with her. Don't you want to know? Wouldn't you like to see her? Do you remember her at all? I don't ever want to forget Daddy and I don't want Lily to forget him either. Why can't you for once give what you know you need even though you didn't get it? Daddy and I have been giving to you and Lily all our lives. And I know you don't feel it or understand it, but for once in your life I need you to give."

CHAPTER 3

Horse Sense

KATY NEVER FORGOT. Every time she brushed her hair back or washed her face she felt it. And anytime she got a quick glimpse in the mirror over her small dresser at home she saw it. Her face was scarred and disfigured and it didn't matter that it was only one side; it was still a constant reminder of that horrible night and the life that chose her. She never knew how the fire started and because she was in such bad shape she wasn't able to attend Jeremiah's funeral.

She felt bad at the time but now any further thought of carrying the Fletcher name made her blood boil.

Her thoughts seemed more muddled than ever before and her mind felt pressed and overloaded. It felt as though the same fire that scarred her face years ago was now burning in her head as she was beginning to process what was real from a lifetime of lies and deception. She was at a loss to understand why it was Jeremiah Fletcher that had been chosen to be her lifelong guardian and pretend father? Why would her father send her to live with a stable manager? Did Lord McLaughton pay him to take her off his hands? The thought of that made her feel even more worthless. If he was at all worried about her wellbeing as Samuel mentioned in his letter to her why didn't he send her to live with a relative or at the very least a home that had a woman living about so that at least she could have had some kind of mother figure in her life? Either he wanted her or he didn't. It just seemed extremely cruel that her fate was to live out her life in and around the stables just so he could watch her grow up. Why didn't he invite her into his home on occasion for tea or her birthday or Christmas or anything if he really wanted a connection? Why didn't he send them both away together? It just didn't make any sense to her. Why would or should the Lord of North Highlands be afraid of a little girl? She never had a crazy thought in her life unless one might think her dreaming to marry Samuel was off a notch. Don't all little girls dream of marrying their very own Prince Charming one day and living happily ever after in their very own castle? This reoccurring, distant dream had just turned into a nightmare beyond anything she could have ever imagined and she knew it was far from over.

She then recalled the visit from Pastor Wynne when he told her that he knew her when she was born. He knew, too. He had to. And she supposed he took this secret to his grave. Her mother was missing and perhaps dead, Lord McLaughton and Samuel were living in another country, Jeremiah was dead and Jonathan was gone perhaps never to return and she really didn't blame him. How would she ever find out why, she just needed to know why?

She knew that Jonathan loved her in his own way, but she always felt like he married her out of an act of pity or simply because of the nature of the man he was, that it was the noble thing to do. And she supposed she was angry at herself for thinking that she had no other choices in life but to accept his proposal. In the world they lived in that was what the women did and what was expected. At least in her crazy dream to marry Samuel she would have been able to travel and have access to a much more comfortable life. Katy had never wanted to live on a farm. She at one time had a mind of her own and wanted to somehow put it to use. But after one miscarriage and two children and no hope of ever having a different life she just felt her mind, body and soul slowly bleeding, and she didn't know how to stop it.

Out of sheer exhaustion, Annie and Lily had slept most of the day and Katy had enough of mentally and emotionally sorting through all the should and could haves. It was now the end of their second day here and time for dinner. They ate on the biscuits and preserves again at the table with Annie and Lily taking turns pretending like they were one of the servants. Annie lit the candles in the middle of the table while Lily scooped the preserves into the small soup bowls. This time when they were finished much to Annie's surprise Katy announced, "You girls can go on. I'll clean up."

Katy knew Annie was dying to put her hands on some of the books in the library and Lily had already asked three times if she could play on the piano. The piano was probably one of the most painful things thus far in the house for her to look at and her nerves just weren't up to the noise of a child banging on the keys. Suddenly she could clearly remember that her mother had been an accomplished pianist and singer and she wanted to keep that memory intact. She figured this way she would be far enough away in the kitchen that it wouldn't be a bother to her.

Annie pulled out and dusted off a couple of thick history books while Lily scurried straight to the piano. She pulled the stool out, plopped down and ran her tiny fingers over the keys slowly and intently one at a time. Then as Katy was drying the last dish and Annie was reading about the Irish Confederate Wars, a magnificent sound of music began to flow through the air flooding the room just as the moon light had their first night there. Lily played hymn after hymn as effortlessly and earnestly as Annie could read the pages of her newly discovered books. It was as though every note she had ever heard played in church had been mentally recorded in her head and was now exiting her body through her fingers. This child that was born premature and had shown little sign that she would ever lead a productive life had just produced the most magical moment of her audience's life thus far.

Katy had moved from the kitchen and stood there with tears streaming down her face while Annie was utterly stunned. And although Annie and Katy were both thrilled that Lily had obviously inherited her grandmother's gift they were also mindful as to what other family secrets would be uncovered in this old house.

That night they slept upstairs in the blue bedroom all in the same oversized canopy bed with each of them having dreams of their own.

When daylight peered through the windows, Katy slipped out of bed, dressed and crept downstairs. She went out the back door, walked out through the meadow and stood there while a soft, slow, cool breeze flowed through her hair and around her body. These were the days she missed and loved the most. The days when she would climb up on one of her four legged friends and ride to the edges of the estate leaving behind her dreary life of servitude. This was the only time she felt free, hopeful and that there was a God. She had a special bond with each and every one and that's really all Katy thought she ever had in common with Jeremiah was their love and devotion for the horses in their care.

Now, Katy remembered just before they left their cottage on the outskirts of North Highlands seeing a couple of wild horses that she silently prayed for God to keep in his care now that the land would be empty and barren. If they were still out there she needed one of them to hear her plea for freedom again. But, it was a different freedom this time. She wanted to be undone from years of deception. So, as she had as a young girl, with the same two fingers between her lips, she blew out a loud whistle and waited. Again, she sent out another shrilled whistle along with a clap of her hands and out beyond a thicket almost a hundred yards away appeared a beautiful gray stallion. She knew in that instant that she had not lost her special bond with these amazing creatures as he walked slowly toward her still and breathless body.

"Always approach these animals from their left side because that's usually their good eye. And never ever let them smell fear. You must always respect them and speak in a firm commanding tone. Then they will respect you." Jeremiah repeated these lessons to her starting when she was just a small girl.

But when he wasn't nearby she would speak gently and softly as though they were the only souls she had in the world that understood her or cared what she had to say no matter how silly or unimportant it may have been. In her mind she thought they would deliver the secret desires of her heart to God since he didn't seem to directly hear or care if she was alive anymore. She would often tell Gallo about her dreams of being with Samuel and now she thinks of how utterly ridiculous all that was. Why didn't Samuel ever share his faint memories with her? There had been plenty of time and opportunity. They could have put old Lord McLaughton in his place. They could have threatened him with the truth. She wouldn't have been afraid. All the lost years, chances at a better life were gone unless she stopped wasting time and pulled herself together.

"Come on boy, good boy." He finally got close

enough for her to reach out and stroke his back and it was as though he somehow sensed she was safe and familiar. Then he willfully followed her back towards the house like he had been waiting for her to bring him home.

Katy knew Annie was right when she painfully poured out her soul. They did need to find out what happened to Jonathan. She owed it to her girls to at least try to find him, but she knew for all their sakes she had to find her mother even more. Maybe she was still alive and maybe she loved her after all. Katy had to make herself believe that her mother didn't mean to try to kill her that night. Maybe she had been overtaken for just a moment of confusion and not the madness she had been sent away for. Lord McLaughton never gave Lizzie a second chance and he certainly never gave Katy a second thought. She hoped he died. No, she hoped he suffered a long time first, like she had suffered. He threw her out into the hands of a stable hand like she was some old half breed dog. And her once beautiful face was now freakish looking. She thought of all the painted pictures in the house and not one of them bore any resemblance of her mother. And when she stood there and studied each one she couldn't see even a slight resemblance in any of those people of herself.

Katy had to believe that this chance connection with her new friend along with her years of experience would be their way out. There in the back of the house was the carriage house and she knew that if she could spend enough time and train him, that it might be possible to hook him up to one of the remaining carriages and perhaps they could make the trip to

Dublin just as Annie talked about. Her daughter always had a plan. She went to bed with one and woke up with one. She always knew what she wanted her next step to be and now Katy had to at least try to map out a plan of her own.

She pulled the latch back and opened the carriage house and to her relief there was one small carriage left and a few bags of feed. The gray stallion was thin but there was enough feed left to bulk him up for a slow ride. The carriage would work well enough for it had a leather top cover and two black leather seats. Annie and she would ride in front together and this would give Lily the back seat to rest most of the way. It would take some time she thought but they could possibly make the sixty or so mile trip in a couple of days. Surely there were maps somewhere around here to help them navigate in the right direction for she had no idea which way was east or west or north or south. Katy knew it wasn't all her fault for not knowing and being so unaware of her surroundings. She rarely left the estate grounds when she was growing up because Jeremiah loathed going into the village and now she knows why. And then the fire had damaged not only her face but her soul and the outside world just looked and felt so utterly cruel to her. And now she knows the people in Highland Way weren't just staring at her face but, they knew, everyone knew except her. The things she should have learned. She could have done better. She could have been a better mother but for sure not a better wife. Jonathan knew. He had to know. His family had to know. And everyone kept it from her. She really didn't care if she ever saw him again even though Annie and Lily would miss him, she already did not.

Annie was the first out the door and then Lily followed looking for Katy that morning. Annie was nervous and agitated for a moment thinking that her mama had taken off again and was quite relieved to find her in the carriage house.

“Mama, where did the horse come from, he’s so pretty! Can we keep him? What’s his name?” squealed Lily.

Katy pointed in the direction across the meadow and answered, “Well, let’s see, he’s been living right over there all this time waiting for us to come back. He’s been lonely and a little bit hungry, so I thought we could take care of him and maybe in return he could help take care of us. What do you think?”

Annie just stood there with her arms crossed and shaking her head. “Mama, how’s this horse going to help us do anything?”

Katy turned and pointed at the carriage and answered, “He’s our ride out of here, silly!”

Lily jumped up and down and asked “Can I call him Miracle, you know, because it’s kind of one that he waited all this time just for us?”

Stunned into silence again for a moment, Katy answered, “Of course, sounds perfect.”

Over the next two weeks Annie and Lily sat nearby and watch their mama work with Miracle and Annie was beginning to be proud of her mama. Katy felt that same feeling of being with the horses again in the riding pants she wore even though they were a couple sizes too big. They had found them rummaging through an upstairs bureau and were certain they belonged to Samuel as he wasn't much bigger than Katy. He had always been a small framed man and never appeared to fill out anything he wore.

For the first few days Katy would just slip a loose rope around Miracle's neck and walk him slowly around the meadow. This gave her the private and intimate time she needed to bond with him. This also gave her the freedom to share her heart hurts out loud to another beating heart without feeling judged. She certainly didn't want Annie or Lily to hear her harsh words toward those she felt had nearly destroyed her. Then when she was sure they had mutual trust she attached the driving harness and carriage to him and they rode up and down the long dirt driveway back and forth.

It was during one of their back and forth trips on the long driveway that Katy surprised Annie with a detour to their small cottage. As expected without the care and interruption of the touch of human hands it had also been taken over with wild vines and weeds. They made one final pass inside the stale and vacant rooms and Annie knew this would be the last time she would ever walk the floors of her old life and it made her sadder than the day they left. But, Katy was for the first time beginning to have hope that she would never again have to live the life of a farmer's wife.

As they walked back to the carriage through the weed infested front yard, Annie reached down and pulled seeds from the dried up dwarf yellow verbascum, snapdragons and forget-me-knots and put them in her pocket. If she had to put roots down somewhere else one day at least she would have a piece of this once perfect way of life with her to replant.

On their way back to the estate Lily giggled as she bounced up and down in the back seat and Annie was in complete awe of her mama's horse sense. She had never witnessed such strength and grace before as she watched her hold the reins and drive the carriage.

And it was this horse sense that would be the start of defining the meaning of that last bible verse that her daddy read to her the night before he left, "...they should mount up with wings as Eagles." For Annie saw what was once Katy's burden in life would become her wings of triumph through tragedy, and it would continue for years to come.

It seemed that the inside of North Highlands grew each day that they were there. They would comb through one room after another, finding some of the most wondrous and curious remains. Annie and Lily were both amused and adventurous in their treasure hunting but Katy was on a mission. She was looking for anything of value as well as any further proof or evidence of her birthright besides Samuel's handwritten letter. Katy also knew they needed money or least something that they could sell to afford the room and board once they got to Dublin. Katy was starting to be both puzzled and physically drawn to those two rooms that seemed to be nailed shut and deep inside she was certain that the contents of those two rooms held the most important missing pieces of the life she once had here.

Katy and Annie had both wiggled the door knobs and pushed all their weight and neither were strong enough to break down or through either door. But, Annie had climbed quite a few trees in her time on the farm and she was certain she could scale the exterior vine covered trellis and gain entry outside through the window. Annie shared her laid out plan with her mama that once she got to the window, she would break the glass and unlock the window. So with a small hammer from the carriage house in her coat pocket, Katy and Lily watched with their hands halfway over their eyes as she slowly crawled up the surprisingly sturdy trellis while carefully feeling each step up with her bare feet. It was only a second story window that was the intended target but she was now several feet from the ground and her nerves were starting to tighten. It wasn't the same as all the trees she had climbed as a little girl because there was always a branch or two to reach out and grab. This feat involved pressing her flat chest up against a hard brick wall covered in a thicket of vines and she felt everything depended on her in this moment. She reached the window that was to her right and she just needed to stretch over, crack the glass, unlock the window and give it a good hard push up. She took the hammer out of her coat pocket and with one hard tap broke the middle glass pane and then continued tapping it out until the glass was cleared. Knowing she would need it again, she put the hammer back in her pocket and then stretched her arm again until the latch was undone. She pulled her body back on the trellis and took a minute to settle her nerves. Then it was one more hard reach over as she pushed the window up and tumbled in head first landing inches beyond all the broken glass in the first mystery room.

Her eyes weren't met with the same sight as when she and Lily stumbled through the library filled with books. This was definitely a room meant exclusively for a woman as the walls were papered with small pink and yellow flowers on a white background and someone had added a soft pale yellow rug. There was a dark wood four poster bed that had what was once white but now a yellowed dust covered crochet cover over the top, a small night stand and a large wardrobe bureau on one side of the room. And on the window side sat a faded light blue velvet chair, a small ladies dresser with a mirror and a wooden bench. None of this furniture had been covered with sheets like all the other furniture in the rest of the house had been. There were inches of dust on everything with cobwebs cascading down and across the ceiling.

"Annie, what do you see, can you open the door?" Katy asked impatiently as she jiggled the door knob.

"Just a minute, Mama, I'm working on it," answered Annie.

"Hurry up Annie I want to see, too!" Lily chimed in.

Annie used the hammer as she pulled and tugged away the boards that had been nailed across the inside of the door. She couldn't imagine why on earth anyone would nail the inside of a bedroom door shut but as she finally freed the last one loose they would all soon come to know as Katy and Lily slowly entered the room. They all just stood there looking around almost afraid to touch anything. For they all knew that time had stood still in this room and this was the last place that they knew for certain that Katy's mother and their grandmother, Elizabeth "Lizzie" McLaughton had slept. How fitting that today was Katy's 34th birthday. Her whole world changed more than thirty years ago and today her rebirth was beginning. She was standing in her real mother's room, and there was the bed she slept in and the dresser she sat in front of and staring back at her on the dresser was a small photograph of Lord McLaughton and his new bride, Elizabeth. She had the same eyes, nose and oval face as Katy with the same thick locks of natural curls pulled up in a loose soft looking bun. Lord McLaughton was dressed in a suit and had the same dark heavy mustache that she remembered seeing when he wasn't known to her as her father. Her mother was dressed in a long, elegant laced dress fitted from the waist up, long full sleeves with a gathering fabric from her waist down and she held a bouquet of daylilies in her hands. They were both standing stiff as though they were in front of a firing squad and neither of them was smiling. Katy just stared and Annie nor Lily didn't dare move or say a word. She was finally having her first look at the mother she had been deprived of for decades and her girls wanted her to have as much time as she needed. And with the closest touch in her furthest memory with the mother that had been torn away from her, Katy knelt on the floor and rubbed her hands over the gold framed photo.

"Mother, I've missed you so much, and I will find you, I promise." Katy said softly.

As Annie was beginning to worry that her mama would need her help again to recover, Katy unexpectedly collected herself and said, "Let's get busy and see what else we can find that belonged to your grandmother."

Lily went straight to digging through the small vanity dresser drawers pulling out strands of pearls and onyx and stringing them around her neck while Katy and Annie turned their attention toward the bureau. Katy opened the doors and pulled out several dresses and formal gowns holding each one in front of her while posing in front of the bureau's built in full length mirror. To her delight and amazement each one appeared to be a perfect fit.

While Annie had found several empty hand bags in the bottom of the bureau her reach for the last one pulled out a small white beaded purse that had a small silver clasp and this one had some weight to it. She sat on the floor with her legs crossed in front of her, pulled back the clasp and inside wrapped in a white linen handkerchief were several pieces of exquisite jewelry. There was a round brilliant cut diamond ring surrounded by two rows of smaller diamonds, with matching diamond earrings. There was also a gold necklace with a large ruby pear drop pendant and two other rings with settings of pearls and sapphires.

"Mama, look, this must have been Grandma Lizzie's wedding ring," as Annie slipped it on and off her ring finger.

Katy threw the last dress onto the bed and reached down for the ring, "Oh, my, yes, it is absolutely stunning. And this is just what I was hoping we would find." But then her interest turned abruptly to something next to the bureau. It was a door knob and it appeared that most of the door had been blocked by the bureau. Katy and Annie used all their weight with their backs pushing up against it to free this new opening. Her trembling hand reached and turned the door knob and she found herself in the last place she had spent the night as a McLaughton. The pink walls had white shelves loaded with dolls and stuffed animals, a large doll house in one corner with tiny pieces of furniture and in the other corner was a small bed. Still in place was her favorite blanket that was passed down to her from her older brother, Samuel. She remembered that everyone in the house called it the sleepy time blanket because it had cut out patterns of yellow moons and stars sewed onto the dark blue fabric and it was always a must for her to go to bed at night. There was a much smaller bureau that Lily had already reached in and pulled out a perfect fitting dress for her along with a pair of fine looking button up shoes. Annie gave her a quick look of disapproval but it was too late. Katy had already crawled into the small bed, pulled herself into a fetal position and all Annie could do was watch her mama cry as fitfully as her daddy did the day he knew that the potato blight had forever ended their time on the farm. And as Annie continued to inventory the room, she figured out that this must have been the room that belonged to the second door knob that wouldn't turn. For the same person that boarded up her Grandma Lizzie's door had also boarded up her mama's.

The next day they filled a large crate with some of Lizzie's clothes for Katy along with Katy's childhood clothes that fit Lily, the purse full of jewelry, the rest of the preserves, biscuits and apple cider, the wedding picture and Katy's childhood blanket. Katy hitched Miracle to the carriage and off they headed down the driveway and away from North Highlands Estate. Annie and Lily were sure they would see their daddy soon in Dublin. But, Katy had the reins and she knew where she had to go.

CHAPTER 4

Mr. and Mrs. Toudle

KATY HAD FOUND tucked away in the carriage house some of the local maps of roads in and around the Highland Way area and there was only one way she could see to the insane asylum. The actual name didn't appear on any map but there was a small notation outside of Dublin that indicated there was a hospital there. She could only hope that it would be The Weatherly House for the Insane as Samuel wrote about in his letter. They would have to head in the opposite direction of Highland Way which would be east for fifty miles and then take a turn south for several miles. And as she carefully mapped out and planned their trip for several days this new found spirit of adventure made Katy feel empowered for the first time in her life. She had never travelled anywhere outside the Highland Way area much less being so much in charge as she was beginning to be. She prayed the weather would stay dry for the most part because she knew the old dirt roads could become hazardous once the carriage wheels were laden with mud and she didn't want Miracle to get hurt. She didn't mention a word to Annie that her head and heart was in finding her mother first. Annie and Lily were just happy they were on their way to the big city to find their daddy. She figured that if everything went well they should be there in two days. But, she hadn't given much thought of where they would stay the night.

Miracle responded well to the tug of the load and Katy was excited that she hadn't lost her touch with her beloved breed. It still made her terribly sad that all the horses that she handled and came to know and love died that night in the fire. The grief of that loss actually stirred her insides more than it ever did for Jeremiah. He was a grown, able bodied man and at that time he was supposed to be her father and safe keeper. Why didn't he wake up and get her and the horses out? For the first time she wondered if the fire had been the result of Jeremiah's reckless behavior. He would often leave their small cottage after he thought she was asleep and drink heavily in the stable until he passed out. Maybe in one of his drunken states he knocked over a lantern and burned to death on his own account. If that was the case he certainly deserved it, but why did the horses have to suffer such a horrific death as she has had to suffer so much to live? There was only a few feet separating their cottage and the stables and with the thatch roof she supposed it only took a few minutes for the fire to lick its way onto their roof. All she remembers was waking up in horrible pain as Jonathan was pulling her out and she has been pulling away from him ever since.

***

The long driveway and estate had left their rear view for hours now. Annie thought she now knew what she had been missing all these years. She always had a full take on what she had with her daddy but even her imagination couldn't place her in that seat next to her mama. Her mama was in charge. She was really for the first time in charge of their lives, their destiny. If all that happened in the past had to be to get them where they were now she thought to herself she would do it all over again just to be here today. The sun was shining and she wasn't carrying, watching or holding Lily's hand. Her mama had the reins and she was sitting on her good side.

Annie was chattering on and on about what she was going to say and do when she saw her daddy again with Lily chiming in with an occasional "me too". Suddenly Katy waved her hand at the both of them to quiet down. Her ears had picked up a faint clippity clop ahead of them. It was as though all her senses were gradually being reborn. Someone else was headed their way. Katy wasn't sure whether she should slow down to avoid what was ahead or hasten their pace. She decided to just stay the course. But in a matter of just of few minutes they all started to also hear the sound of something banging.

Gradually coming in their view was an old man walking with his horse's reins in hand and the old four legged fellow was burdened with pots and pans strapped on either side. As Katy's carriage caught up, they both stopped. He tipped his old black worn out hat and introduced himself. "Hello there, Mr. Toudle here, Madam."

Annie immediately thought that his name somehow fit his frame perfectly. He was just as short and round as the name sounded but his disposition already reminded her of good old Pastor Wynne. Their trip was already looking to her like it was going to end well.

"Hello, my name is Katy Ewing and these are my daughters, Annie and Lily," replied Katy.

"Yes, yes, nice to meet you, where are you headed out here all alone?" asked Mr. Toudle.

"We're on our way to visit relatives in Dublin," answered Katy.

"Well you've got a good ways yet and night fall will be on you soon. Not a good place for all of you to be out here all alone at night. Mrs. Toudle and I have a place not far from here. You're welcome to stay the night. I'm sure the Mrs. will be glad for the company," offered Mr. Toudle.

"Well, I suppose it wouldn't hurt if you're sure Mrs. Toudle won't mind," answered Katy.

"What are you doing with so many pots?" asked Annie.

"Well, I used to forge and make them, now I just repair them for my old customers. Not many left around here anymore to make for. The last few years have been really hard. I had a booming business at one time when all the estates and surrounding farms were full and working but I'm lucky now to make a pass and pick up a few repairs. I mostly picked these up the last couple days in Preston and Highland Way. I never wanted to work for anyone but myself and now you see what happened to all those poor folks who lost everything because of the potato crop going bad. Who would have ever thought? But I was able to keep my place right up here and the Mrs. and I do alright. She'll be real pleased to have some women company," answered Mr. Toudle.

The town of Preston was familiar to Katy because that was where she had been told was her birthplace. Now she knows that was all a lie but she was still a little curious about Jeremiah's previous life, that's if he had one, before his move to North Highlands.

Annie quickly hopped down and tied his horse to the back of the carriage then insisted Lily join her mama up front. She couldn't wait until the two of them settled in the back seat to pick his brain.

He was rather elderly, had a genuine smile and seemed harmless enough. Beside they did need a place to stay for the night and pulling over and spending the night outside in the cold wasn't their best bet. Katy knew that Mr. Toudle coming along as he did was no coincidence, that in spite of her years of unbelief, perhaps her head and heart was opening up to the notion that God may have sent this kind old man to help them.

Meanwhile Annie was continuing to decipher that

last bible verse on her own "....the Lord shall renew their strength..."

They straggled along for the next few hours eating on the preserves and biscuits and talking about how things use to be. But the conversation was mainly between Annie and Mr. Toudle, because neither Katy nor Lily had little contribution or appreciation of the good old days since they both for the most part had been physically and emotionally absent. And Annie felt like she did in the days when she would walk along with her daddy and Pastor Wynne but this road home was different because her mama was in the picture now.

The four continued on their way as the sunshine of that April day began to fade and the familiar cool wind of the night started to blow. Then as Mr. Toudle directed, Katy made a turn off the traveled road onto a narrow dirt road that seemed to head directly into a heavily wooded area. There in a small clearing they saw a short, thin gray headed woman that appeared to be cooking over an open fire pit. With the pots clanging over the sides of Mr. Toudle's horse she didn't look up or even notice the extra guests until they were almost upon her.

Mr. Toudle announced, "Mrs. T, we have company for the night!"

She stood up, threw her gray hair back and with a beamed smile said, "Oh, it's been so long since we've had any visitors. Please, come on over here, have a seat," as Mrs. Toudle cleared off a bench by the fire pit.

"Mrs. T, this is Mrs. Katy Ewing and her two lovely

young daughters, Annie and Lily, they're on their way to Dublin," explained Mr. Toudle.

"Katy Ewing, you mean, Katy Fletcher, on my dear Lord, is that you?" Katy had just climbed from the carriage and suddenly she froze in place. "My little Katy, oh, I don't believe it, I can't believe my eyes, I never thought I would ever see you again, why it's been too many years to count," Mrs. Toudle said throwing her arms up and down in complete disbelief.

Katy's chest tightened. How did this woman know who she was? Confused and nervous, Katy asked, "Ma'am, how do you know me?"

Mrs. Toudle reached out and pulled her close and hugged her tight and through her quiet sobs, said "I took care of you when you were a little girl. I was your Nanny Mae when you were a child at North Highlands. Don't you remember me at all?"

Night had fallen and the light from the fire lit up the faces of these two long ago constant companions. Annie, Lily and Mr. Toudle stood by Miracle and the carriage not wanting to stop or interfere with this unexpected reunion.

Katy pushed her away and said, "I don't believe you, you're crazy!" then she turned to Mr. Toudle and said, "Did you know, did you know who I was, who we were back there when you offered us a place to stay?"

"No, ma'am, but you know I believe our Maker works in mysterious ways and maybe our meeting today was just meant to be," he answered with a quiet confidence.

Katy gave in reluctantly to the strangers and sat on the bench while Mrs. Toudle sat beside her and took her hand.

"Please tell me, what happened that night? Were you there? Did my mother really try to kill me? Was she insane?" as questions spilled from Katy in a rushed and trembling voice.

"Oh, for goodness sake what a horrible thing to say, who told you that?" asked Mrs. Toudle.

"Samuel did, he wrote and told me as much, that my father caught my mother trying to suffocate me, so he sent her away," Katy said as she fought back tears.

"Lord McLaughton was a terrible man for what he did to you and your mother. There was nothing wrong with her that treating her right wouldn't have cured. He was so jealous of anyone even looking at her. They had parties and such in the beginning of their marriage but he stopped all of it because he just couldn't handle all the attention that would surround her. She was so talented with her singing and playing the piano. And she seemed to have another gift that I've never seen since. It was almost like she could see inside of you. It was more than a sixth sense it was as though she knew what you were capable of when no one else did. People were so completely captivated by her intuitiveness and talents that he gradually started shutting her off from everyone from the outside world. So Mrs. Lizzie just started spending more and more time at the stables with the horses and Jeremiah. I guess she just needed someone to talk to and he was there for her. You know he never married because I think his heart belonged to Lizzie. You see she was going to leave him that night, she told me that much. Jeremiah and her were going to take you and Samuel and they were going to run away. She wasn't trying to hurt you and she certainly wasn't trying to kill you.

She was just covering you up good to keep you warm to go out into the night when Lord McLaughton walked in and caught her. She had even hidden some of her jewels that they were going to sell. He beat her real bad that night and then he had her committed and sent you to live with Jeremiah. I guess he suspected that you were Jeremiah's daughter, but he had no proof. I think he just wanted you close to see you grow up but far enough away not to have to live everyday with the guilt of what he did to your mother."

Katy just sat there for a moment listening to how her life had unfolded and at least for now finally knew part of the reason why. Who her father was, was now in question again and she still wasn't sure she wanted to belong to either one of them. She saw no resemblance in either one of herself although she had to admit that she did just begin to realize that she shared a lot of the same outward appearances as Samuel. But, she knew the picture they had taken from Lizzie's bedroom was the spitting image of her, that she was sure of. Now she just wanted to spit in Lord McLaughton's face and tell him what a horrible and evil man he was. Then she wanted him to die and leave this earth. Her feelings kept going back and forth, but if she had to choose she supposed it would have been the man that her mother had come to lean on and trust. He may have been rather cold to her but he never once abused her. He never told her he loved her but he did take care of her. She supposed he loved her mother that much that he gave up his life to take care of this little girl that belonged to the only woman he ever loved, never knowing whether she was his or not.

"If you really cared for me then why didn't you expose him for what he did?" pleaded Katy.

"Oh, believe me, I tried. I told anybody that would listen but nobody wanted to cross him. Everybody around here depended on him to make a living. It was really hard, but I stayed on for a short while and cared for Samuel. Mr. Toudle was coming around a lot back then and it seemed like every time I was in the servant's hall, he was there. I talked to him about it a lot and we just got real close and one day he asked me to marry him and here we are. You know it was Pastor Wynne that married us and we would hear bits and pieces of your life from him. I was so sorry when we heard about the fire and Jeremiah's death. But then I was grateful to hear that you and Jonathan married, he was such a fine young man," said Mrs. Toudle.

Annie and Lily were now standing behind Katy. Annie was thinking about the purse full of jewels she found. Her grandmother had a plan years ago to use the jewels in very much the same way they had packed them up to do, to start a new life. Annie was sad for this woman that she never met and sorry that she didn't make her planned escape. But she was thankful that her mama did and even more so, that it was her daddy that was there that night to save her.

Mrs. Toudle was cooking a stew in a large black iron pot and the smell made them realize just how tired and hungry they all were. She could see their hunger was equal in their minds and stomachs and was glad that she had been able to change her little Katy's last memory of her devoted mother.

Annie glanced around looking for some sign of the cottage that they were going to sleep in for the night but only caught a glimpse of a couple wagons that resembled part of a gypsy caravan that she had seen in town once. Were they in the midst of some kind of band of gypsies and fortune tellers? Mrs. Toudle did resemble the women that she saw in a gypsy caravan one day in the village. Her clothes were of colors rarely worn by dignified women, she had bangles of silver and gold around her wrists and big earrings hanging from her ears. She also had her hair down and not put up or pulled back in any proper way. How could this woman have been a nanny to her mama?

Annie couldn't hold it in any longer and finally asked, "Are you and Mr. Toudle travelers…fortune tellers…gypsies?"

"Oh for goodness sake, no dear," Mrs. Toudle fell out in a loud cackle. "All this I wear was left over there in those two caravans. I no more believe in fortune telling than, well, that Mr. T's horse can talk. See we really did just find this place. We were actually on our way to Dublin, just like you are. Pastor Wynne had just married us, God rest his soul. We thought we would make our way to Dublin and Mr. T could start his business there. We pulled right in here for the night and found all this that you see, just as it sits, all laid out and not a soul to be found. So we decided to rest here for the night and have been here ever since."

Lily finally said her first words, "I'm hungry can we eat now?"

Mrs. Toudle laughed again, filled their plates to the brim but she made sure to serve the child that she was entrusted to care for years ago first.

Katy, Annie and Lily slept in one of the caravans that night. While Katy dreamed of seeing her mother tomorrow, Annie drifted off hoping to share another story with her daddy about how they met their new friends.

The next morning Mrs. Toudle prepared some potato bread and gave Annie and Lily some of her silver and gold bangle bracelets to wear. She pulled their faces in her hands and kissed their cheeks. Annie knew that it would have been fine even if this woman had been a gypsy and was sure that she had been a wonderful and kind nanny to her mama.

Then Mrs. Toudle turned to Katy and said, “I hope what I’ve told you will give you some peace. We don’t always have control over what happens to us in life, but we do have the last say on how we learn to live with it. Don’t let what your father did to you keep you in the same kind of prison that he put your mother in. It’s your life and I pray that you will find the freedom from all your past hurts that have weighed you down for so long.”

Annie knew they would be fine and Katy had more strength than ever to go on.

CHAPTER 5

Weatherly House

MR. TOUDLE MADE sure that Miracle was fed and had plenty of water. And after a night's rest he was full of energy and was able to pull Katy, Annie and Lily along at a brisk pace. Katy just had another chapter of her life emerge in a way she never expected. It was as though one minute she was regaining her youth and the next minute she felt she had aged twenty years. Since receiving the letter from her brother she felt as though everything that she thought was true was now suspect and even now the truth seemed to change day to day. She was really trying to hold her own throughout all this not wanting to burden Annie another day with any more breakdowns and her hopes were mounting on the final leg of this journey for the rest of her unanswered questions. She ached to see her mother and she was more desperate than ever to know who her father was.

***

Annie's head was so full of new family tree connections, trying to decide if she wanted in or out. After all, Lord McLaughton sounded like a horrible bully who not only neglected his wife, but beat her, had her imprisoned in a mental institution and then put her mama out when she was just an innocent child. And what kind of brother or uncle for that matter was Samuel? Even after he grew into a man, never once did he speak out about the terrible injustice served on his mother and sister. Even if her daddy knew the secret of where her mama came from Annie felt sure he kept it to himself to protect her. After all, what was so terrible about where and how they lived? Her daddy always treated her mama with honor and respect and she was the love of his life. If she had to choose which life she had wanted, it was no contest. She was glad to have been a farmer's daughter and she was even more thankful that she did not have to ever again set foot in that horrible house where the men once lived that hurt her mama.

Katy let Annie take the reins on this day as she was constantly pulling out the map in her anxious attempt to find any sign of The Weatherly House for The Insane while Lily was riding in the back pointing to what few living creatures were left. In the time they pulled away from the old gypsy camp of Mr. and Mrs. Toudle she had counted four rabbits and two deer. Annie thought if her daddy had been with them he would have killed enough for them to eat well for weeks.

With every turn of the wheels on their carriage along with every clop of Miracle's hoofs, Katy felt her insides get tighter and tighter. Had she made the right decision to detour this way without saying a word to her daughters? What if her mother was dead or just marginally competent and doesn't even remember that night much less who she was? She wondered whether she should just follow the road straight into Dublin rather than expose herself and her girls to another chapter of her dysfunctional family. Then she heard the same sounds that once again let her know that they weren't alone on the road. This time the clippity clop was behind them but at a much faster pace than the gentle gait of Mr. Toudle's horse the previous day.

Once in sight, this enclosed carriage was twice the size of the one they were riding and it was being driven by two horses of a much larger stature than Miracle. This driver was indeed much different looking in that he had a black top hat with a black coat over a red vest and white pants with black boots up to his knees. A quick look by Katy and Annie as they flew past only exposed the passengers to be two women and one man and they both seemed stunned as to where these well-dressed folks were heading in such a hurry. Most well to do folks simply took the train from one town to the next and there didn't appear to be anything around that would have brought them this way other than the hospital. Then as though all their lives depended on this next move, Katy clinched her daughter's hands in hers and said, "My darling Annie, I love you and Lily more today than I ever thought possible. Please understand this is what I have to do not just for me but for all of us". And with that, Annie let go of the reins for she knew what their next stop would be. There on the right side of the road was an old weathered sign. The large black printed letters sounded close enough:

WEATHERLY HOUSE > 1 MILE

This was Katy's journey for now and like it or not, she was going to follow through. Maybe there were two houses, one for the insane and one for when you're weren't anymore. She had no idea who decides who's crazy or not anyway because as things have been going lately she felt like everybody in the whole world could use a good mental evaluation.

It was situated in the middle of a sea of tall grass that seemed to be as wide open and as far as the eye could see. The carriage that had passed them had already arrived and was empty of its occupants and there were several other carriages all lined up along the massive circle driveway in front of this unusual looking house. It wasn't made of stone of any kind but rather had a wooden exterior that had been painted bright white with a large porch wrapping completely around the front and both sides. The windows had sea blue shutters on either side and there were at least a dozen high back rocking chairs painted the same blue placed here and there on the porches. The women that were standing about on the porches had on long dresses that were drenched in beautiful spring colors that Annie had only seen before in their flower garden. And the men that were gathered about had on suits in shades of blue, yellow and white and they were divided in small groups playing quoits.

Katy had no idea what this place was that seemed to appear out of nowhere so she made the bold move to pull their small carriage to the rear while she gathered her thoughts for a moment. She knew they wouldn't fit in with the arriving crowd since she and Annie had unintentionally decided to wear the gray button up matching outfits that the kitchen servants had left behind at North Highlands. It had really been Annie's idea to do away with their old clothing since all of it was worn so thin that it offered little protection from the cool evenings and Lily was able to fit snugly in one of her mother's old play dresses. Buying her daughters a few new outfits was on Katy's list of things to do once they got to Dublin. But, she was worried for now, how would they blend in with this crazy colored clothing crowd?

The mystery of what happened to Katy's mother and their grandmother quickly deepened. What kind of place was this? Were these people visitors to a fancy inn or had they all been committed as lunatics as Elizabeth McLaughton had been? They all appeared to be happy and wandering about without any guards or hospital staff in sight.

Suddenly a voice called out, "You're late, get in here right now and put your things away. They didn't tell me you had children. You're just going to have to share one bedroom. I don't have time to make changes and the older one can help in the kitchen but you need to keep that little one out of sight, do you understand?"

The stern command made Katy and Annie quickly unload their things and follow the short stout woman through the back door into a long kitchen much like the one at North Highlands except this one was buzzing with life and there were huge portions of food laid about on the counter tops. Before they could blink they were walking down a long hallway and the woman opened the door to a small bedroom with just one bed and nothing else.

The boisterous woman finally gave them their first clue as to what they had just gotten themselves caught up in, "For the duration of this weekend you will refer to me as Mrs. Molly. I'm in charge of this house, this party and making sure that all the guests are served properly. I'll see what I can do to make up some bedding on the floor for the children but you'll only be here for three nights." Directing her look at Annie and Lily she continued her tone of disapproval. "I still don't know why you brought them with you." Molly closed the door behind her and Katy, Annie and Lily just stood there looking at each other wondering where in the world their feet had landed.

A few minutes later they heard a soft knock on the door and there stood a young woman with their white starched aprons and head scarves.

"Mrs. Molly said to make sure I get these to you and I'll take the little one out in the back garden. She can play with the other children that aren't supposed to be here either. By the way my name is Hattie and if you please Mrs. Molly this weekend she might let you come back. You know, the owners, Mr. and Miss Fletcher have these big parties twice a year, one in the spring and again in the fall around the end of October.

And if they are impressed with your service you might get to come back. The pay is good but it's not really about the money so much as the people you might get to meet. There are some real important people here and you never know how your luck might change. One lady I know got a real good job as a nanny for a bank president in Dublin. I've been serving at this house for these gatherings they host for the last two years and I'm hoping maybe this time my fortune might change." Katy could barely contain herself as Hattie shut the door as a flood of tears flowed down her face. The door flew back open and Hattie said, "Oh yeah, I'm sorry, I need to take the little one out of the house, now."

"Her name is Lily," said Annie.

Katy quickly wiped her face with her apron and said, "You go ahead, there are other children for you to play with. I promise to check on you in a little bit." And surprisingly without any hesitation Lily skipped down the hallway with Hattie.

"Did she really say Mr. and Mrs. Fletcher or Mr. and Miss Fletcher? There's no way they could have pulled off their planned runaway. Jeremiah is dead, you said so yourself. And Grandma Lizzie got sent away years ago. And besides if it's really her then why didn't she call her by her real last name of McLaughton?" Annie reasoned.

Katy felt her head spinning and she thought at any moment she was going to throw up. Her stomach, head, heart and every part of her body swirled and ached and this sensation was becoming more common every day. Had they just abandoned her completely? Had she really come this far to have to experience another gut wrenching betrayal? After all, she was told that Jeremiah had died in the fire that night. She was badly burned when Jonathan pulled her out and she never saw Jeremiah again. Any signs of the stable and the cottage they lived in were gone and she never returned to the estate until the day she received the letter from Samuel.

Annie finally spoke again, "Mama, I know this all sounds peculiar, maybe it's just a coincidence or maybe it's God's hand that's been leading us here the whole way. You did find out from Mrs. Toudle that your mother never meant you any harm. That she was just trying to get you and Samuel out of there. Didn't that make you at least feel a little better? We're here and I know you need to find out what happened just as much as I need to see Daddy again. So, let's just try to pull ourselves together and go out there and do whatever it is that this Mrs. Molly thinks we're here for. I know you'll know her when you see her or least once they see you, there's no denying you then, right? Look at it this way, so far this had been one crazy and exciting adventure after another. Who knows what will come of it. You may not get the answers you want but isn't the truth what you really need?"

It had become evident that they had somehow been mistaken for hired help when they arrived. So, they needed to take advantage of how they got their foot in the door and do as they were told to stay for however long it took to get to the bottom of all this. Katy and Annie wrapped their bodies with the long white heavily starched aprons, covered their heads in the scarves and headed down the hallway. Annie knew her way around a kitchen really well for she had cooked for her and her family since she was just barely tall enough to reach the kitchen counter. And then she would just pull up a chair and take the bowls off the shelves and be the proud "big girl" that her daddy often called her. Katy however barely knew how to boil water so she just hung close to Annie and followed her lead. Katy was sad that she had not been the kind of mother to her girls that she should have been but was quite proud of her daughter for being so strong and resourceful. She had to start giving back. But, first she had to get her own wounded and shattered world in order. There had to be a reason for all this.

Mrs. Molly shouted and waved her hands over and over again as plates and bowls of soups, roasts, baked chicken, casseroles, breads, and the like kept leaving the kitchen in the hands of white gloved stiff looking young men that heaved them up on their shoulders and returned with empty trays. They followed the recipes and cooked things they couldn't pronounce much less have ever eaten. There was almost an excitement in the room of finishing one dish and taking on another. The desserts were fit for a king. There were overflowing dishes of fresh fruit and enough cakes and pies to feed an entire town. There was no doubt these people were well off and had no problem sharing it with others. Katy heard the muted words and laughter of the guests but couldn't pick up even the faintest hint of Jeremiah's voice. She thought she would remember it but it had been years. She had just barely turned fifteen when Jeremiah told her good night for the last time. She thought about the day she married Jonathan. She was just a few days shy of her eighteenth birthday when she married and twenty when Annie was born. But what choice did she have? Who would have her?

And here she was standing alongside her daughter possibly working as hired help for her parents? Was this some kind of sick, cruel joke? She shook herself from the possibility of such and started washing the dirty dishes.

After what seemed like hours, all the cooking and cleaning was finished and Mrs. Molly bid them an abrupt good night and directed them to retire to their rooms in the same commanding tone that she had brought them in under. But, Katy didn't want to go to their room. She had been there all afternoon within a few feet of two people she desperately needed to meet. She was certain that this Mr. and Mrs. or Miss Fletcher had eaten what Annie had helped to prepare and she probably had washed the very dishes that they had touched and ate out of. Those old feelings of not being good enough were showing their ugly head and Katy couldn't afford to lose it now. Annie had somehow managed to show so much strength at her age for all that she had experienced thus far and Katy knew she had to try to do the same and make herself calm down and wait at least one more day. So, she stood there and waited for her turn for the one bathroom they all had to share which seemed inconvenient to her already as it was only the second time they had used an indoor bathroom, the first being at North Highlands.

Lily had always stayed close to either Katy or Annie but something happened today. She finally let go and played with the other children and Katy didn't check on her one time. Lily didn't know the exact time and date that the feeling swept over her, but she was beginning to feel safe and secure that her mama would be there waiting for her to come back to. And Katy felt it too, as soon as she walked in the bedroom. Lily had already been put down in her make shift bed on the floor by Hattie and she seemed quite content with a peaceful smile on her little face.

Katy crawled into the small single bed while Annie curled up next to Lily on the floor. The thin one inch mattress and worn quilt bedding was no more inviting than the feeling they got from Mrs. Molly when they arrived. But, at least they were still together and Annie wouldn't have cared if they were sleeping in a cave. In her mind, she was just one day closer to finding her daddy.

It seemed so long ago when Annie had to leave her perfect room that she shared with Lily in her perfect world on the farm. Then to have to live cramped together with Mrs. Beaker and her children in that awful flat in Highland Way. And now this week they had slept together in a large canopy bed in the great estate of North Highlands, then last night they slept in an abandoned gypsy caravan. And now tonight they would be sharing one small bedroom in the servant's quarters at a place called Weatherly House. But, what had happened to the place called The Weatherly House for the Insane? How or when had it been transformed and when were they going to finally get to meet the owners? And once they got to Dublin where would they live there? And then Annie finally faded out into a deep sleep.

As Annie was starting to feel the lump of Lily in her back, they were all jolted awake with a heavy knock on the door. "Time to get up, it's six a.m. and we have to have breakfast ready by eight a.m. sharp." It was Mrs. Molly, taking her turn on each door down the hallway. When they first arrived Annie had counted four doors on each side that must have housed the help of all the women workers. She wasn't sure where the men slept but there had to be at least that many rooms for all the young men she saw whisking in and out of the kitchen yesterday. They arrived just in time to prepare the evening feast and she couldn't imagine what a full day of work in the kitchen would entail. They got dressed and Lily was the first up and out the door like she had a plan of her own without mentioning one word about breakfast. This time Katy would see to it that she checked on Lily at least once. Hattie had assured her that sandwiches had been sent out to the children the evening before but this would be a full day outdoors for Lily and her new instincts told her that this was not something her youngest was accustomed to.

Katy had a plan of her own today as well. Somehow she would have to leave the kitchen unnoticed and find her way into the crowd of guests. She couldn't conceive how they would ever be lucky enough to meet any of the guests as Hattie had mentioned since Mrs. Molly had such a tight guard on their comings and goings. And she couldn't afford being fired after they had miraculously gotten this far. She thought that maybe she and Annie could hatch some kind of plan that wouldn't upset the entire staff. Maybe she could get Annie to help her write a short note to the unknown Mrs. or Miss Fletcher and convince one of the servers to slip it to her. Surely, one of them would know who she was. After breakfast was done and they had everything cleaned up she would get Annie to help her come up with something smart to write.

As they headed down the hall back to their room Katy asked Mrs. Molly for a writing tablet and pencil. She told her she just needed to send a note home to let her family know that they were doing well and would see them soon. Mrs. Molly grudgingly ripped a couple sheets off her small desk situated off the hall and said, "I don't know why you're going to the trouble because you're going to be home long before any letter will have time to make it."

"What do you mean? I thought we would be here for a few days?" Katy asked.

"No ma'am, remember I said this is the weekend spring party that the Fletcher's have every year. After tomorrow all the guests will be heading out and there won't be any need for you or the others again until we hold our fall celebration. For the rest of the year it's just me and my husband, Albert, who serves as the butler. You know this place use to be a hospital for certain kinds of special people."

Katy finally found the opening she had been waiting for and asked politely, "So, what happened to all the people that stayed here when it was, you know, a hospital for certain kinds of special people?"

And before she could answer Annie had enough and didn't want to waste this opportunity for full disclosure on Mrs. Molly's part by being polite and proper. "What are you talking about? I thought this place use to be called The Weatherly House for the Insane. When did it close and what happened to all the patients? Weren't they all sent here because they were insane? Did they all get better at the same time or did they move somewhere else?"

"Well, we don't use that kind of language around

here young lady!" snapped Mrs. Molly. "I don't know why I'm telling you any of this because it's none of your business really but Miss Fletcher's brother just showed up here about twenty years ago to visit her and together they began to change the lives of everyone that lived here. They told me one day that the poor folks that were sent here were for the most part quite sane. They had just been put here because their rich families either didn't want to or didn't know how to deal with their troubled souls anymore. That's all they really were. Some were kind of slow in their minds, but Mr. and Miss Fletcher just taught them how to live a better way. Anyway that was all before my time. My husband and I came to work here only after it was renamed Weatherly House and that's been almost ten years now. Mr. and Miss Fletcher had already been here for about that long when we came on here. Ok, so I've told you enough and don't say another word if you want to finish out the weekend."

Katy knew at any moment she would burst and hurried down the hallway with Annie running behind. When the door to their bedroom was shut her eyes popped wide open with this revelation and she started spit shouting to Annie the way old Pastor Feil did at the First Presbyterian Church, "Did Mrs. Molly say that it was Miss Fletcher's brother and he showed up twenty years ago? Annie, that's exactly when the fire happened and everyone thought Jeremiah died. He must have gotten out somehow and found his way up here. But, how did he know where she was and why did he go off and leave me like he did? I just don't know what I would say now to either of them. I can't think of any good reason at all for this."

"I know Mama. But, like I said and you know this. You have to find out why, whether it's a good reason in your mind or not. And you still need to know who your real father is. So let's finish what we started," Annie replied.

So, together Katy and Annie wrote this short note.

Dear Mr. and Miss Fletcher,

Would you be so kind to honor me with a few minutes of your time? I believe that we might share some distant relatives from the area of Highland Way. You have been spoken highly of and I was asked to give you their regards if we should meet.

Sincerely yours, Katy Ewing

After the letter was written and she read it, Katy stood there again feeling like her whole world was again spinning out of control. This was a do or die moment. Either she would win big or lose everything she had hoped for. What if they weren't Jeremiah and Elizabeth? What if this was just some bizarre and strange ill-fated coincidence of someone having the same last name. After all, Fletcher was a pretty common last name in that area. She didn't care about being sent on their way if she was wrong but her heart raced with the notion that she might be right. What would she say? What reasons could they possibly have for not taking her with them? Lord McLaughton threw her away and now to think that Jeremiah and her mother had intentionally abandoned her as well was more than she could mentally and emotionally bear. Maybe that's why Jonathan never told her. Maybe he was just trying to protect her from more hurt. Suddenly, she needed him there. He had always been there to hold her up. It wasn't fair to ask Annie to. Whatever the answer was, she was going to take Annie and Lily to Dublin. In an instant her heart had changed. Suddenly she didn't know why she held him responsible for the life she had before. He had always meant well for her and the girls and if given the chance, she knew she had to give back to her husband and be the wife and mother she should have been. They all deserved better.

She folded the note and pressed it into the hand of the kindest face of all the men. He was the youngest, probably around the age of twenty and had been the most patient of all with the women. Katy begged the young man to hand the note only to Miss Fletcher and that she would take full responsibility if there was any trouble from it. He was eager to comply like he had a bit of mischief about him as well.

He tucked the note inside his sleeve and out the door with the beginning of the midday tray of meals propped up on his shoulder. She hadn't seen Lily all day and thought this would be a good time to excuse herself and go outside, get some fresh air and find her. For what little she was contributing she thought no one would miss her. Annie continued cutting up the fresh fruit trays and had her own prayers for an end to this. She just prayed, "Dear Lord, please let my mama find the truth today, so she can start to heal."

Then suddenly she heard Mrs. Molly holler out her mama's name.

CHAPTER 6

The Family Tree

"YOU THERE, WHERE is your mama. I don't know what she's done, but Mr. and Miss Fletcher want to see her right away. I'll tell you one thing for sure, if there is any problem here, I promise that all of you will be sent on your way before the sun sets. These are good and decent people and I hope you or your mama didn't do anything to upset either of them," threatened Molly.

Annie frantically called her mama inside and followed her down the hallway until Mrs. Molly stopped and motioned her back down. Molly continued, "The Fletchers only asked to see your mama. You stay put. And while you're at it you might as well pack your things. I can't see where this is going to turn out well. If either of you have brought any shame or bad blood in this house I will personally see to it that you will never work here again or anywhere else for that matter."

Mrs. Molly escorted Katy through a small gathering in the large parlor and out onto the side porch. Sitting in one of the dozens of high back rocking chairs in what seemed like her own quite segregated area was a thin, auburn haired delicate looking woman that at first glance, Katy knew. There was absolutely no doubt that she had finally come face to face with her long lost mother. Even in her sitting position with only a side view she had the exact profile that had almost been erased from Katy's memory. The wind was blowing through the porch in an almost cleansing sort of way. She was dressed in a pale yellow long linen dress and had a light blue crochet wrap hanging loosely around her shoulders with a pair of spectacles propped on her nose. As her wobbly legs moved her directly in front of the matriarch of the house her long awaited look into her mother's eyes were shadowed by the dark colored lenses that only served to reflect her own. The little girl in Katy had dreamed of this heavenly reunion many times where her mother would come running for her with outstretched arms and pick her up as she swung her around in midair. But, this scene being played out was different. Not only did her mother not rise to the occasion, her first spoken words in the company of her daughter were to excuse her devoted and loyal friend.

"Everything is fine here now Molly. Can you just make sure that we have some time alone out here?"

Lizzie spoke softly, "It's a beautiful spring day today, don't you think? Can't you just feel the beauty of it all around? Come closer dear." And as Katy bent down for a closer look Lizzie reached up with her hands outlining Katy's every feature trying to acquaint herself with her new visitor. Then she heard the voice of the man that she had strained to hear through the walls from the kitchen.

"Hello Katy," Jeremiah said and in that instant his arms swept up this once abandoned young girl as her legs collapsed beneath her and placed her in the chair next to Lizzie. He then pulled up another to make a circle of three.

It was all over and instead of feeling relieved Katy felt completely paralyzed. She felt as though every bone and muscle in her body had stopped working and that at any moment her heart would stop beating. The only thing left working was all above her neck. She could still see and hear but her brain started to feel numb again and then without caring whether she lived or died she vomited her need to know out loud.

"I don't understand, how, why, is this woman my mother and I thought you were dead!" Katy sobbed and wretched in between her words, "What was wrong with me that I was so unworthy of your love to abandon me so long ago. Please, please help me to understand."

"Oh Katy, I'm so very, very sorry. I wished so many times that things could have been different for you, for all of us. I've rehearsed in my mind for years what I would say if we ever met again, and everything I thought I would or should say just seems so empty and unforgiving now," Jeremiah said. Then he turned and directed his voice toward Lizzie and said, "Lizzie, do you remember me telling you about our little Katy, well she's sitting right next to you. And she's every bit as beautiful as the day she was born."

"Yes, my little girl is with me again. It's a miracle, isn't it? And I could feel every bit of her perfect and unspoiled beauty in my hands," answered Lizzie.

"What do you mean by feel, can't you see me?" asked Katy.

Lizzie turned her head away as though she couldn't find the right words. Jeremiah replied, "No, Katy I'm afraid she can't," he sighed, "She's completely blind. That beating that Lord McLaughton gave her that night took not only her sight but it also took her memory."

"No, no, no, she looked at me, she did. I saw her look my way. You see me don't you, Mother? Please say you can see me, please! And you can't take someone's memory away, that's impossible!" cried Katy.

"Yes, I'm so, so, sorry. But, not only is her mind empty of what happened but unfortunately she has no memory whatsoever of you, Samuel or even me before then. In other words she remembers nothing from her life at North Highlands. I'm so sorry that we didn't tell you all of this sooner. It wasn't because I didn't care about you. I just figured you were so much better off where you were. And knowing about all the evil in that house would have served no purpose."

Katy sat there stunned and motionless. It wasn't a choice in her mind of whether she wanted to laugh or cry, it was a matter of if she wanted to keep breathing. All these years she had fought back any memory of her life as Jeremiah's daughter because it was just too painful. And now she's hearing that fight was for nothing because she was never really born. If your own mother has no recollection of bringing you into the world then why does it even matter. The fight was over. Her dream was over.

"Katy, my darling, I'm so sorry to let you down in such a terrible way like this. I know it's such a shock and disappointment. If I had a choice to change one thing it would be to remember you. I'd take that beating all over again and a thousand times more if I could see your face again and remember all the moments we shared. Jeremiah has told me every detail of your life from the minute he took you in until he felt it was time to go," said Lizzie.

"Time to go, you said time to go. Did you plan all that, Jeremiah? Please tell me you didn't start that fire? Please tell me it was just an awful accident? And tell me whose body did they find that night? Because somebody died." Katy snapped back.

"Well, it was Rudy that died that night." Katy's hazy memory began to clear. It wasn't Jeremiah that drank until he passed out. It was Rudy, the old blacksmith. She remembers now the arguments that Jeremiah would have with him when he would find his empty whisky bottles. But she still felt betrayed.

"You know how he used to drink until he passed out. I went out to the stables like I usually did every night to check on things and I saw him over in the corner sleeping it off again. Then I don't know after that, it all just happened so fast. I was knocked out and when I came to, the whole place was up in flames. I just crawled out and the next thing I knew, I saw Jonathan pulling you out and it looked like you were fine and I was sure he would always make sure you would be taken care of. There was nothing left for me with the house, stable and horses all gone so I just made the decision in an instant and just took off."

"Just like that, I looked like I would be fine, so you just took off? Well, I wasn't fine. I almost died that night. And look at my face! This is my permanent souvenir of my wonderful life at North Highlands. I've spent years trying to get over that night. And all those years that you let me pine over Samuel just makes me sick. And who were you to make the decision as to who would make sure I would be fine. Shouldn't I have had some say so on with whom and where I should live?" Katy shouted.

"Katy, don't be so hard on Jeremiah. None of this was his fault. He took care of you when I couldn't and I will be forever grateful. If you need someone to be angry with let it be me if you want, but I beg you not to hold anything against him," pleaded Lizzie.

"He could have told me the truth. If I hadn't gotten that letter from Samuel exposing all the lies I would have never known any of this and God only knows where the girls and I would be right now. His letter sent me here and it's going to take us away from here until I find Jonathan!" exclaimed Katy.

"I would have and I wanted to but it just wasn't my truth to tell. I know it sounds selfish but I was sure that you would blame me for the whole mess and hate me for losing all the horses. I knew you had a gnawing emptiness all about you and it wasn't hard for me to see that you needed to get away from that awful place and I was certain that you would be taken good care of. Your mother needed me. It was time for me, for us, to move on and I just thought it would be better if you thought I was dead," Jeremiah explained.

"How did you even know she was here when Samuel didn't even find out until he found the commitment papers when they were moving? And why does Mrs. Molly keep calling her Miss Fletcher? Did you two get married or something? She said something about you being her brother. And what do you live on out here? Where does the money come from if there are no longer paying patients here? None of this makes any sense."

Jeremiah went on to remind her, "Remember the day that Pastor Wynne showed up and you were worried we would have to leave. Well, he came to tell me that he found her. It seems that when the old man dropped her off here as some sort of lunatic he signed her in under the name of Elizabeth Fletcher. Apparently, he didn't want the whole world to know that a McLaughton was committed to an insane asylum. And it was her money that he used to pay for her stay here. It seems that he really only wanted her for her money anyway. It was her inheritance that propped up the estate for years and once I got here I made sure it came back her way or I was going to expose him. So, I'm sure Pastor Wynne's visit with Lord McLaughton didn't go well. Because he told me that he let the old man know that he had been up here to see her. I don't think it was a coincidence that I was knocked out that night and the place set on fire. I believe it was Lord McLaughton trying to kill me and you too. That's when I knew we both needed to get out of there," said Jeremiah.

Katy had one remaining question, “Jeremiah, are you my father?’

“No, Katy, your mother and I were never together that way. It’s not that we didn’t love each other deeply. But, she was too afraid of what would happen if we were ever caught. Our plan was to run away, she would get a divorce and then we would marry and start our lives together. I had no idea where she went either. For the first few days I just thought she left on her own because she changed her mind. And then one afternoon Nanny Mae told me about the beating,” answered Jeremiah.

“Why didn’t you make him pay for what he did?” asked Katy.

“Oh, don’t think that I didn’t want to. It’s probably one of the hardest things I had to do, that is, not kill him with my bare hands. But, then what do you think would have happened to you? After your mother disappeared he showed up at the stables with you and a small suitcase. He made it clear that if I didn’t take you he would make sure that your mother would never see you again. I just always held out hope that one day she would find her way back and I wanted you to be there when she did,” answered Jeremiah.

Lizzie finally spoke again softly and said, “Katy, I’m so very sorry we lost one another so long ago. I wished I could have been there for you. But Jeremiah told me that you married a wonderful man and had two beautiful daughters of your own. I didn’t want to burden you with things that just couldn’t be changed”.

Katy sat there for a moment staring at these two people that had long ago moved on with their lives without her while she had languished for years in a constant state of anger and depression that literally prevented her from building a life with her own family and bonding with her own two daughters. She now knew her mother had little or no accountability for her circumstances other than blindly falling in love with a greedy, jealous, abusive and wicked man. And Jeremiah who had no real connection to her other than his wanting and waiting for her mother made her sad for all the years she had withheld her love and affection for Jonathan. She knew she had unwittingly blamed Jonathan as well. She supposed that Lizzie could be bitter for all her losses but she instead had such a peaceful and serene presence that could have only come about by choice. She now finally for once and all knew her biology. That horrible man that almost killed her mother and sent her away was her father. And just like her daughter insisted, as bad as it hurt, she finally knew the truth. And even though she didn't understand why God would allow so much pain to enter their lives it was now her choice to let go or hold on to, as her mother said, to "things that just couldn't be changed." She couldn't rewrite her history, her mother's or Jeremiah's. But she could start new and appreciate her now and look forward to all her tomorrows with the people that just wanted to love her and maybe just start giving back a little in return.

Katy finally spoke, "Lizzie, can I call you Mother?"

Lizzie answered, "Just because I lost my memory doesn't mean that I ever lost the heart that God gave me to share with you. I will always be your Mother."

Then Katy got up and rested her head in Lizzie's lap and she felt complete in a way she never thought she would. With the simple touch of her mother's hand as she stroked her hair, she knew without a doubt that somewhere deep inside this woman her mother's love still remained.

When it seemed as though everyone had bathed and rested in their own truths, Jeremiah interrupted with one still standing deception, "You know when I showed up I just told everyone that I was your mother's brother. The hospital manager at the time just hired me on as a handy man and gave me a place to stay. It took some time to gain your mother's trust, then I just slowly started giving her a few pieces of her old life. I'm not really sure why she accepted or believed me except she just had a way of seeing what was real in her head. We hired Mrs. Molly and Albert and as far as they know I'm still her older brother. To this day they know nothing of what really happened or the circumstances that brought us here and I think it would be best if we just kept it all between us for now."

Katy picked her head up and asked, "What happened to The Weatherly House for the Insane and when did it all change? And what are all these people doing here?"

"As beaten down as your mother was when she got here it was as though she had some kind of special gift. Her sight was gone but she had an insight into what people could be just by listening to their stories and where they came from. She gave them hope and prayed for and with them and one by one they would leave." Jeremiah pointed down the porch and said, "You see that man over there holding a cane. He was so grateful to your mother for how she helped him, he bought this whole place just for her. And since then, it's kind of been of retreat of sorts for all of them to come back every year and celebrate the life that Lizzie gave back to them."

Katy asked Jeremiah, "What did Mother do for him?"

"Jarvis Williams was fifteen when he arrived here with a terrible stutter. The sounds that came out of him were quite beastly and his parents couldn't handle him anymore. His inability to communicate made him fly into uncontrollable rages. So as a last resort they sent him to live out the rest of his life here. And Lizzie spent hours and hours teaching him to calm his throat to breathe correctly when he spoke. When he left here at age twenty, his first job was as a bank teller. Now he is the President of Dublin City Bank. She has been the driving force for changing the lives of so many others that went on to become doctors, ministers, teachers and even artists," answered Jeremiah.

"I may be blind, but I can hear just fine. So, would you two stop talking about me as though I wasn't sitting right here. Now, when am I going to get to meet my granddaughters?" Lizzie laughed.

They didn't have to leave after the weekend or that night as Mrs. Molly had threatened. Instead, Katy, Annie and Lily moved upstairs and took over two of the splendid guest rooms that came with their own private bathrooms.

Their time there spilled into the summer as Katy spent endless hours getting reacquainted with Jeremiah and Lizzie. And the Ewing girls delighted in getting to know their grandmother and the man who sacrificed so much. Katy was certain now that the long wait was worth this time with her mother and Jeremiah. And Annie thought her Grandma Lizzie was a lot like her daddy in that she had in her own way stirred a revival of justice for the patients that had been sent here to wither away and die. Katy, of course, hung on to her every word trying to deposit every minute of their time together as a family in her heart and mind all the while wishing Jonathan was there with them and wondering what he would think. And then finally Mrs. Molly and Albert were enlightened to the family tree connections while they were all under the same roof.

Even as well as their visit was going and as happy as Katy was, she knew Annie was getting anxious about their stay. It was time for her and for them to move on.

Annie was excited and sad that tonight would be their last night together. Her mama had finally found her way and now it was time for Annie to find hers. She missed her daddy and thought about him every day. She found herself pushing back any negative thoughts of her daddy's fate. After all it had now been over six months since they last saw him. It was a bitterly cold January morning when he left them with Mrs. Beaker in that awful flat and she worried then how the two men would survive during that long trip to Dublin on foot. Annie had written to Mrs. Becker on several occasions and still no word came of what happened to the two men. But her daddy's strength and positive attitude filled her with still one small ray of hope. She knew her daddy had a plan. He always did. And she was sure that he had to have been working really hard all this time building a new life for them.

That night as they gathered for their last dinner that Mrs. Molly had prepared, Katy finally decided to ask for her mother's parting insight for each of them.

"Mother, what do you believe I have to offer? What I mean is you've helped so many people that were considered hopeless. And I lived in such hopelessness for so long...."

"Katy, I believe that because you have suffered so much in the depths of your soul, that your words will truly be an inspiration to the world one day," answered Lizzie.

"What about me Grandma Lizzie?" asked Annie.

"Well Annie, you have shown such a tremendous amount of mercy and strength in your short life I would have to say that's your calling," answered Lizzie.

"My calling?" asked Annie.

"Yes, the needs of others are very important to you," said Lizzie.

"Grandma Lizzie, I just want my family back together," said Annie.

"I know, but it's going to be bigger than that one day, you'll see," promised Lizzie.

"And me, I'm too little, huh?" asked Lily.

"Oh no, do you know what Lily means?" asked Lizzie.

"Flower?" answered Lily.

"Yes and purity, a pure and good heart," said Lizzie.

"I'm so proud of my girls and I know each of you will find your way," Lizzie finished.

Jeremiah just sat and smiled and was so thankful just to have a seat at the table.

Katy could clearly see how Lizzie had inspired so many others to greatness. Her blindness in this cruel world had actually become her gift. She couldn't see Katy's scarred face, Annie's tired and gangly body or Lily's frailness. She seemingly only saw through into their good and kind hearts.

Lizzie gave them her blessing for the sale of her long forgotten jewelry. And Jeremiah promised to take good care of Miracle while insisting on finishing the last leg of their journey with them. He would hitch his driving horse that he had appropriately named Gallo to their carriage. He knew the way well into Dublin and he felt he owed Katy. Dublin was a big city and he thought he should at least help them make the rest of the trip and get them settled somewhere safe. He knew a few people from his time at Weatherly House. And he thought with his contacts they could perhaps locate Jonathan more quickly, that is, if he was still alive.

They promised to return and Lizzie promised she would be waiting.

CHAPTER 7

Dublin

AS GALLO PULLED them along Katy was finding herself grateful for Jeremiah's presence in her life again. Even though she now knew he wasn't her father she felt safer that this selfless and honorable man had the reins, as the bright, unfamiliar gas lights of Dublin began to appear. He had taken care of her so many years ago when her father had abandoned her and now in a strange twist of events he was helping them along their way to find her husband and her children's father. How foolish she must have been to think that she could have found her way in a place that was already appearing larger than life. She had spent her entire life in and around North Highlands Estate and other than the visit to Weatherly House she had little knowledge or experience of the outside world. They had all heard stories of women and children being kidnapped and sold as slave laborers abroad and that alone shook her to her core. Annie had the same thoughts running through her head that although she had gained this newfound confidence in her mama, she was also thankful that this time it was Jeremiah that was in charge.

As the lights became brighter so did the noise of the night life swirling throughout the streets of this strange and enormous city. It was as though a thousand voices were echoing in their direction. And for the first time in months Lily reached over and took Annie's hand as they got closer and closer.

Annie wondered out loud, "How in the world will we ever find Daddy in all this chaos?"

There were dozens of teams of horses pulling everything one could imagine. There were large four wheeled open carts loaded down with bags of flour, coffee beans, cabbage, turnips and bales of cotton while other wagons had only human cargo of men ending their work day in the factories and ship yards. There were enclosed carriages filled with people dressed in everything from top hats to sequin dresses and all this activity was at night. Even the large warehouse factories still had thick gray smoke billowing from the multitude of smoke stacks as though they never went to sleep.

Annie's discomfort in their new surroundings

continued to grow with each passing block of buildings that seemed to be all shoved together. She could only recall one pub in Highland Way and so far she's seen one on every corner for the last six blocks with men staggering in and out. She hoped that they would not have to live in a place such as this and was almost certain that her daddy would never allow it. Then it suddenly struck her that this was perhaps the reason why he had not sent for them. She knew it. She knew her daddy had a plan. It was just taking him longer than he thought. This city was too big, too noisy and too dirty for his family and all his hard work here would provide the means to settle them somewhere else.

Lily whispered, "Why is everyone up so late and how do they sleep with all the noise?"

"Well, some of these folks work long hours and when they get off work they don't always go home. This is how the big city is. They have restaurants and pubs that grownups like to go to," answered Jeremiah.

"Well, I don't like it. When it got dark back home everybody went inside except for the animals and even they would settle down for the night," Lily said.

Jeremiah, Katy and Annie all laughed at the youngest mind of the bunch that had just echoed out loud what they were all thinking.

Jeremiah had no plans to stop until he got to Jarvis' house. Once he had become President of Dublin City Bank he built a beautiful home for his wife and children and Jeremiah knew they would be welcomed there. He just had to find 200 Canal Street. All the fine homes on this main street stood directly across from a canal that ran straight through the city.

For the first time since they left the farm, Annie was sure she wouldn't be confused for either a farmer's daughter or a servant. Mrs. Molly was so remorseful for her ill treatment that she made her three new outfits while they were there and she cried and kissed each of the Ewing girls as they loaded up that morning. Today she had on a pink and white gingham short sleeve top with pearl buttons down the front and a crisp new pink matching long skirt. She had pulled her hair up in a soft bun that she and Mrs. Molly had worked on for days trying to copy her Grandma Lizzie's hairdo. Her feet had grown enough so that she and Katy could share the several pairs of shoes from Lizzie's old bureau. And for her trip to the big city she slipped on a couple of the silver and gold bangle bracelets that Mrs. Toudle had given to them.

Lily sat up and pointed, "There it is, that's it!" She knew they were looking for some place that was safe, familiar and inviting and it was. There in the middle of an entire block of splendid brick and mortar homes was an exact replica of Weatherly House. Even under the flickering gas lights it had the same stark white boards, blue shutters and wraparound porch. It was as though Jarvis Williams had picked it up and planted it on 200 Canal Street. The only difference here was they had a smaller yard that someone had filled with color and installed a three foot white picket fence and at first glance looked almost identical to their tenant farm front yard. Annie had a sudden ache for her daddy because it had been almost a year since the summer they had picked bouquets of flowers from their own yard for her mama.

Jeremiah pulled up, got out first and secured the

horse's reins in a small ring hanging from a post. Katy, Annie and Lily followed through the white picket gate onto the porch and after a couple knocks a small heavy set woman dressed much like Mrs. Molly opened the wood and glass beveled door. Annie immediately remembered Hattie's story about one of the workers being hired by a bank president in Dublin.

Jeremiah announced, "I'm sorry we're here so late. My name is Jeremiah Fletcher and we're not expected but should be welcomed here. Mr. Williams is a good friend and he told me that if I was ever in town to stop by. So, I'm here, um, we're here. Would you please let him know?"

She disappeared and before Annie could count the stair steps halfway up in the foyer, Jarvis was slapping Jeremiah on the back and moving them into the parlor.

Not only had the outward appearance of the girls changed but the time spent at North Highlands and Weatherly House had refined their manners. Even Lily walked, stood and sat with a great deal more confidence and assuredness. They all sat together on the curved, buttoned back, ivory velvet sofa with their hands in their laps like they knew a fresh cup of hot tea would likely be served soon. Jeremiah, on the other hand flopped in a familiar looking large brown oversized leather chair.

"What a wonderful surprise and it's good to see you again so soon. You'll stay for dinner, right? My wife Emma and daughters Ellie and Marie will be down shortly," Jarvis said as he smiled and rubbed his hands together. And as though he had introduced them in perfect timing, Emma flowed down the staircase with Ellie and Marie right behind her. What a perfect looking family, thought Katy.

Jeremiah apologetically explained their unannounced visit, "Sorry to drop in on you like this. Let me introduce Mrs. Katy Ewing and her daughters Annie and Lily. You might be interested to know that Katy is Lizzie's daughter. They've been separated for years by circumstances beyond their control and have just recently reunited. You may remember seeing them during our last spring event. Anyway, I've accompanied them this far along but they need help in locating her husband. He, along with their neighbor, came out this way several months ago to work at the harbor and they haven't been seen or heard from since and I was hoping you might have some suggestions on where we might start looking?"

"Well you know how I feel about Lizzie. So, you're welcome to stay here for as long as you need and I'm certain if Mr. Ewing is here in Dublin, I can find him, guaranteed," answered Jarvis.

"Well that's kind of you Jarvis, but we had no intention of staying the night," replied Jeremiah.

"Oh no, you absolutely must, I won't hear otherwise. Besides Katy and the girls will be good company for Emma and the children," Jarvis insisted.

Annie's face lit up "Mr. Jarvis, sir, can we start looking for my daddy in the morning? His first name is Jonathan, he has black hair, almost as tall as you are and he is probably working on a fishing boat."

Jarvis replied, "Why Annie there are probably hundreds of fishing boats here. But I'll get someone on it straight away in the morning. It may take some time but I'm sure one of the fishermen or dock workers here will have heard of him. These guys are part of the same kind of family. They don't just live and work together. They fight, eat and drink in the same pubs, too."

Ellie was ten and Marie was seven but they took Lily in like she was one of their own that evening. Annie was full from dinner but couldn't remember what she ate. She just kept trying to remember what her daddy looked like. She could see him in her head but his features were becoming a little vague and that was upsetting her as she laid with her eyes wide open most of the night in yet another strange house, bedroom and bed. She had prayed every night that tomorrow would be the day. And even though she was grateful for all the firsts they had experienced she just couldn't imagine her life without her daddy.

The next morning after breakfast Lily shot off upstairs with Ellie and Marie while Katy had to endure Emma's constant chattering all day long about nothing really. She lived the life of the social elite planning one event after another while fretting about what she would wear to each one. Katy thought she had probably rescued Jarvis more than he had them for the next few days and she guessed it wasn't the perfect family after all. It just looked like one. Katy was both surprised and perplexed that someone like Jarvis that had suffered the way he did would have married someone who had so little to offer to their actual life together. She didn't mention her husband's name a single time and rarely spoke of her children except for their school lessons that seemed to annoy her. But, then again, hadn't she been the same way? Jonathan was a wonderful, kind and hard working man who had for years settled for an empty and loveless marriage to her. What had she contributed to their life together? He had single handedly put food on the table and raised Annie and Lily while she just sat around and listened to the constant chatter in her own head about how she somehow deserved better. She thought about Lizzie's old room that had been frozen in time with all the dust and cobwebs and the door nailed shut for years. That had been her life for so long and she felt like she was still clearing away all those cobwebs in her heart and mind while opening the door for the first time for all the new experiences that lay waiting for her as a wife, mother, woman and human being. She wished she had the time and felt comfortable enough to share her story with Emma, but not yet. Lizzie did tell her that her words would be an inspiration to the world one day, but she still felt timid about giving anyone advice and thought she still needed more time to grow into her new skin.

Annie spent most of the day on the front porch waiting on some news of her daddy's whereabouts while Jeremiah had disappeared in the early morning hours with instructions from Jarvis on where to go and who to talk to. She kept thinking of her grandma's intuitiveness of her special gift which sounded too much like the burden she had been carrying for too long. She wasn't interested in filling someone else's cup anymore. She wanted and needed someone to take care of her or at least someone to lean on for a while. And even though she saw her mama standing stronger than she had ever before, she was tired. The people she so dearly treasured and admired were gone. Why had Pastor Wynne and her daddy been taken and the likes of Lord McLaughton and Samuel were living rich and full lives in America? And why had her mama missed out on being a part of her own mother's life? And poor Jeremiah was still waiting for the love of his life to remember what he meant to her and how they fell in love. None of her painstaking new discoveries in this crazy family tree seemed right or fair and she hoped things would take a turn for the better soon.

Without the knowledge of the Ewing girls, Jeremiah had volunteered to Jarvis to be the one to look for Jonathan. He had a huge stake in all of this. He knew all too well what it felt like to wait for someone to come home and even though he wasn't Katy's real father or the girl's grandfather by blood he still wanted to do right by them. So he spent hours walking through the fishing and shipping neighborhoods talking to as many fishermen, dockhands and bartenders as he could trying to get any little piece of information.

On the evening of the third day Katy had enough and pressed Jeremiah for answers. "Jeremiah, I know you've been looking for Jonathan every day. I can see it in your eyes when you come in."

"You're right. After dinner tonight I'll tell you everything that I've found out," confessed Jeremiah.

That night Jeremiah and Jarvis gathered Katy and the girls in the parlor. He motioned them to take a seat and said, "I've got some news about Jonathan today and I'm sorry it's not what you hoped for. It seems he was hired on as a deck hand on a passenger vessel called The Rosewood bound for America. It docked back here two months ago and he wasn't on it. They made a call out before it pulled from the harbor in New York City and he just never showed back up. The

Captain remembers him well. He said he was a real hard worker, probably one of the best he ever had. He clearly remembered how he talked about his family and how he needed to make enough money to get all of you over here to Dublin. The Captain even said he had a place already picked out for all of you when he got back. And to this day, nobody knows what happened to him."

Not being the optimist that Katy expected, Jarvis added, "I have a few friends over there. I can send out some letters of inquiry to all of them. But you have to understand, New York City is a real big place and unless you go over there yourselves, I'm not sure what else we can do for now but wait and see if he makes it back. You're welcome to stay here for as long as you want."

Annie pressed her face in her hands and sobbed. Lily, rubbed her back and said, "Don't worry Annie, he'll be back, please don't cry, you know Daddy always keeps his word."

With those words Katy tightened her scarred face, rubbed her forehead and said, "Well, I guess we will just have to go over there, then won't we."

Katy thanked Emma and Jarvis for their hospitality and told them and Jeremiah that they would be leaving tomorrow. She later pulled Jeremiah aside and said, "I need your help to pawn some or all of Mother's jewelry tomorrow. Then I need you to get us a hotel room and find out when The Rosewood is scheduled to leave again for the same trip. I want to sail on the same ship he did. Maybe ask around to some of the hired hands. Somebody is bound to know something. People just don't vanish into thin air. If Jonathan didn't get on that ship there's a reason."

The next day they packed up and loaded their carriage to head to the hotel that Jarvis recommended. He said, "I wish you would stay awhile longer, but I understand. You know I owe your mother my life and if you ever need anything, just let me know. Everybody around here knows who I am."

Katy smiled and thanked him again. She suddenly became incredibly envious standing there looking at his family all together. This outsider had his life changed in such a remarkable way by the mother she lost years ago. It just wasn't right. Here he had his whole world completely intact, mindless and chattering wife and all. It didn't matter that his parents gave up on him. God had used a total and complete stranger to help make him whole and she wondered when and if he would do the same for her.

CHAPTER 8

The Lottery

ANY THOUGHT THAT KATY had of capturing that long ago life she once had with her mother was finally dead and buried. The only thing she could hope for was to wash away the past and start building on her future with the sense that every relationship would be different now. And that difference was already making her realize just how much time had been wasted on her own personal self-imposed famine. How ironic that it took a plant malady for her to see the abundant life she had all along right in front of her. She had to almost lose everything before she found out what was truly real and important. She couldn't wait for Jeremiah to find the hotel so she could have some time alone with her thoughts and the man who had raised her.

Jeremiah finally broke the silence. "You still have that same look on your face that you use to get when you were a little girl. What are you dreaming about now? Are you sure this is what you want? You know that we can turn around right now and head back to Weatherly House."

Katy replied, "No Jeremiah, this time it's not a dream. Like it or not I have found my truths and it's time for me to let go and move on. Annie and Lily need me. They need me to be their mama. I'm sorry that so much was put on you all those years ago and I know you did the best you knew how. After all I wasn't your daughter, but you did take good care of me and I will always love you for that. This is our journey now. I mean, for me and the girls. Jonathan was a good husband and father and if we have to go to the ends of the earth to find him then so be it. He has waited so long for me to love him, and I guess this is going to be my first step. I allowed this scar on my face to be a constant reminder of what I thought was the worst day of my life. But, the truth is, it was actually the best thing that ever happened to me. Jonathan saved me that day and I owe him my life."

Katy decided outright that no matter what, she was going to keep two pieces of Lizzie's jewelry. She wanted to hang on to the diamond ring for Annie and the ruby necklace for Lily. Whatever they got for the rest would have to do. She not only wanted but needed her daughters to have something tangible from their Grandma Lizzie.

Jeremiah left them in the carriage and took the diamond earrings along with the pearl and sapphire rings into Maker's Pawn and came out with five hundred pounds. Not as much as she expected for such incredible pieces but it was still hard times, even in Dublin. Thankfully, she didn't have to follow through with the new outfits for the girls as she had promised since Mrs. Molly had sewed for all three of them.

They soon found the place that Jarvis recommended called The Manship Inn. It was a little more elaborate than she thought they could afford, but a place in time she would soon realize that they would all need. They took two rooms for a week, one for Jeremiah and one for the girls and were surprised and delighted to find out that Jarvis had already covered their bill in advance.

Katy wanted to know where Jeremiah came from and who did he leave behind in Preston? These were subjects that she didn't want to talk about or mention in front of the girls or her mother. They also needed to secure passage on The Rosewood's next voyage to New York and she had no idea when they could expect to leave or how much three tickets would cost. She just hoped their timing was such that they wouldn't have to wait long.

Lily quickly got involved with children of her own age at the hotel while Annie found a small sitting area off the lobby littered with books.

Katy spotted a small white gazebo that seemed suitable for a quite intimate visit across the street. There, she and Jeremiah could finish their reconciliation without an outside audience of any kind this time. At first Jeremiah wasn't very forthcoming about his life before North Highlands as it was difficult for him to talk about because he had been scarred too, but in a much different way.

"Katy, I'm really sorry that I lied to you about so many things. But, never once did I have to pretend to love or care about you. I always tried to do what I thought was best for you, I just didn't always know how to show it the way you needed. I just didn't have any experience with children before the old man brought you and dropped you off that day. He didn't even as much bring many of your clothes much less the things you were familiar with. If it wasn't for Pastor Wynne and Nanny Mae dropping by in the beginning, I don't know what would have happened to either of us. I just hope that you have a few good memories to take with you," Jeremiah said.

"Don't worry about that anymore. I promise. I didn't bring you over here to talk about me. I wanted to talk about you, Jeremiah. I know you mentioned that you were born in Preston, but what about your parents? Where are they and what made you leave everything behind there?" Katy asked. This was the beginning of what would be many firsts, for her to actually think that someone else might have a past, too.

"Well, none of it was good except my father did teach me about horses. He was a horse trainer at this place called High Meadow Park. It was a place that bought and sold horses all over Ireland and I started working there when I was a small boy. But, my father drank a lot and while he was at it he knocked me around a lot, too. I don't know why or what made him that way because I always did just what he told me to do but it just seemed like I was never good enough. You know that's why I got so angry with Rudy about his drinking. I guess it really wasn't any of my business except I didn't want him around you like that. And my mother would just sit there and let my father beat me and never said a word. So one night rather than take another beating, I just took off. I guess I was around fifteen or so going from town to town doing odd jobs until I wound up at North Highlands." Katy figured this was about all she was going to get out of him when he suddenly changed the subject and started rambling on with stories of Katy when she was a little girl. Things she had forgotten until now. How they would ride together and laugh about the horse making her bounce up and down and the times he overheard her talking to the horses when she thought he wasn't around. He explained the real reason why he quit going into town was when he started noticing some of the woman gathering about and pointing at them. He wasn't sure if it was real or imagined that everyone knew but he wasn't willing to take the chance to have her hurt and disgraced any further.

Katy assured him that she now understood completely why he needed to protect both her and her mother and how difficult it must have been for him. Her eyes were beginning to open to the ugly truth that everyone had something to overcome. And she knew now that by hanging on to what could have been had kept her from being the person she should have been. And for this she hoped and prayed it wasn't too late. They engaged in much lighter conversation with Annie and Lily during dinner and retired to their rooms for the evening.

Jeremiah slept like he hadn't in years. The weight of so many years holding back the truth had finally fallen away. He not only felt loved and accepted for whom he really was but he now knew that everything was forgiven. He was the first one awake and downstairs waiting for the Ewing girls that were there with him because they wanted to be and that made him feel like the luckiest man in town.

When daylight streamed through their bedroom window Lily were eager to see yet another new menu but Annie had another thought on her mind so they all headed down for breakfast. As soon as Annie and Lily sat down, Annie asked, "Mama, do you know what today is?"

"Well let me think. I believe today might be Tuesday," replied Katy and Lily giggled.

"That's OK. I know you've got a lot on your mind right now. But, anyway, it's my birthday today. I'm fifteen today Mama. Isn't that great! Me, you, Lily and Jeremiah are all sitting here in this fancy place. This is my birthday breakfast, right. I mean, it couldn't be better, except if Daddy were here. I bet he's wishing me a Happy Birthday right now, wherever he is. Anyway, I'm not worried. I think he probably got busy helping somebody that day over there in New York City. You know how he is. Always helping someone and he just lost track of time and missed the ship. He's very resourceful you know. He's probably working around there somewhere waiting for The Rosewood to return. And you know even if he we able to send a letter back home to us, we weren't there to get it. You see, we've been missing too in a way. He's probably worried about us too," Annie said decisively.

Katy suddenly felt another pain of disappointment in how self-involved she had been. How could she have forgotten Annie's birthday? Then she wondered how many others she had forgotten or even when she knew, she just failed to acknowledge.

"You're right, Annie, it did slip my mind. But, I think I know just the perfect gift for a young lady on her fifteenth birthday," said Katy.

After breakfast Katy made a quiet inquiry at the front desk then turned to Annie and said, "Off we go." Annie squealed with delight with Lily right on her heels.

Jeremiah headed out to The Rosewood while the girls only had to walk two blocks into the shopping district part of the city. The sign read "Monty's Beauty Parlor." Mr. Monty washed, trimmed and curled Annie's thick long straight hair. He then pulled the curls up loosely into a perfect up do with small bobby pins that were pressed deep enough that even she had no idea how he had performed such perfection. She couldn't believe her eyes when he turned her chair around. That plain gangly looking girl that she saw in the mirror at North Highlands was gone. And in its place she was beginning to see someone special.

"Oh my goodness, you look absolutely stunning, just stunning. I know I haven't told you enough but if it hadn't been for you, I don't think I would have had the courage to make this journey. And my darling Annie, I will always be grateful for you being the kind, wonderful and generous young lady that your daddy worked so hard to raise. I'm just so sorry that I had very little to do with how you turned out." Katy said, as she was starting to finally give. She was giving back what she needed so long ago when her hands were callused from working in the stables and her hair was in braids. She was beginning to understand.

In the meantime, Jeremiah had managed to gather a little more information from the officer in charge of The Rosewood, Captain Julius. He again spoke well of Jonathan but mentioned this time that his friend Mr. Beaker was a bit of a hot head. "He was always stirring up trouble and Jonathan would intervene just before fists started flying. I wonder now if old man Beaker may have gotten in over his head over there and Jonathan may have gone down with him. Because now that I think about it, he never showed back up either" Captain Julius continued on, "Anyway, there's not much room left on this trip out, so if your friends need to travel with us they need to make arrangements quick. We'll pull out of here at nine a.m. Saturday morning and as of now we're almost booked up in our first class. The rest of the folks wanting passage on this trip will be given a number and drawn from a lottery and I believe there are only eighty of those. That just gives them a bed below deck and I'm telling you right now that it's pretty rough down there. You know I don't own The Rosewood; I just navigate it back and forth. If it were up to me I wouldn't allow the women and children below deck but rules are rules."

By the time Jeremiah got back to the hotel and they returned to purchase the tickets there was only one first class cabin left with a two person capacity. The first class tickets at one hundred fifty pounds each would have to be for Annie and Lily and the only option left for Katy was a thirty pound ticket below deck in the steerage section. She would just have to take her chances in hopes that her number would be called from the lottery drawing on Saturday morning. For most of her life she just assumed she had been the victim of bad luck always drawing the short straw. But for once she knew there was no way that they had come this far for her not to have a place on board The Rosewood. It was all or nothing. They would all go or have to stay and wait for months for another chance. She was going to stand firmly on her new found faith. They would pack their bags and be ready to board this coming Saturday morning.

***

The names, Annie Ewing and Lily Ewing had been neatly hand written on their first class tickets. They had already boarded with the rest of the first class passengers and were weaved in this new world standing on the outside deck while all the others were waving to the crowds below. Annie and Lily were still in Katy's sight while they all waited for her number to be called. Annie prayed with her whole body while Lily just crossed her fingers. The hundreds of men, women and children gathered on the dock, waiting on this last chance, had been given tickets with a number hand written on it. Some were gathered in small groups all holding on to one another with their tattered handbags and suitcases and off to the side was a group of men with only small duffle bags. The air was as still as the water and the sound of deep coughs bellowed throughout this unfortunate crowd.

With only eighty beds available it appeared that there would be way too many shattered hopes and dreams for a better life in America. However, Katy knew that she just had to be one of them. For days now she had prayed for God's mercy and grace and she just knew that even against all odds her number would be called. It had to. Then the crowd grew quiet and still. An old bearded gray haired man dressed much like Jonathan in a heavily worn white shirt and suspendered brown pants stepped on top of an old stump and began calling out random numbers from a small basket. The first number was seventy two, then one hundred sixty and the next number was two hundred forty five. The chances of an entire family boarding together were almost impossible. He called the numbers quickly as though he wanted no part in this dreaded chore. Cries from the crowd melted in with shouts of joy as one family member heard their number while others waited breathlessly. And after what seemed like an eternity Katy heard the number forty two. She was in! She waved her lucky number in the air and blew kisses to her darling girls. Things would work out after all thought Katy, Annie and Lily. Again, why else would they have gotten this far? It didn't matter that she would be separated from Annie and Lily for six weeks. How hard could it be? So far in her lifetime she was born at the North Highland Estates, lived and worked in the stables, on a farm, that horrible flat in the village, slept in gypsy wagons and a converted insane asylum. She was sure it couldn't be any worse and would be over in no time. And it was a small price to pay for all of them to be together again one day in this new country called America, that was full of opportunity, wealth, freedom and Jonathan Ewing.

Jeremiah held a small neatly wrapped package in his hands and knew he only had a few minutes in what could be their last time together. As he handed it to Katy he said, "I know I've missed a lot of your birthdays over the years, too. But I always wished nothing but happiness for you on each and every one. You know when you really love someone to the depths of your soul like I've loved your mother all these years anything is possible. I'm telling you this because I believe that's the kind of love that Jonathan has had for you since he was a young man. You know he came to see me one afternoon when you were off riding."

"He did, why?" asked Katy.

"He wanted my permission for your hand in marriage one day. He said that he knew where you came from and why you were there and none of that mattered. He knew from the minute he saw you that day when he helped you up that you were his soul tie."

"What's a soul tie?" asked Katy.

It's what I know I have had with your mother all these years. It's a forever connection that no force or hand of man can come between. I knew Lizzie was morally and legally bound to Lloyd McLaughton in the eyes of God and the law. And I swear that I've never laid one finger on her to this day. I don't ever want to do anything that will bring any more harm to her or you for that matter, because somehow I feel like we all paid for the horrible consequences of us trying to run away that night. So, only when he dies will I ask her to marry me. Until then I promise to keep a hedge of protection around her as her husband should have done. I'm a patient and God fearing man and I know our day will come. So my dear sweet, broken hearted Katy, go to the ends of the Earth if need be. Take your daughters and find your husband and know that goodness will be your tailwind. Let your faith be in seeing what you believe. So, if you see Jonathan Ewing standing on the shores across that big ocean, then go and I promise he will be there waiting. This gift is from me to you to record your journey."

Katy opened it, smiled and wept. It was a journal book and all the pages were empty. It would be her journey book and it was up to her to fill the pages with the new chapters in her life.

Jeremiah waved. And Katy promised she would write.

CHAPTER 9

The Voyage

THE NIGHT BEFORE THEIR departure Annie had carefully sewed the ruby necklace inside the waistband of her blue skirt and the ring was stitched inside the band of her white dress skirt. She just didn't want to take the chance of someone going through their things and perhaps taking off with the only remaining possessions that belonged to her Grandma Lizzie. Tonight she would wear the white blouse and skirt as she thought it would be the most appropriate outfit for dinner. She wasn't sure what to tell her companions on board about her mama. Would she dare mention that she was travelling alone with Lily or would anyone even notice. There had to be hundreds of passengers milling around on deck before they left Dublin and not a single person looked as lost as she felt. After she learned how to keep up her new hairdo that she got at Mr. Monty's she could probably pass for Lily's nanny. A very young one, but she could pass. So Lily and she decided that if anyone asked for the next several weeks she was, in fact, Lily's nanny and she was simply bringing her back home to her parents who were wealthy socialites.

The ship had yet to move an inch toward its destination and Annie was already feeling more overwhelmed than she had even been, even when she was totally alone with Lily walking late that evening toward North Highlands, not knowing where her mama was. And she was also experiencing a new and strange kind of torn feeling of guilt and entitlement at the same time standing in the middle of her first class cabin. Her daddy was somewhere all alone over there in a place she had only seen in pictures in their World Atlas while her mama was going to be sleeping and living below deck. She was sure she would be fine, just perhaps not as comfortable as her and Lily. Katy insisted that it be this way or they would have to wait months for The Rosewood's next trip. Annie didn't feel like her mama owed them this however she was grateful that her mama made the decision to put their comfort over hers and she didn't have to share space down below with total strangers for the next six weeks. And the best part of this trip would be that she would soon see her daddy. She, at least, had some kind of end date to all this. Surely she could find things to do to pass the time until they arrived in America.

It wasn't the same as their visit to Mr. Jarvis' house. There they were just guests in someone's house that owed her grandma a special favor. Here, their room was paid for by their inheritance and the tickets had their names on them. Would she be referred to as Miss Annie Ewing or Miss Ewing? She didn't care. She just knew she would feel privileged to answer to either one. And Lily had not only grown a few inches over the last few months, but she had become a great deal more secure with her surroundings. She hardly whined anymore and quit sucking her thumb at night while they were at North Highlands.

The room wasn't as big as any of the bedrooms they had slept in at North Highlands, Weatherly Place or the Jarvis'. But it was certainly larger than the one she grew up in and shared with Lily. It had a set of twin beds made of dark wood and the heavy bedspreads were a quilted sea blue. Apparently these were made to keep the passengers warm on what would be some very cold nights out at sea. There was one small bureau that she quickly stored their things in. The floor was covered in crimson red carpeting and they had one small round window that she could still clearly see the dock they had just walked on. She had no idea how fast the ship travelled and guessed it would take some time before there would be water all around them.

As they entered what would be their home at sea on the walkway up she counted four rows of windows stacked on top of each other and a large deck area on top. But once inside going through the many hallways and staircases she had completely lost her bearings and for now had no idea what floor they were on nor could she figure out just where her mama was staying. They would have plenty of time she thought to investigate all the ends and outs of their floating hotel. In the time they spent living in Highland Way she figured out where everything there was so this shouldn't be much of a challenge. The thought even occurred to Annie that if they were really clever they could probably sneak her mama in their room. What would it matter anyway? It wouldn't be stealing, after all the room was paid in full.

Lily had already curled up on the bed and passed out. This sight made Annie think for a moment that either Lily still needed her naps or this was just her way of staking her claim to the bed she wanted just like she did when they still had their cottage back at North Highlands. Either way she would let her sleep as she stood there at the window and watched the sights and sounds of Dublin and the country that she loved so much fade away. Another leg of their incredible journey was underway. There would be no way after all this that she wouldn't see her daddy again. All of this was for him and because of him.

Katy had only one small bag that contained a few articles of clothing, her book of empty pages, pencils, her hand sewn childhood blanket and her mother's wedding picture. She knew it was silly to pack the blanket but she really thought she could still smell comfort in it. Katy wanted Annie to have all the really nice clothes and she also didn't want to have to worry about someone stealing her things either.

***

Jeremiah begged Katy not to travel this way, "What point are you trying to prove? The Captain said if it were up to him he wouldn't allow you down there. So why put yourself in that kind of place if you can just wait for the next trip?" Jeremiah pleaded.

"I'm not going to make Annie wait another day, Jeremiah. Anyway, I believe I do have something to prove. Annie has been the strong one for so long and it's the least I can do after all the terrible things I put her and Lily through. Besides, it's only for a few weeks, how bad can it be?" Katy replied.

Just like Annie, Katy had the same mindset that she might be able to possibly interact back and forth with the girls on occasion but no one, not even Jeremiah, knew what was ahead.

Katy followed the steward along with dozens of others. It seemed like they walked for miles. With each hallway he opened the door with a key and then she heard it slam behind her. It was an eerie feeling and she was already beginning to wonder if she had made a bad decision. Were they all going to be locked away like some kind of prisoners? She knew they would be somewhere below deck and not invited or entitled to the first class perks, but she had no idea they would be so isolated. The men were sent in one direction while the women and children were herded another way. That gave her some comfort that the men and women would be separated since she didn't like the way some of them were looking at her during the lottery call. They had to all line up and show their ticket one at a time before they were allowed to board.

Annie and Lily had already boarded an hour before hand. She guessed that was part of the first class privilege. She had never gotten comfortable with the glares and stares that she got before in Highland Way. But at least she knew these were either because of her family's secret or later on because of the burn scar on her face. These looks from the men were a little different. They weren't looking at her face but were giving her a sinister up and down look that made her skin crawl. It suddenly occurred to her that her daughters were all alone upstairs. What was she thinking? She just prayed that God would keep them safe. And then finally the last door was opened into a dimly lit room that was just big enough to hold four rows of ten cots. She would be sharing this room with forty other women and children.

***

Lily woke up just as Annie heard a knock on the door and the steward said, "Dinner served in thirty minutes." Annie's hunger was gnawing at her by now as she let Lily sleep through lunch and most of the afternoon. She couldn't understand how Lily had always managed to escape her discomfort by sleeping through it while she had to do all the worrying by herself.

Annie washed her face and helped Lily clean up. Then she dressed in her yet-to-be-worn white layered skirt and blouse. She had saved this outfit for a special occasion and she thought now was as good as any. Mrs. Molly told her that this fabric had been shipped in from Paris as a gift by one of their returning guests, Mrs. Roberts. This was yet another story of Lizzie helping a broken life. Mrs. Roberts arrived in a deep state of depression and her husband was frantic she would one day be successful in her attempts to kill herself. Again Lizzie had such a gift of words and encouragement that Mrs. Roberts was able to leave and join her husband. Annie ran her hands up and down the skirt thinking about all the events that had to unfold for her to be standing there wearing it while feeling the bump of her grandma's ring hidden in the waistband. Lily had slipped into one of the dresses that Mrs. Molly had made with her skilled seamstress hands. Her outfit for tonight would be an ankle length dark emerald green velvet dress with long sleeves and ivory lace around the collar. Annie couldn't believe how beautiful she looked even as a child with her long auburn curls draping against the dark green fabric. She would certainly pass for a child of socialites tonight. Annie decided not to add the silver and gold bangle bracelets as her accessories because even she knew that it would not look suitable for her age.

By this time the halls were lit up and she and Lily just followed two couples in front of them to dinner. They walked down the long hallway, out a set of double doors, up two flights of stairs and out onto the deck. The moon was shining on the black sea and as far as she knew they were in the middle of nowhere. By this time she had a good hold of Lily's hand for both of their sakes. She was shivering all over and didn't know why. She just wished that her mama was there. She needed an adult. Annie was certain that she was way in over her head when they turned the corner and saw the dining room through the glass windows.

The room appeared to be the size of the spread of land that they use to have at home or at least it felt like it. It was full of round tables covered in white tablecloths with large overflowing vases of flowers as center pieces on each one. And, the seating at each was filling up with families and couples already enjoying their first night on board. She quickly counted six chairs at each table and envisioned that she and Lily would be sharing this meal with four strangers and she had no idea on what or where the conversation would be or go. Annie had been alone plenty of times in her life but this would be the first time that she would have to sit alone in a crowd such as this. The waiters made several passes to their table with entrees of roast beef, grilled mutton chops, baked chicken and pork tenderloins. They chose the roast beef along with fresh potatoes with onions and squash. In addition to the meat trays were baskets of fresh bread, unlike anything they had ever tasted along with platters of fresh fruit, chocolate, strawberry, lemon cakes and pies. The food just kept coming in an endless flow and they all ate like it was their last meal. They were seated with two couples that carried on as though the girls weren't there never once acknowledging them and they drank as much as they ate. This scene reminded Annie of the dismissive looks she had grown use to from Lord McLaughton and Samuel. And with that, Annie made a mental note to avoid this seating arrangement the next day.

***

Day 1 – Journal Entry

I was at a loss to understand how so many families made on board here together. Then as we were walking down I overheard some of the ladies mention that many of the so called "winners" simply just turned around and sold their tickets for double the price. It seems that many of the folks down here have been in Dublin working for months just to save up as much as they could for this voyage. The famine had pushed so many into the cities all over Ireland and there were ships heading out of every dock making their own journey abroad. And today they believe, as I, that we were the lucky ones. We were the chosen ones. We were the winners. There was, no doubt, that their days of hunger, sickness and poverty would soon be behind them.

It is more obvious now that we are confined together the affects that the famine has had on all the women and children down here. Many of the women have gaunt facial features with barely the strength to carry their own pathetic bodies much less carry their small children. I immediately felt out of place not because of any social standing but because I had my health as well as my two wonderful daughters sleeping somewhere just above me. My stomach was still full from the bacon, eggs and biscuits we had for breakfast this morning at the hotel. I quickly found a cot next to one of these frail women with a small child. We shared only our first names. Emily seems pleasant but nervous and somewhat beaten down by something more than hunger. Her adorable little blonde haired boy, Matthew, appears to be about three, and he would have no part of anyone but his mama. One of our allotted beds was suddenly missing and since he was so small she was told they would have to double up together. I feel bad for their discomfort but a little bit jealous that she has her child with her and I do not. We had chicken liver sandwiches for dinner and a cup of apple cider. It's really cold and damp down here and they've only given us one blanket each to cover. There are only two wash basins and buckets for toilets. I'm starting to feel sick to my stomach with waves of nausea. KE

***

Annie and Lily woke up to another knock on the door announcing that breakfast would be served in thirty minutes. They were both still so full from the mountains of food they had the night before they decided to skip breakfast.

Annie decided this morning that she needed to find her mama through the maze of hallways and stairways. The people here were rude and pushy and no one so far had made any eye contact with her. The idea that someone would think that they had a higher value in life based on how much money they had, had always irritated Annie. And her mama's wanting of that kind of life had almost finished them off. But now, here and now, it was that very same woman, her mama, that was the most valuable person to her on the ship. Because of her mama's courage they were on their way to see her daddy, whom she figured was the most valuable and honorable man in America. They got dressed and followed the same path from the night before to the outside deck.

"Pardon me, sir, how do I get below deck. I mean, how do we go downstairs to the steerage area?" Annie asked a young man in a white sailor looking suit.

"No ma'am, I'm sorry but that area is off limits. Those people are not allowed up here and only a couple of the stewards are assigned to work that area. Why would you need to go down there anyway? That's a low class bunch down there. Not a place for a young lady like you. Let me show you our library and sitting room. I believe you and your friend might find some books or a game or two to pass the time," answered the young man.

Just because they couldn't afford the first class fare they were considered low class? Suddenly she was overcome with a rage that she had never experienced and wanted to slap that highbrow young man in white across the face. But, she tempered herself down quickly and followed him grudgingly not wanting to risk a confrontation with someone that she might need later over his poor choice of words.

Once in the library, Lily quickly spread out on the same crimson red carpeted floor and engaged in checkers with a little dark haired girl. While Annie was searching through their small library a bearded middle aged man who spoke perfect English approached Annie and asked if she would be interested in a book he had yet been able to publish. "Here, might I interest you in this. And if you could give me your opinion I would greatly appreciate it". The book was titled "Moby Dick" and his request garnered her interest, so she immediately immersed herself in his unbound manuscript in her attempt to distract herself from her failed plan to find her mama. That night Annie tossed and turned as though her bed was on the open sea fighting through a terrible nightmare. Then when she awoke she remembered more of the dream that Lord McLaughton was chasing after her and Lily on board and while running away Lily fell overboard and was instantly swallowed up by a whale. With no one to share this with, it took Annie all morning to shake it off.

***

Day 5 – Journal Entry

Emily and Matthew didn't sleep very well last night and neither did I. He coughed and cried most of the night. It seemed like we rolled with every wave of the ocean all night and there is a strong smell of vomit in the air. I don't want to think about food right now. KE

***

It's been a constant up and down, back and forth to the dining room, library and their first class room all week. Annie didn't feel so first class anymore. She just wanted to be with her mama. This great adventure didn't seem so great anymore. Her nerves were shot and she was more exhausted now than she had remembered being since their life in that flat in Highland Way. She was tired of entertaining Lily and watching her every movement. There were guard rails all around but the thought of Lily getting out of her sight were not the same as if they were on dry ground. One wrong move and Lily could wind up in the Atlantic Ocean swallowed by a whale and be gone forever. She wished she had never read that stupid book and hoped she could avoid the stranger for her opinion for the rest of the voyage. They had a pond on their farm back at North Highlands that she and her daddy would spend their rare lazy afternoons fishing but this much endless water was just too much. She wasn't sleeping well at all and they still had five more weeks before dry land.

***

Day 14 – Journal Entry

We haven't seen daylight in days and no one really knows what day it is or if it's day or night. I assume its day fourteen as we have been brought fourteen sandwiches of one kind or another. We've all complained to the steward when he brings our pathetic meals but he just keeps telling us that he'll take us up tomorrow. Matthew's cough is getting worse and the other women are losing sleep as well because of it. I heard one woman say that he needs to go. What a horrible thought. Poor Emily is sick with worry and she can't get word to her husband about his condition. They were among many that were separated once boarding. I've begged the steward to get a message to Captain Julius for me and either he hasn't as yet or he isn't the kind man Jeremiah said he was. Oh how I regret the years I wasted feeling sorry for myself. KE

***

Annie decided to take matters in her own hands as she had to do so many times. She'd let go of her taking charge of things when her mama had finally awoke to her surroundings. But, three weeks of this was enough. She had to get downstairs to her mama. She had to get her out. She didn't want to be this pretend like nanny anymore. She was tired of all of it. She just wanted to rest in the arms of her mama. She had noticed a few shy weak smiles from a young steward and though she had no idea how to, flirtation was her only option.

His name tag read Daniel and Annie called out to him that morning. "Daniel, do you think that perhaps you could show us around sometimes? I've become quite bored with all this. My charge and I would like a tour," Annie said as she tried to bat her eyes.

Daniel made a quick glance up and replied, "Well, I suppose if it's ok with your folks, I don't want to get in trouble, maybe later on tonight I can show you only what I know."

"You or I don't have to answer to my folks. You see I'm here alone with this child. I'm to deliver her to her parents. They are very important people, too important for you to know. However, I'm sure they would be very pleased with your generous time and favor," answered Annie.

Rather than drag Lily along she put her to bed and dared her to move. Annie had never spoken to Lily with such force before but her mood was slowly changing. She knew her mama meant well with the layout of this voyage but it certainly wasn't working in her favor. Lily had her but who did she have? It was like old times again. She was in charge and her mama was again missing from the picture. Annie was becoming angry and resentful now and her mind was slowly starting to place tricks on her. She had started to think that her mama was probably enjoying her peace and quiet. Things were going to change tonight.

Daniel met her on the first floor deck as promised and the moon was just a quarter sized. Annie was in new territory here. She had never used her girly charms before to get her way, simply because she didn't think she had any. He had his hands stuffed in his pockets and swayed back and forth giving out what little knowledge he had of the ship all the while staring at her raven hair and fluttering eyes. He was smitten and she knew it just by the way he stuttered. Jeremiah told her that she would turn heads one day soon after her new up do. "Well, Annie you have gone and done it now. You're all grown up looking with that new hairdo, just wait and see. The first time you meet a young man that sounds tongue tied that will mean one thing only. He's got an eye for you."

"So, one of our maids settled in below deck and I really need to see her. Do you think you can take me down there for just a minute or two?" asked Annie.

"Oh, no Miss, I would have to have the keys to get down there." answered Daniel.

"Keys, what do you mean, are they locked in below?" Annie asked nervously.

"Well, yes, those folks down there aren't allowed to mingle with the upstairs guests. Captain Julius wouldn't have it. You see, they are just common folks like me which was why I'm surprised you even spoke to me at all. I could get in real trouble for even being alone with you right now," said Daniel.

And without thinking her impulse had her leaning toward him with a quick kiss on the cheek.

"I'm as common as you are, Daniel," and then

Annie felt she had no choice but to pour her soul out. She told him about their plan. How her mama had won her place below with the lottery and they used what little money they had for them to stay in first class. She was tired of taking care of Lily and wanted her mama to join them in their room.

"Annie, your mama didn't win anything. I hear it's horrible down there. They are in the belly of the ship, might as well be in the belly of a whale for the conditions down there," replied Daniel.

Annie thought why did he have to say in the belly of a whale? A horrible wave of nausea, fear and grief tumbled over Annie. She knew her mama had made great strides over the last few months. She had come a long way emotionally, mentally and even physically. But, if they were locked in or up like some kind of unwanted stowaways how would she survive? All of sudden she felt horrible for thinking her mama was down there enjoying herself. If Daniel couldn't help her, then she had to find a way to Captain Julius. He would know who they were. He knew her daddy and spoke well of him. Once he found out that Jonathan's wife was below deck living in filth and his children were wandering about up here alone, surely he could and would rescue her.

***

Day 21- Journal Entry

Matthew has gotten very weak as he can barely lift his head. We have repeatedly begged for medical attention but have been refused each time. Emily even placed her son at the steward's feet shouting that only he could save him now. And this stupid heartless man just stepped over him and said that the boy is probably just sea sick and will eventually get over it. But, his head is hot to the touch and he hasn't eaten much in days. I'm afraid he's not going to make it. Emily cries all the time and the other women have totally isolated us. They think he has the fever and I'm beginning to think so too. KE

***

For all Annie knew her mama might be dead. What would they do then? Oh God how many times must I live through this nightmare of being alone with no one to turn to? Why have you forsaken me? They were in a strange and hopeless predicament. Her mama was close by but she couldn't reach her. She couldn't see her. She couldn't talk to her. And her daddy was God knows where doing who knows what? This was all just too much. She was right back where she started months ago. Two steps forward and four steps back. Where would she start once they landed? What story would she tell and who would believe her and worst of all who would be willing to help her? She was going to find Captain Julius even if she had to bust through his door. She knew she had that much left in her. Like the time she climbed the wall at North Highlands and busted the window and climbed through. She climbed into bed with Lily that night. She had to draw her strength from someone as she prayed for God's perfect timing on her next harrowing adventure at sea.

***

Day 28 – Journal Entry

It's been four weeks and the rot and stench down here has become unbearable. I don't think Matthew is going to be with us much longer. What are we going to do if he dies? Poor Emily will probably die with him she is so distraught. They were going to America for a new life and a fresh start. They had lost everything just like we did during the famine. And they fought and scratched their way to get on this ship that will probably be their little boy's coffin. I've constantly prayed with them and for them. I've given Emily my blanket, as much of my food and drink as I could bear to do without and tried to be as hopeful and encouraging as I could. I wish I had the gift that my mother had here. She must have been some kind of saint with healing powers unknown to man. How was she able to change the lives of so many people? She was blinded by a severe beating that she couldn't remember getting. I wish I could erase my memory like that. Maybe that's how she survived. She had absolutely no memory of anything, good or bad. I would be glad for a beating right now. KE

***

Annie put on her best dress. She had only worn it a couple of times out to dinner. For the most part she had made arrangements for her and Lily to eat in their room. The loud chatter and laughter had long ago pushed them away. She and Lily were just not use to this kind of living or way of life. She much preferred her life back at North Highlands. And she hoped that this place called New York City would be a small and quiet place like Highland Way. There were way too many pubs, noise, street traffic and the like in Dublin. She just wanted to get settled with her daddy, mama and Lily somewhere on another farm. But today she was determined to find Captain Julius.

It was just after their in room breakfast when she took Lily downstairs to the play room that she had gotten comfortable in. "You find yourself something to do right here. Do not leave this room or I'm going to give it to you good when I get back. Do you understand me? And if you find yourself in any trouble make sure you ask for Daniel. He promised to look in on you for me," said Annie.

Daniel had given Annie a hand drawn map of the entire ship, as much as he knew of anyway. He had gotten his job as a steward just over a year ago. He made the trip to America with Jonathan and remembers speaking to him only once or twice. And he also remembers what a heavy weight old Mr. Beaker was but didn't want to mention it to Annie. He thought as they all did that Jonathan was either dead or in jail somewhere because of him.

Annie followed the hallways and stairs all the way up to the very top deck. She felt like this was God's perfect timing in that she didn't pass a single white uniform along the way. There was no one to stop her this time. She opened the wood and glass door and it appeared she was on top of the world. What a glorious sight to see. And then she heard a man's voice.

"Hey you, Miss, what are you doing up here. You're not supposed to be here. Come this way right now." This man dressed all in white was heading in her direction.

"I'm just on my way to see Captain Julius." And she ran up the last few steps and blew into his door just like she fell into her grandmother's room through the window.

"Captain Julius, please, please, I need your help, I'm Jonathan Ewing's daughter, Annie. My mama's down below in the steerage and I'm wondering, well I'm hoping you can help us. You see by the time she got back to buy our tickets there was only one first class room left. And because of me she didn't want to wait months before we could make the trip together. So she just got her ticket through the lottery and went below. And I thought that maybe somehow if it didn't matter or hurt anyone that we could move her up with us. What would it hurt? It's been over five weeks and I'm worried about her. Could you please help us? For the sake of my daddy, please?" Annie cried.

He stood there and stared for a moment as though he was seeing the ghost of Jonathan Ewing. He had no idea why he was moved but something inside him had to get involved. "What was your mama thinking young lady? I warned Jeremiah that traveling below was a bad idea. Come on, of course she can stay with you."

Victory at last!!!! This was it. Their trouble was finally over. They were going to rescue her mama and finish their trip all in first class. Just a few more days and they would all be together at last in this place called New York City.

***

Day 38 – Journal Entry

All the doubts that I had about making the decision

to travel below deck are gone. There was a reason for me to be here. I had silently prayed for God to use me just as he used my mother. I wanted to be a healer too. I wanted to help change the lives of the broken. But this was not at all what I bargained for. God had used me all right. But it was my purpose to sacrifice and suffer with Emily. I believe that God's reasoning was twofold. He wanted me to see suffering, true gut wrenching suffering. And he required me to be a comforter at the same time. I know now more than ever before just how truly blessed I have been for so many years with a kind and loving husband and two healthy daughters and I squandered it. And from this day forward I promise to never again take my family for granted if you just give me a second chance. KE

***

The further down they went the darker the hallways got. And then suddenly the stench hit her like a brick. The air was cold and damp and smelled like death and raw sewerage. Captain Julius knew it all too well. He rarely came this way because it was just so unfair and he knew there was little he could do to change the way life served the different social classes. It took him years to make his way out of the streets of Dublin onto this very ship. He started out as a young deck hand and gradually worked his way up. He was determined to work his way to the top and five years ago he finally did. He knew there were rules even though he disagreed internally. Why must these people be treated this way? The owner was a strict business man and profit was his bottom line. He knew he was taking a risk but he had taken plenty before and those had always paid off.

The sign read STEERAGE ROOM 6, WOMEN AND CHILDREN ONLY. Door must be kept locked at all times.

Captain Julius pulled out his keys and unlocked a horror of all horrors. There were emaciated bodies of women and children everywhere. Their skin was pale and their eyes hollowed out. Annie hadn't seen the likes of such since they had sat behind the rows of orphans at Highland Way Presbyterian Church. But at least those children were washed, clean and free.

Katy was sitting there holding on to Emily who was holding on to Matthew. His little blonde head was buried in her lap. She was stroking his hair and softly singing to him. But he could no longer hear his mother's voice. Neither could he raise his head and look at her. His eyes were closed and Matthew O'Connor would never see the other side of the ocean.

Captain Julius and Annie froze. There had been a few occasions of passengers dying on board but never a child. He knew what he needed to do, what he had to do. And he couldn't bear to think in that final moment, how he was going to pull little Matthew from his mother grasp. But for the sake of everyone on board it was a necessary evil.

Annie was overwhelmed with grief for Emily and at the same time desperate to get her mama out of that hell hole. How could they allow such poor treatment to all of these people? Even the homeless vagrants in Highland Way and Dublin didn't match the looks on the women and children's faces.

"Oh Mama, what have they done to you?" Annie cried.

"My dear sweet child, it was meant for me to be here. Emily and little Matthew needed me. Don't cry for me. I've missed you and Lily so much and I promise from this day on to be all that God intends me to be. I've wasted so many years feeling sorry for myself and cheated you, Lily and your daddy out of the time we should have had together," as Katy choked on her own words.

Captain Julius ordered the steward to escort all the women and children to the first floor deck. I want this place cleaned top to bottom and these people for the remainder of the voyage will be allowed on top deck twice a day. I don't care what anyone says. You can tell old man Victor whatever you want. This little boy's death is on my hands. And I pray to God that he will have mercy on me for I know I will surely pay for this one day.

He wrapped Matthew in his arms as Emily, Katy and Annie followed.

They located Mathew's father, Roy, in the men's quarters and at nightfall prepared his body for burial at sea. Emily was inconsolable swatting away any effort to pull her little boy from her arms. Matthew's father told her it was over, pulled him away and told the Captain, "You better do right by my boy and give him a Christian burial." Katy took her childhood comfort blanket and cocooned his little body in it while Captain Julius began the only prayer he knew, "We commit his body to the deep..." Then in a moment he was gone. Matthew's body was dropped in the dark waters of the Atlantic Ocean. And through the tears of her own heartache, Katy softly cried, "Good night and sweet dreams our darling little Matthew." And in total breathtaking and unspeakable silence they all stood there and watched until the image of the floating yellow moons and stars disappeared.

Annie had retrieved Lily from the playroom and together they held on to each other as though they were suddenly afraid one of them could be next. Annie wanted to turn the hands of time back like never before. She wanted to erase that horrible image of this innocent child being dropped in the cold water like he was waste from the ship. And Katy wanted to burn the image forever. She didn't want to ever forget. She would forge ahead from this day forward with such an undying determination that she would do whatever she had to do to make the world a better place just like Lizzie. For it was Lizzie that told Katy that her words would be an inspiration to the world one day. Several nights later in their first class cabin she wrote her last journal entry.

From the moment of our first breath until the day we breathe our last

We spend our time together trying to forget the past

They try to change us, break us and even rearrange our lives

For some of us the pain we cannot hide

To some of them we have given them their names

While others make us want to forget from where we came

Some of them steal our joy while others make us want to stay

Passengers

Some leave sweet fond memories while some scars never fade away
We've had too many tears of pain and sorrow
And for some they will not see their tomorrow
We are all passengers giving and taking along the way
Brothers and sisters in more than one way
We are all passengers from the moment we open our eyes
Bound with each other until mourners stand by our side
God gave us our choices to make whether foolish or wise
And these too are the passengers in our lives

When the sun broke through their window in the morning Katy got up and looked out and saw the beginning of her first new day and land.

PART TWO

CHAPTER 10

New York City Haystack

IF THEY COULD WALK on water they would get there sooner. For Katy, Annie and Lily it felt like they were crawling at a snail's pace. In actuality the ship had decreased its speed in order to navigate into the New York City Harbor. Annie just knew that in no time she would find her daddy. But Katy knew it was going to be difficult if not impossible. In the weeks she spent in the belly of The Rosewood she heard a myriad of stories of people travelling abroad and just disappearing. There was one mother who hadn't heard from her son since he left two years ago. And another whose husband had written about how the city was not fit for animals and she hadn't heard a word from him since. But, Captain Julius promised he would not abandon them. His ship would dock this time for a month for much needed repairs and he knew a place they could stay that would accommodate them.

Captain Julius had done a lot of living before he arrived as a young boy on what he made claim as his ship now. He had seen things that he thought human beings shouldn't be capable of. But this was one thing that he felt would haunt him for the rest of his days. Matthew's death and burial at sea had left him scarred. He knew Emily and her husband, Roy, would never be able to visit their little boy's grave. There would be no headstone with his name chiseled or a place for flowers. Sailors have been buried at sea since vessels began to travel on water. But this sweet little boy deserved a proper resting place. He should have been spared such a tragic end. He wasn't certain he wanted to captain this ship again or any other for that matter. Maybe the layover would change his perspective. What would he do if he didn't? After all, this had been his life for so many years. He came from nothing as a child of gypsies. The wandering life blood was in him but not the fortune telling and slight hand of tricks that he had witnessed all too many times. He started out as a stowaway and when discovered was put to work to earn his passage and he hadn't left the water since.

***

Annie's eyes were sore from stretching along the coastline. This was not at all what she had hoped for or envisioned. It was the worst of the worst. The buildings not only appeared to be shoved together but on top of one another as well, along with scores of people everywhere. And unlike Dublin where for the most part everyone was Irish but spoke mostly English, she knew from talk on the ship that there would be many different languages and cultures here. During their voyage she picked up one book and tried to learn a little Italian but repeating the words out loud made her sound silly and stupid. What if they couldn't understand the language? Or worse, what if no one could understand them? How would they begin to find her daddy? For the first time since she boarded, she felt safe on The Rosewood and didn't want to get off.

The youngest of the Ewing girls had made a gang of friends and didn't want to let them go. Because she had always been content to cling to her mama, Lily never had any friends and she had patiently worked hard to carve these out. She cried pitifully "Mama, will I ever see them again?" as they were packing their belongings. "I'm certain if you don't, there are plenty of children here for you to play with, I promise," answered Katy.

Out of nowhere they felt a hard shift from outside their room and knew it was over. New York City and Jonathan Ewing were waiting for them. Annie was certain that her mama would lead them through this maze. She had watched her as she knelt and prayed not only with them but for them over the last few nights and knew it was real. She knew her mama had in the worst way but for the best possible reason learned the value of life and family and how quickly things could change. And this horrible event was the cement her mama needed to never again take off the shoes that only she was meant to wear.

Captain Julius met them on the deck and together with their belongings they piled into yet another carriage ride into a crowded city. From all outward appearances The Grand Hotel was much larger than The Manship Inn in Dublin. Matter of fact everything so far appeared to be larger and dirtier. The streets were wider, the buildings were taller and most of the people were crusted in dirt from head to toe. Annie thought, "*How could this possibly be a better life?*" and knew in an instant that her daddy would not have voluntarily chosen to stay here. They had already witnessed several fist fights even dodging a few taking place in the middle of the street. But, the two young men at the door put Annie at ease when they opened the heavy glass doors and said, "Welcome to The Grand Hotel," in perfect English. However, they were all quite startled when the couple walking behind them were pushed back and told by these same greeters "Sorry, the hotel is full." Annie was convinced that it must have been the Captain's fine tailored white uniform that allowed them in and she was hopeful that this same uniform would continue to open doors for them in their hunt for her daddy.

The large open lobby was well appointed, but in a much more modern way than The Manship Inn. Here there weren't any gas wall lights for lighting but rather there were elaborate looking three tier chandeliers with hundreds of pieces of cut glass that filled the room with prisms of light. The floor was covered with white inlaid marble and there were tall lush indoor green plants the size of small trees. The oversized gold framed mirrors didn't cause or create any inadequacy in Annie's mind this time as she had weeks of young men flirting with her during their voyage. The curved, white marble staircase had several young men dressed in black caps, red jackets and white gloves, running up and down, smiling and tipping their hats at each passing guest.

"Mama, I can't wait to see what's upstairs!" said Lily, as she had become quite fond of running up and down them during their North Highland stay.

One of the young men instead motioned them into an open box fixed in the wall. It was just barely large enough for all of them to stand shoulder to shoulder. He pulled a lever that slowly closed the doors and the box moved upwards. Not one word was said until he pulled the same lever and the doors opened on a new floor. Captain Julius knew they had just moved inside a new fangled invention called an elevator but the girl's eyes were as big as saucers. They had no idea what they had just experienced but for the moment delighted in its magic movement.

They had been given two rooms side by side at the Captain's insistence. He made it quite clear at the reservation desk that he would not leave much distance between them for some time. He had hoped to care for Roy and Emily O'Connor in the same manner for a few days but they quickly disappeared into the city. He knew there was little he could do other than try to make their stay here a little more comfortable. But Roy had made it clear only an hour before they left the ship that he needn't ever forget. "You're going to pay for my boy's death one day, you'll see." And even though the Captain knew Roy was drunk, it still made him pause and look over his shoulder along the way. Katy tried to ease his lingering guilt with her words, "That poor little boy was feverish and malnourished on their very first night. I'm not sure there was anything that could have been done even if he was moved." But the Captain still felt that he should have not turned a blind eye to the ill treatment of the poor working class down below but Victor, the ship's owner, was adamant about who got what kind of service. "They're just ship rats anyway, put them and keep them down below where they belong."

They agreed to clean up, rest a while and make dinner plans later. For now, food was the last thing on Katy's mind. She clearly remembers the horrid look on Annie's face on the day of her rescue. Her hair was no longer auburn but a matted mess of black filth. And since no one was allowed to bathe or wash their clothes along with their squalid living conditions created the appearance of near death for everyone. Fortunately, she was in remarkable health when she boarded The Rosewood. Other than dark circles under her eyes and the loss of a few pounds she wasn't suffering any health issues other than the feeling that her skin was crawling. The whole area below deck was infested with mites and bugs and even though she bathed and cleansed thoroughly many times once she was moved upstairs she still felt the need to scrub down again. She found some soaps and creams in a gift basket on the table and lathered her entire body until she felt she had finally removed the last physical remains of her time below deck. And before she knew what was happening she felt her mind and body caving in together with the kind of grief she had yet allowed herself to experience. She could still clearly see Matthew's little body tightly swaddled in her own blanket, with all the hand stitched moons and stars floating for a few minutes before the ocean swallowed him up. Katy cried for not only Matthew's suffering and his parents' broken hearts but for the life he missed out on. He would never be a husband or father and she was sure he would have made a mark in this world. She hoped that his brief time here would never be forgotten.

Annie and Lily had fallen asleep and Katy was at peace. Her children were safe and sound and in her care and she would never let them out of her sight again. Her heart ached for Jonathan. He was now the man of her dreams and she was determined to find him. Just as she had gazed out her tiny window near the stable and longed for Samuel, she found herself looking out their window at The Grand Hotel into the City of New York longing for Jonathan. In just the few blocks from their departure of The Rosewood to the very spot she was standing had almost been as intense and overwhelming as her journey across the ocean. How would they begin to find her husband in this sea of lost and broken humanity?

While they were resting the Captain went downstairs and disappeared into the city. Later on that evening, he sent one of the young bell boys out for a surprise he purchased for his newly adopted family. The young man returned with three large boxes that were sent up to their room. From each box Katy pulled new, fine outfits for each one of them, with a note that read, *"Dear Mrs. Ewing, it would be an honor and privilege to escort you and your lovely daughters to dinner tonight. Kindly accept with my sincere fondness." Captain Julius.*

He was proud of the dresses he had carefully chosen at Adele's Dress Shop. The Ewing girls had pointed at and admired the dresses on the mannequins in the windows as they passed by and with the help of the sales lady had picked out a perfect fit for each one. He had feelings he had never experienced before in wanting to be not only their rescuer but their provider.

Katy couldn't remember the exact moment when she stopped being self-conscious about her scarred face. Maybe it was the gradual healing in her soul that had lifted her head high without any thought of those old second glances. Or maybe they were never there in the first place and it was all in her head. She had clearly learned all too well these past few months that life at times could rear its cruel and ugly head. But now she had a new weapon, one that had been with her the whole time. And that new strength and armor against anymore personal setbacks was given to her by her mother. She wanted to follow her mother's path in life. Lizzie, who couldn't see at all, was still able to see the best in everyone and had the ability to infuse that positive flow into the lives of so many. She was sorry for Samuel that he was neither an old or new memory for their mother. Then suddenly Katy realized something that had been lost from her thoughts. It was her brother that had started all of this with his letter and she had completely forgotten he was here along with the father that she wasn't sure she ever wanted to see. Someday she would have to forgive him if she ever wanted Samuel back in her life, but not today.

Katy woke the girls and they giggled and shrieked with their new dresses. Lily's was a dandelion yellow long dress that fell to her ankles and once again her auburn hair added the only accessory she needed. The shoulders were gathered and puffed up and the sleeves gradually tightened to her tiny wrists. There were a dozen buttons up the back covered in the same silky fabric. Annie's outfit was a two piece deep cobalt blue. The bodice fit her chest tightly but the ingenious gathers in the front gave her the mature look that her body still had not. The long skirt was full and swirled when she turned. Katy's dress was more divine than anything that they had confiscated from Lizzie's bureau. It was an ivory dress covered with lace that could have easily passed for a wedding gown which is what was apparently on Lily's mind when she spouted out, "Mama, are you and Captain Julius getting married tonight?" Lily had already made Annie angry earlier that morning as they were leaving the ship when she whispered in her ear that she thought he was handsome. Although she liked him and appreciated all the effort and the risks he took, which could possibly cost him his job, she didn't like him that much. No way would anyone take her daddy's place. Starting tomorrow, it seemed like it's always tomorrow, they would find him. After they dressed and Katy powdered her face, Annie made a couple of cuts in the waistbands of her skirts and pulled the ring and necklace out. She insisted her mama wear the ring in honor of being Jonathan's wife while she draped the ruby necklace around her neck.

The Captain lightly tapped on their door and patiently waited in the hallway to escort his brand new reason for living. He continued to envision a life with these three who, only a few days ago, he had no connection to or with, other than Jonathan's shared stories. Now he understood why Jonathan had so much passion and devotion for his family. What he didn't understand was why Jonathan would allow himself to get mixed up in anything that would keep him from returning home. He was certain that he had met with the same fate of so many others and was buried in a pauper's grave somewhere.

Katy opened their door and as Annie and Lily followed, the captain's outlook on life changed in that very instant. He wasn't sure what he had done to deserve so much happiness in that moment, but he knew that he had never before felt so complete. Katy slipped her arm into his while Annie and Lily followed into the box in the wall, the doors closed and down they went.

As they crossed the lobby Annie again noticed several sets of eyes on her and she was certain that it must be the dress along with her new hairdo that was turning heads. Or maybe it was her imagination or these new lights or the Captain's uniform because even though she felt different on the inside now, she still didn't equate that with how her looks were changing on the outside. She hoped she hadn't taken on her mama's negative self- image and made a mental note to ask Lily for her honest opinion, which was surprisingly starting to matter to her.

It wasn't the same kind of seating arrangement that she and Lily had to endure on The Rosewood. Here, Captain Julius just said a few words to a man clad in a black suit and instantly the four were escorted to their own private table. Tonight they ordered their food one at a time from a printed menu and baked fish was everyone's favorite.

When Annie closed her eyes that night, her thoughts rambled on again, from the farm to Highland Way, the North Highland Estate to the gypsy camp, Grandma Lizzie's, Dublin and finally her last thought was Moby Dick. Lily curled herself almost into a fetal position pushing her back against her mama who finally had real genuine warmth for her while Katy actually longed for the life she had long ago wanted to be rid of.

Captain Julius was awake most of the night wondering where to start looking in this big city to find an Irishman that had already absorbed thousands in the last few years. He hoped for the girl's sake that he was alive and well but for a minute thought he could be with them forever. He had missed out on being a husband and a father. All the years at sea didn't give him much opportunity to court much less marry and have a family and he was growing very fond of the Ewing girls. He found himself pretending that they were his family at dinner and as far as anyone else knew, they were. After all, Katy had a wedding ring on and they were all dining together in public. Back in Ireland a married woman would never have been seen alone in public with a man unless he was a relative and he just assumed the same social rules applied here in America. While watching Katy move with such grace across the lobby that night he just couldn't imagine her living the life as a farmer's wife or being the daughter of a stable manager. And Annie had such a quick wit and charm about her with wisdom far beyond her years it seemed to him that she could have had the same exposure to proper schooling as anyone he had come across from the first class passengers. But it was Lily that truly tugged at his old, seaman's heart. That evening when they left the dining hall, she smiled up at him then slipped her sweet, little hand into his, and without skipping a beat, proceeded to lead the way down the hall.

Before the sun rose the noise from the street below started. Annie could hear the horses clattering on the brick streets and the street vendors were already setting up. The activity they left on the streets of Dublin was much more organized than this chaotic new-found land. And, many of the voices she heard on their ride here were foreign tongues which frightened and intrigued her all at the same time. She thought about the stories she read in the Highland Way News of the travels of Lord McLaughton and Samuel and considered that they had probably fit right in. "Mama, do you think that perhaps Uncle Samuel might be able to help us find Daddy? I mean they've been here awhile now and maybe they've seen him." Annie pleaded. "I don't think so and anyway I'm not sure I'm ready to see him just yet. Besides the Captain seems to think we need to go back to the harbor and ask around there. But I need you and Lily to stay put. He said it was not a place for young girls like you to linger around," replied Katy.

"Mama, no way, you can't possibly think, well I

mean, stay with Lily, really? She exhausts me, Mama," Annie pleaded.

"I know, my darling, but just be patient a little bit longer. I promise that I'm going to do everything I can to find him. I miss him, too," answered Katy.

After breakfast Annie took Lily up the stairs this time back to their room while the Captain rented a carriage to take him and Katy back to the harbor. On the ride there it seemed to Katy that very little thought was put into the layout of things as the city was being carved out. The randomness of the buildings and streets made little sense to her. Once again she thought she would have been in way over her head if it had not been the Captain with the reins in his hands. Without him she wouldn't have known where to begin. They got out and the Captain questioned one man after another with Katy staying a few steps back. So far, no one had ever heard of a Jonathan Ewing but two of the working dock hands had a few unmentionable words for Mr. Beaker. It seemed that Jonathan's friend had a habit of making bets and not paying up. Or, he would drink too much and pick fights with someone always bigger than him and things would quickly turn into an all-out brawl.

"Well, it seems that they both just disappeared in thin air. We can take it further over a few more blocks ,but that's an even rougher area. I'd rather you not be with me," said Captain Julius.

Then it occurred to Katy that Samuel and her father had traveled many times and the Highland Way News would publish articles about where they went and who they met.

"I know, why don't I put something in the paper?

There should be a local paper that we could write some kind of, I don't know, 'Do you know this person or have you seen him' article. I can talk to the girls and I'm sure they wouldn't mind if we take my mother's last two pieces of jewelry and pawn them. They're bound to be worth a pretty penny and we can use that money to offer a reward of some kind to anyone that has any information," Katy said.

"I don't know Katy. That's a mighty big risk to take. You'd have all kinds at your door with God only knows what kind of tall tells and lies. I know how that kind of stuff works. My folks were gypsies and they were awful good at convincing people that they knew things about people when they didn't. I'm sure this city is full of cons and thieves just doing what they can to survive. Maybe you could just put a message in the paper that only he would understand and leave out the reward thing," answered Captain Julius.

It was called The Irish Settlers News and the owners who were also Irish immigrants themselves had set up shop just for the purpose of keeping the Irish folks informed of what was happening back home and amongst each other there in the city. The Irish people had not been accepted well and most struggled in the lowest paying jobs if they had one at all. The immigrants that were beginning to fill the city's landscape had come abroad by the thousands and pocketed themselves in sections all over the city. There was a settlement for the Germans, Italians, Irish and even Chinese. The owners, Mr. and Mrs. Clayton were gracious and welcomed them just as Mr. and Mrs. Toudle did back on their road to Weatherly House.

After Katy told her story, Mrs. Clayton shook her gray haired head and said, "Dear child, we've heard this story too many times to count. You can write whatever you want and we'll be happy to print it for a very small charge, but don't get your hopes up. Many a man has met his last day here. The graves are full of unknown men, women and children who died and there was no one to claim their bodies. It's just a fact of life here. It's like finding a needle in a haystack."

Upon returning to The Grand Hotel, Katy decided not to share the dock hands opinions of Mr. Beaker or pessimism of Mrs. Clayton. Instead she told Annie that she found a newspaper that had some success in connecting people to one another.

That night, Katy, Annie and Lily spelled out how they wanted it to read without sounding desperate and for the first time while writing the letter, Annie felt a connection starting to forge again with her daddy that she hadn't experienced in almost nine months.

Dear Jonathan,

I arrived here in New York City a few days ago and have not been able to get in touch with you. I visited the last address I had for you and your neighbors weren't aware that you had moved so suddenly. Funny thing is they just thought you had gone back home to North Highlands for a visit and would be returning soon. I traveled over on The Rosewood with my friends Annie and Lily. We would love to see you. We are presently staying at The Grand Hotel and if we should relocate before you make contact I will be sure to leave a forwarding address. I have so much to tell you and miss you terribly.

Sincerely, Katy Ewing

CHAPTER 11

The Irish Settlers News

THE IRISH COMMUNITY that surrounded the newspaper was massive. It seemed that the onslaught of Irish immigrants into the city of New York was in the thousands and growing every day. Katy and Annie had yet to see anyone they recognized but the faces and sounds of their voices were bringing some comfort to the Ewing girls. Annie desperately missed the wide open space that she grew up on and the people here were much rougher around the edges. Most of the newcomers had arrived with their meager belongings after many had travelled much the same as Katy had in the underbelly of the ships. So, for the most part, the arrivals had shifted into survival mode and it had become essentially, every man for himself. Lily was overwhelmed with the new city and had little interest to find or make new friends and was beginning to tug and hang on Katy or Annie again for her emotional support.

Before the ink was dry on their so called "search and locate" article, Annie was confident that her daddy would see the small personal article right away. She was so confident that she felt a sense of urgency for her mama to purchase their tickets for their return home. She knew her daddy loved to read and reading The Highland Way News back home was part of his daily ritual and that any day he would read their notice and appear at the newspaper building or be waiting for them at the hotel. However, Katy had the sense all along that something was and had been holding her husband here and any premature thought of going back to Ireland would be unrealistic. She was standing there on their wedding day hearing the words "for better or worse, till death do you part" and even though she had not, for one day, followed those vows she knew Jonathan had and the likelihood that he was still alive was growing dimmer for her every day. She had just started to gain Annie and Lily's trust and forgiveness and she wondered if she would ever get the chance to earn Jonathan's. And even though she knew God had already forgiven her, she didn't know yet how to forgive herself.

They all needed some kind of normalcy in their strange new environment so they set themselves into a routine with the Captain reporting back to the ship to oversee the repairs every day while the Ewing girls headed to The Irish Settlers News building. Mr. and Mrs. Clayton were quickly becoming their extended family as they waited for any news of Jonathan's whereabouts. Annie knew it wasn't polite or proper to ask but she guessed that their new friends were probably old enough to be her grandparents. Mr. Clayton's long lean body was topped with a grin and balding head while Mrs. Clayton had to stand on her tiptoes just to peck his cheek with a kiss. Annie felt a sense of warmth and connection between the two that she had longed for between her own parents every time they finished one another's sentence. And they shall become one. That's what marriage was supposed to be. Maybe this was yet another chapter in their journey. She now knew that her mama didn't have the same upbringing as her daddy and her heart was never prepared for what marriage should or could be. Maybe this long separation between her parents was God's way of pulling her mama out of her darkness towards the light of day. And perhaps their time here with the Claytons would show her mama how to be the wife her daddy deserved. She had certainly proved herself as their mama since they left Ireland and maybe this was the last leg of her learning curve. At least she hoped so, why else would they be here? She knew there was no such thing as coincidences in life and there was a reason that things were falling into place such as they were.

The Clayton's lived in one of the duplex apartments over the newspaper where they had eaten lunch every day for the last two weeks. It was a sparse but clean two bedroom apartment that only had a few personal furnishings of photographs and books. Annie noticed a framed photograph of a young man that appeared to be not much older than her and in a moment of both curiosity and genuine interest asked, "Mrs. Clayton who is that photograph of?"

"That's our son Robert," answered Mrs. Clayton.

"Where is he now?" Annie continued to dig.

The Clayton's had travelled over several years earlier before the famine tore Ireland apart searching for their son. Robert Clayton was a deck hand on a much smaller supply vessel that was part of a growing import trade into America. And much like Jonathan he left the shores of Ireland and never returned. So not wanting to send Annie into a state of hopelessness, she glanced over to Mr. Clayton and he answered for both of them, "He's working out of the city right now. And just as soon as he gets back we'll be sure to introduce you. I'm sure he'd be glad to meet all of you one day." And Mrs. Clayton was sure that he would be proud that they had a hand in helping another family find a lost one much like they had done since they arrived. This was not the first time they had placed an article in the newspaper for a missing loved one but this was the first time they had opened their doors and invited the waiting in. There was something different about this little family that Mr. and Mrs. Clayton just wanted to stay with. Maybe it was their hope or maybe it was their bold faith. The Clayton's just knew that they wanted to be a part of their journey. If for no other reason but to help them to move on from their heartache of not knowing what happened to their beloved son, Robert.

Katy, Annie and Lily became such fixtures at the newspaper that they put themselves to work doing anything they could to pass the time. Mr. Clayton patiently took the time to show Annie how to typeset and roll the ink over the letters to form the pages for the paper while Lily was in charge of counting and handing out bundles of papers to the neighborhood paper boys. Katy grew to trust Mrs. Clayton so much with her deepest thoughts that she shared her journal of filled pages of their tumultuous and heart-breaking voyage. Mrs. Clayton was so impressed with Katy's writings that she handed her the reins of writing a small advice column for women. Ironically in this column she would print recipes from Mrs. Clayton, advice on child rearing which she learned from watching Jonathan and cleaning tips from Annie. Other than their recent voyage she had no real sense of sacrifice or words of wisdom or so she thought. But, after Mrs. Clayton's urging she began her own personal column. In addition to "Katy's Household Hands," she added another column that was truly hers called "Words of Hope for the Day" by Katy Ewing. This would be her calling. To offer hope to the hopeless and impassioned pleas to the faint of heart that God was and still is the way through all suffering. She knew first hand that only through suffering did we find our true strength and compassion for others just as Jonathan had suffered a loveless marriage and Lizzie had suffered a brutal beating. She too had suffered the loss of knowing her true past but, she would never again, not forget to appreciate and feel blessed with her "now."

Captain Julius had not received any notice to resign from the incident, but he still wasn't sure if wanted to go back to his life as Captain of The Rosewood. As hard as he tried to push back, his heart was growing more and more attached to Katy. He knew that not only Katy's heart would have to be broken in two for him to become her husband, but Annie and Lily's as well. Jonathan would have to be dead and what a horrible way to find the woman of his dreams. He took some comfort that, at least for now, their time together was innocent enough. He was their guardian and caretaker and this temporary self-appointment was more fulfilling than any day or night at the helm of The Rosewood had ever been. He didn't have to share his thoughts with Mr. Clayton as he saw it in his eyes just as Jeremiah had seen that faraway look in Katy's.

"Look Captain, you're doing right by looking after the girls here. But, are you willing to give up your life as Captain of The Rosewood?" asked Mr. Clayton.

"I would go from here to Ireland and back again a thousand times just to be in their company. All I ever wanted or thought I wanted was to be in charge of guiding The Rosewood wherever it needed to go. But I've never felt as alive and necessary as I have being with Katy and the girls. You know I never had a real family to speak of and I do feel a bit guilty of wanting after someone else's. But, I'd be willing to take that chance. You know, just in case, he's dead. I met Jonathan and I'm telling you that something bad must've happened to him or he'd have been back home a long time ago. There's no way he would have abandoned his family. There was just too much of them in him. All he wanted was to make a better life for his family and if he can't, then, God willing, I will."

It didn't help the Captain as he tried to mask

his feelings when one evening at dinner, Lily asked "Captain Julius, what's your real name?"

"Everyone just calls me Captain, why?" he answered.

"No, I mean, what is your birth name. Like my name is Lily Ewing, what is your daddy's last name?" Lily asked with her head turned sideways.

"Julius, just Julius," was all he could say as he turned himself inward.

"Ok, then, can I call you Uncle J?" Lily asked with a turned up smile.

"Of course you can," answered the Captain. He was more than happy to go along with her new endearing name for him. Katy just smiled and was glad that Lily felt safe and comfortable enough to engage with him in that way. But, Annie, on the other hand, was not thrilled with the idea which clearly showed in her face when she clinched her jaw in instant disapproval. Annie certainly did not have feelings for him in that way and wasn't sure that she ever wanted to. But, she had to admit to herself that she was thankful for his presence in a city that seemed to swallow up the innocence of every new arrival. She found herself becoming a bit hard hearted toward the beggars that camped out around the newspaper building holding out their hands as if she had something to offer.

"Why don't they get a job or something? Don't they have any pride at all? I mean on our worse day we didn't hang around waiting for handouts from total strangers!" Annie said in a fit to Katy one morning as they walked from the hotel to the newspaper.

"Annie how could you?" admonished Katy. "Have you already forgotten all the strangers that helped us find our way over here? And what about before we ever left? As bad as we all felt toward Mrs. Beaker at times, even she fed us when I did nothing but sit around and feel sorry for myself. If you want to be angry with someone for not helping themselves, then be angry with me for all of this."

Annie felt an instant pain of remorse and shame. "I know Mama, I'm sorry but it's just that we're going about our lives like this is all there is to do. Isn't there more that we can do to find Daddy besides helping to run a newspaper? It's been over a month now and we've not heard a word."

"Well, if you haven't notice, my advice column does read, "Words of Hope for the Day" by Katy Ewing. My name is in the paper every week. If he's somewhere around in the city I believe that he'll eventually see it or someone who knows him will. All I know is that for now we are staying put. This is the last place that we know your daddy was and I'm standing on that for now," Katy answered firmly.

"I know, but it just seems like there should be more that I could do. I need to do more than just sit and wait for him to maybe show up one day. I want to go out there and look for myself," answered Annie.

She had no idea where to begin and who would be willing to help her. Over the last few weeks Annie found herself pulling away from the Captain and it didn't help that Lily was calling him Uncle J. He wasn't related to them in any shape or form and even though she knew Lily was just trying to create her own little make believe family unit, she did not. Everything in her mind had just turned into the ugliest family tree that she just wanted to shake every rotten limb free. She had lost all interest in meeting or engaging with her real uncle much less take on a pretend like one. Even her own mama hadn't made any attempt to contact him or her grandfather, the great "Lord Byron McLaughton." And yet she wanted her to stand still for Lily calling this stranger Uncle J.

Even though Mr. and Mrs. Clayton had offered the empty duplex across the hall many times they were still staying at The Grand Hotel. And everyone there had become familiar and she was certain one of the young bellboys would be willing to be her guide. After all, she had used her charm once before on the ship to get help from that young steward. Even though he didn't make the first move, Daniel had been her first kiss. She had never told anyone and was sure she never would. It was a daring move but one that did pay off. Did she want to use herself again in that way? It did seem wrong to behave so unladylike. She knew her daddy wouldn't approve, so she decided to try mending fences with Captain Julius.

That night at dinner Annie asked, "Captain, if you have time do you think we can travel around the city some?"

"Well, I think most of the repairs on the ship are just about finished. What did you have in mind?" The Captain asked with some glimmer of hope for a much needed connection here.

"Does that mean you'll be leaving soon?" Suddenly Annie was horrified at the thought that their friend, companion and safety net might soon be gone.

"I'm not sure yet Annie. You know I just want to be where I can do the most good now. I've been doing some growing up since I got here. You know it's never too late to swallow your pride and admit when you're wrong. And I've been wrong in what I thought was most important. I always thought that this uniform made me the man I am. But, it's really the man that makes the uniform. In other words, I wasn't a very good Captain. I turned a blind eye to the way people who didn't have much money were treated and for that, a little boy died. And that will haunt me for the rest of my life. So, just tell me what you need and I'll do whatever I can to help," he answered.

Annie knew in an instant she had been put in her place. She was the one that had become so prideful and closed minded. She had been so busy trying to keep her guard up by not allowing this kind man in her life, she had become blind to his generosity and steadfast commitment. She was trying to push away the person that not only rescued and reunited her with her mama, but quite possibly saved the lives of so many that left below would have surely met with the same fate as Matthew. She had been keeping score for so long over all the wrongs and ill treatment she received she had forgotten the thing she most admired in her daddy, to admit when she was wrong. She could no longer use the excuse that she was just a child and didn't know any better. For when you feel the nudge of conviction, you've crossed over from the innocence of childhood to the accountability of adulthood. And reluctantly she felt it and knew it. She was coming into adulthood and God had given her, her own personal cross to bear. And it was up to her to carry it for however far or long she needed to. As the last verse that Jonathan left with Annie replayed in her head, she felt her wings begin to unfold.

“Uncle J, I need your help,” Annie finally said.

It was as though his own words of truth had rewarded him instantly. For it was not the uniform on the man that just opened this door, but the man in the uniform. This was his opportunity to spend more time with Annie and show his genuine good intentions. He would rent a small carriage, pack some sandwiches from the hotel restaurant and spend the entire day going up and down every street they could safely travel. He would also bring his revolver, just in case.

CHAPTER 12

Matthew's House

THE CAPTAIN DRESSED down that morning as much as possible because he didn't want the vagrants to direct any of their misplaced anger toward him or Annie. He actually had to borrow some work clothes from Mr. Clayton that were a little snug. Annie had reached a point of complete and total frustration that they had travelled thousands of miles to find her daddy and waiting for news to come to them was no longer an option. After all her Grandma Lizzie had lost her memory from a beating and who's to say that the same thing hadn't happened to her daddy. He could perhaps be living and working only a few blocks away possibly mentally imprisoned having to perform some menial job not knowing he had a family desperately looking for him. Katy was a bit apprehensive about Annie leaving the Irish settlement neighborhood for some fruitless search but the Captain assured her that he would not take any chances with their safety. After all, for the most part, the people they would be talking to were mostly working class immigrants that shared the same hard times as they had all come from.

The deeper they traveled into the crammed tenement neighborhoods the more the air reminded Annie of where her mama lived on the ship for weeks. Here they had entered into the same atmosphere, more or less, except, while these people did see the light of day, there was no light at the end of the tunnel for a better life. Annie had seen the same fatal look in their eyes too many times in her short life. She remembered the words of old Pastor Feil that morning when he blamed the famine in Ireland on the sins of their fathers and wondered if those sins had followed them all the way across the Atlantic Ocean. This just didn't seem fair. She knew she didn't yet understand the connection between parents and their children but she knew full well how much she loved her daddy and mama. Her young maturing mind had to believe that all their motives for coming here had been pure and genuine. They all just wanted a better life for their children and here they appeared worse off than before. If they had all stayed home at least things would be familiar. There was a chance things could go back to the way they were before. There were wide open landscapes of hills and valleys with green grass, trees, lakes, rivers and streams everywhere. All she could see around her now were gray board buildings with rags of clothing hanging in the air, and filthy children running about the sewer covered streets and alleyways.

"Captain stop! Please, please stop right here!" Annie yelled.

She wasn't sure if she was seeing things or if she had just experienced some sort of strange wide awake nightmare. A little blond-haired boy had just flashed before her eyes, circled back around and disappeared into a nearby alley. She knew Matthew was gone. She was there when his lifeless body was slowly pushed overboard into the ocean that night. But she knew instantly that she had to find this child. She jumped out of the carriage with the Captain right behind her. At the end of the alley hidden in the garbage was the same sort of small frail body of a little boy. But this one still had a heartbeat. This one still had a chance. His name was Nicholas. That's all he knew. "My name is Nicholas and my daddy is in prison and my mama is dead."

"So where do you live? "Annie asked.

"Anywhere and everywhere, I do ok, my daddy will be out soon and we're gonna go down south. Maybe Virginia, you got anything to eat?" Nicholas asked as though that was his normal first and only question. He didn't care who Annie or the Captain was or even what they wanted.

Annie ran back to the carriage and grabbed the lunch basket. She pulled out one of the sandwiches and before their eyes children came running with their hands out to just have a crumb. It was as though they were suddenly encased in a pack of wild hungry dogs. They broke the sandwiches into as many parts and pieces as they could just to give each child a bite. These were not like the orphans that sat on the front rows at Highland Way Presbyterian Church with a bed to sleep in, clean clothes and at least one good meal a day. These children were all obviously living on the streets and the youngest of the bunch appeared to be no more than three or four years old. What kind of society was this that allowed children to fend for themselves? Where were their parents? There was no famine here to have killed them all off. Was this a famine of a different kind? How could the people of this city be so indifferent to the needs of the weakest and most vulnerable? She didn't think it was possible for her heart to hurt more than it did the night they buried Matthew at sea. This is not how human beings are supposed to live no matter what kind of catastrophe envelopes the world, whether it's man made or not. Annie knew right then she had to do something.

Annie and the Captain had to leave. It was getting late and even he knew they needed to find their way out of this part of the city before dark. As they drove away, Annie promised the children she would be back with more food tomorrow. And with this promise she had no idea just how many times she would be returning.

They rode back to The Grand Hotel in total silence. The Captain thought he had come from nothing as a child. This was beyond less than nothing. These children were living in a black hole of sorts that they climbed in and out of just to grab hold of whatever they could to survive. He could see the wheels turning in Annie's head on the way home. And whatever her plan was, he knew he was in. His career as Captain of The Rosewood was over, this would be his retribution.

Annie had a plan alright and she couldn't wait to share it with everyone that night at dinner. Her mind reeled within her new sense of seeing, for the first time, the kindness of all the strangers that had helped them along their way to where they were right now. It was kind old Pastor Wynne that literally prayed himself to death for the souls of his flock and Jeremiah who had raised her mama even though there was no relation there. There was also Grandma Lizzie, Mr. and Mrs. Toudle, Mrs. Molly, Jarvis Williams, Captain Julius and now Mr. and Mrs. Clayton. God had placed all these people in their lives at just the perfect appointed time. However, her daddy was still the missing piece of their family but at least they were all together in the same city. She knew it as she could feel it in her bones. He was here somewhere. And it was his spirit in her that reminded her that she needed to give again. Remember, to give what you need and one day it will come back to you. This was it. If she gave to these children somehow, someway, she would find her daddy.

During their dinner together that night at the hotel Annie made her plea, "Mama, it was awful, just awful, those poor children have no one. And I think it's our calling or my calling to help them. I think we should accept Mrs. Clayton's offer to move upstairs in that vacant apartment. We can't keep living off of the Captain. We can earn our keep there and Lily would be right upstairs while you and I work. You know we still have those pieces of jewelry from Grandma Lizzie. I don't care to own or ever wear anything like that. You said they were our inheritance. Shouldn't we be able to do what we want with them? They would just remind me of Lord McLaughton anyway. Lily, would you care? I want to sell them and use the money to pay our way and help the children. We can buy sandwiches or biscuits from the hotel kitchen and the Captain and I can feed them. I mean, Captain, would you go back with me again? They have no one else, Mama. They all looked like Matthew," Annie pleaded.

"You can sell the jewelry, Annie. I want to help, too. And I can be their friend. If their parents don't think they matter, then I will." Lily chimed in.

Katy didn't know if she wanted to laugh or cry. It was Jonathan's voice. She was looking at her daughter but all she heard was Jonathan's words, his plea for justice for those that been treated unjustly. There was no way she could deny what they would do next.

***

It was closing in on almost a year ago since the Captain had met Jonathan Ewing for the first time and now this stranger's family had become soaked into his soul in a way that being the Captain of The Rosewood never could. They weren't just talking the talk. Katy, Annie and Lily were all in ready to walk the walk. He had come across hundreds of deck hands in his life and this one man would forever change his life. He had no idea if Katy would ever be his wife, but his passion for helping humanity was suddenly on fire. And there was no risk. This was an absolute. The only risk would be if he didn't get on board. Because, for him this was no longer a need as one needs food or water but it was the new air he needed to breathe just to be worthy of the rich life God gave him. When he returned to his room that night he wrote his letter of resignation as Captain of The Rosewood. The next morning he delivered it to his First Mate, cleaned out his room and walked off the ship free from the shackles of his wandering life. He now knew that his real purpose was not in standing still on a moving ship but it was to move forward on still ground. And he had a lot of ground to cover if he wanted to be a part of this new family and country.

They didn't have to go far to sell the diamond ring and ruby necklace. When mentioned to the desk clerk that he would be paid a small fee he quickly found a willing buyer right there in the hotel. It was a wealthy tobacco farmer and his wife on a return trip that had admired the jewels on Katy and Annie that first night they wore them in the dining room. In all they ended up with two thousand dollars, which astonished them that they had so much value. It really didn't matter what they got for them in the end, they were just glad to finally be rid of them.

Over the next few days Annie and the Captain made their rounds back and forth to the same neighborhood bringing the children as many biscuits filled with meat and jam as they could. The kitchen staff at the hotel would only agree to bake four dozen biscuits each morning as they had their other guests to accommodate. Annie knew they needed a kitchen of their own and tomorrow would not be soon enough. So Katy, Annie, Lily and the Captain delighted the

Clayton's when they moved their belongings and set up house at the newspaper building. There was a small room in the back on the first floor that Mr. Clayton quickly offered to the Captain which made him happy just to be under the same roof. It wasn't nearly as spacious or comfortably appointed as the cabin he had lived in but he had a warm bed and the location was perfect, Katy and the girls would be right upstairs.

The kitchen was small and the living area was even tighter but they seemed as happy as they had ever been for they all had something to do, that would truly make a difference. Katy worked on the paper every day writing her two columns, although she knew it would mainly be read by the more privileged section of society. She was beginning to realize that the working class barely had enough money to survive, much less buy a newspaper, but she hoped she would have some kind of impact on those of means to reach out and help the less fortunate. When Mrs. Clayton encouraged Katy to write an article on the Captain and Annie's work feeding the orphaned children in the city, it did. Money and donations poured in from everywhere like manna from Heaven. And deep inside Katy knew that Jonathan's hand was somewhere in all this. He was, after all, the reason they were here. The biscuits that Annie and Lily got up early to make, suddenly became sandwiches already put together and donated by a handful of restaurants in the better part of town. It just became a matter of Annie, Lily and the Captain picking them up and distributing them to the children living in the same area where they had first met Nicholas. After a few weeks, clothing was starting to be dropped off for the children as well. Katy had placed the money she received in an account and before she knew it there was over six hundred dollars in addition to their proceeds from the sale of the jewelry which they barely had to touch.

Annie and the Captain felt that they still had to do more than just fill the children's bellies. They were sleeping in the alleys and abandoned buildings with no supervision, emotional support, or protection from the weather. Annie could barely close her eyes at night without worry that the next day would bring news of one of them being beaten, kidnapped or killed. They had to get the children off the streets and sheltered somewhere. So Annie and the Captain started looking for any kind of building that was the least bit habitable so they could have a safe place to lay their heads at night. That's what it was all about for the two of them now. They couldn't save Matthew from his death and burial at sea but together they could perhaps save some of these children from an almost certain premature death from life on the streets and the finality of an unmarked grave.

On one of their morning outings, the Captain spotted what he thought would be the perfect place. He had very few fond memories as a child, but one of them was climbing trees. And as a child of gypsies he learned very early to disappear and became quite efficient at scaling even the tallest ones. It was a small abandoned warehouse that needed a lot of work but it had two large oak trees on the side that would make for the perfect playground. When they met with the owner, the Captain and Annie felt as though they were standing there revisiting the worst part of The

Rosewood. For the inside of this abandoned building looked much like the rough underbelly of the ship that the little blond haired boy named Matthew had died in. This building would come to save children, hundreds of them. They paid three months rent in advance and for the first time in a very long time Annie wasn't thinking about finding her daddy.

Annie returned to The Grand Hotel and didn't use her charm but rather pleaded with the bell boys to help with the cleanup while offering a few dollars for their time. The Captain returned to the docks where he was still well respected and gathered a few heavy hands and backs for hauling away trash and erecting a few walls.

Katy wrote an extensive article about their new charity work and again the donations began to pour in. Brinkman's Furniture Store donated forty beds along with a couple dozen small dressers. From the money that was donated, Katy purchased from the same store ten tables and forty chairs so that many of these children would have their first real sit down meal. One of the factory owners donated enough towels, sheets and blankets to accommodate all the new expected occupants and a local soap factory made sure they would be the cleanest children in the entire city by donating enough soap to last an entire year. Annie felt so overwhelmed with the city's outpouring of generosity she felt guilty from her earlier thoughts of how indifferent she thought the people here were. Maybe all their parents were really dead. And maybe she and the Captain were truly the first to realize just how skillful these children had become in hiding in plain sight. Whatever the reason for it all, she thanked

God every night for this miracle that was unfolding right before her eyes. In a matter of two months they had accomplished the unthinkable. It would be the first privately run orphanage in the City of New York.

It was a Grand Opening like no other. People from every walk of life, young and old, rich and poor showed up. Annie, Lily, Katy and Mrs. Clayton scrubbed and bathed sixteen little girls and dressed them in their donated dresses and shoes while the Captain and Mr. Clayton wrestled with twenty four little boys that rarely if ever had a bath or wanted one. The Captain said after that morning "I've sailed the oceans since I was a young boy and have never been wetter than I was today."

They gathered all the children outside while giving the Mayor a few moments in the spotlight. It was not something Annie wanted to share with any politician but knew that they might need a political favor or two later on.

"Ladies and Gentlemen it is with great honor that I have been asked to speak here today. Let me just take a few moments to share my feelings on this great endeavor by these fine folks. All our children are valuable citizens and I want all of you to know that I will work as hard as necessary to make sure this place succeeds."

Annie couldn't take another puffed up word about his feelings and what he promised. Without anyone looking she pulled the large white sheet covering the front door that abruptly ended his long winded speech.

And the sign over the door appropriately spelled out in large letters, "MATTHEW'S HOUSE." Annie knew she couldn't retrieve his body from the ocean or bring him back, but Matthew's short life would come to matter and his death would bring the cause for breathing new life and hope back into the world. And planted on both sides of the steps to this new home were dwarf yellow verbascum, snapdragons and forget-me-knots that broke ground just in time from the seeds that Annie carried over in her pocket.

CHAPTER 13

Prisoner #1225

NICHOLAS HAD BECOME quite fond of Annie and she hadn't been able to let him out of her sight. The Captain and Annie had started taking turns rotating the day and night shifts at Matthew's House while looking for dedicated volunteers to staff the house twenty four hours a day. Their long term goal was falling into place making it a full-time home for the children instead of a place to just serve meals and sleep. She had worried about them so much and felt some relief that for now their trials and tribulations of living on the streets were coming to an end. For the most part many of them had been on their own for years and really had no sense of right or wrong. If they stole something it was purely for survival sake and that was one thing that some of the children couldn't let go of. So it really broke Annie's heart when she found food stashed under Nicholas' bed.

"Nicholas, you don't have to steal food, or anything else for that matter, anymore. I promise we are here to make sure all of you have three good meals a day along with anything else you might need. There's enough food here for everyone," Annie said.

He looked up at Annie with his little blue eyes filled with tears and mumbled "Miss Annie, I'm real sorry, please don't be mad. But it's not for me."

"Well then who's it for?" asked Annie.

"It's for Daisy," answered Nicholas.

"Honey, who is Daisy, I know all our girls here and I know no one named Daisy?" asked Annie.

"She's not here yet, she's still out there," as Nicholas pointed toward the front door.

"Well you take me to her right now!" Annie exclaimed.

Nicholas took her hand and out the door they went. After several blocks he pulled her down the very same alley she discovered him in. There was a makeshift bed made of straw with a small tent covering of a discarded soiled gray wool blanket. This had been his home, their home for as long as he could remember. It was their special place in this cold, cruel, world. And she was his friend that he needed to come back for. That he had to come back for, because she had been abandoned, too. She had been thrown out just as he had. She had that same look as all the rest of the unwanted.

Annie stood with her hands now on her hip like the mother she had become and said "Where, where is she, Nicholas there's no one here?"

"Yes ma'am, right over there. She found me awhile back and you know, we've just been sticking together ever since. I can't leave her now. She was really all the family I had out here," Nicholas pleaded as he pointed to the tent and inside was a shaggy, brown haired, four legged mutt that already knew how to hold an audience by sitting straight up.

Annie had always wanted a dog but Lord McLaughton wouldn't allow half breeds on, near or around the estate, so it was an easy yes for her.

"Oh, for goodness sake, pick her up and come on. She'll need a good bath first though. And she cannot sleep in the house. We'll get Uncle J to make her a nice dog house but she's going to be your responsibility to take care of," answered Annie.

Lily had on the other hand made plenty of friends just like her mama had promised when they left The Rosewood. At Matthew's House she had not only made an abundant amount of friends but she had also become quite a leader and extraordinary teacher in her own way. Not only was she a talented pianist but she could read far beyond most well educated adults. And it was this gift that she used to teach the children how to read and write.

"No reason for them not to be brought up right and proper," said Lily in a surprisingly grown up and maternal voice. She would gather the children around her after dinner and read aloud from "The Swiss

Family Robinson" and the newly published "Moby Dick" which Annie could still barely stand to hear. But Lily especially enjoyed reading from the Book of Genesis and Exodus. The building of Noah's Ark and the parting of the Red Sea were probably her favorites. How fitting that these children were circled around her, soaking up two of the best stories of faith, hope and trust.

They were very thankful that the first warm days of May had finally arrived and they had not lost a single child to the bitter winter cold. The Captain had long since collected his final check and emptied his cabin of all his belongings. New York City was his home now and he was investing himself emotionally, physically and financially. With no family to spend it on he was surprised to see that he had saved quite a sum of money over the years. It had been his intention all along to buy a place back home in some quaint village in Ireland once he was no longer capable of being Captain of The Rosewood. He thought how remarkably his dreams and priorities had changed. Never in a million years would he have imagined himself sitting here in this warehouse turned children's sanctuary waiting for the rain to stop so he could go outside and finish the play yard he hoped to have finished soon. It was going to be his special gift, to have a safe place for the children to play. They all called him Uncle J, following the nickname that Lily had started months ago. It didn't bother Annie at all anymore, matter of fact she would direct the children to go find Uncle J when they had a question she couldn't answer or needed help with a problem she couldn't solve.

They all had become well known in the city as well.

The Mayor had even taken the time, albeit for his own personal political gain, to visit Matthew's House quite regularly. On the morning of the dedication, during his speech that Annie interrupted, he had talked about how important it was to help the less fortunate, then had his photo taken and left without any mention of what the city could or would offer to help. But, Annie was certain that things would work out just like they always had since they left her childhood home. As she looked back it always seemed that when they were in the midst of a storm the calm afterwards made things clearer and brighter than she ever thought possible.

With all the commotion of setting up living quarters for the children and the fanfare of the formal dedication, Annie had almost forgotten the need to locate the children's parents, if they had any. Nicholas would be the first on her list. She knew how badly she missed her daddy and if there was anything she could do to bring this father and son back together she had to see it through. Unfortunately that meant visiting the dozen or so prisons in the city. More than likely he had probably been jailed for some petty crime. She knew that people were picked up every day and hauled away just for being a nuisance. It was cheap labor for the city and unless you had family that had the money to bail you out, men and women could spend years laboring in the fields outside the city while being locked up in the city's jail cells at night.

"Uncle J, do you think you can still fit in that fine white uniform?" asked Annie when he walked her to the carriage. It was his night to stay and she thought this would give him time to sleep on her new mission.

“I don’t know, I suppose, what’s the occasion?” asked the Captain.

“Well, I was thinking that we might possibly have a better chance of getting in the prisons with Nicholas to find his daddy if you looked real important and all. You know that magic suit of yours has opened doors for us before,” Annie replied.

“Well I suppose it’s worth a try, but do you even know his name?” asked the Captain.

“He just said his name was Nick, like his, but they moved around a lot, changing their last name from one place to another. The last name he remembers using is Smith. I’m sure he’s no stranger to the law. He said he got arrested for pick pocketing so he just ran off and hid and that was the last time he saw him,” answered Annie.

“You’ve always got some kind of plan going on in that head of yours. Just go ahead and count me in because even if I tell you it’s a bad idea you’ll just find another way. I just hope this one doesn’t backfire on us. Anyway it looks like we have some volunteers coming next week. The article that your mama wrote of the Mayor’s visit turned out to be a good thing. Some men and women from a mission church want to give us a hand. They said we were doing God’s work here and wanted to be a part of it. So let’s plan on heading out next week,” the Captain replied.

He called on the Mayor and got the information they needed about the prisons and where they were located throughout the city so they could set their plan in place. They would schedule their time to visit three a day if they were allowed in and within four days perhaps they will have located Nick. Depending on his mental and physical state, his criminal record and the money that it would take to bail him out, the hope was that Nicholas and Nick would be reunited by the end of the week. Surely, he would recognize his father or Nick would recognize his own son and hopefully he would want to start fresh somewhere with his son, given the opportunity.

When Annie and Lily got home that night, Katy was sitting in their living room crying with a hand written letter in her hand. Annie didn't understand her distress as she had received hundreds of letters from her readers and none of them had moved her quite this way.

"Mama, what's wrong. Did somebody write something awful again? Is it one of those busy bodies telling you that you don't know the first thing about raising children again?" asked Annie.

"No Annie, it's from Samuel. Here read it for yourself."

My Dearest Katy,

Again, it seems like it has taken me another lifetime to write you. I read your letter in the newspaper that you had written to Jonathan months ago. I wish I had some news of his whereabouts, but I have rarely left our home since we arrived. Father has been ill since we arrived and I regret to tell you he passed away last week. He was a very difficult man and caused a lot of heartache during his years here. I felt it was my moral duty and responsibility to take care of him but I must admit that the loss is not very deep. I'm not sure what I will do next but I'm very proud of you and the girls for the incredible work that I've been reading about that all of you've done for the children. I'm so ashamed to have contributed so little in my time here on this earth. I allowed our father to have such a sinful chokehold in my life as though I owed him just for being born. I must admit that I often dreamed not of different parents but that our parents would have been different people. You seem to be so much stronger than our mother ever was. Were you ever able to find her? I have continued to write but have never received any answers of her stay at The Weatherly House for The Insane. Please know that throughout our time here I prayed earnestly for his soul but I regret that I never saw any change in him even on his death bed.

It may take some time but I have started the process of finding someone to buy North Highlands Estate. There are too many bad memories there and it is much too big for me to manage. I know you probably don't care to, but I would very much like to see you and the girls. You don't have to answer me right away, but please give it some thought.

Also, I'm prepared to give you half of proceeds from the sale. It is, after all, your due.

I will be your loving brother forever, Samuel

"Oh Mama! Your letter worked, don't you see! Maybe Daddy didn't see it, but Uncle Samuel did.

And because of that letter you're going to see your brother again. God works in mysterious ways, doesn't he? I mean, who would have thought. But, I don't understand why it took him so long. And he's going to give you half of everything? Are you going to write him back? When are you going to see him? You've got to Mama. Just think about it. Maybe one day soon we'll see Daddy, too. I know it. I just know it," Annie said.

"Annie, this is hard. I just need some time to absorb it all. I don't want to get too sidetracked here. We all have a purpose now. What would I say to him anyway? I don't know anything about him. I mean I'm not angry with him at all anymore. We both know it's because of his first letter that we're here right now. What if, I don't know, he just sounds so weak. I just don't know if I have room in my life for someone who doesn't know how to stand up for themselves and for the people they care about," Katy responded.

"I know. I use to feel the same way about him, too, but, Mama, you use to be like that, remember? And look how much you've changed. Maybe he just needs to be with family. You know real family that can help him feel whole and worthy. He is worthy, you know. We all are," Annie answered back.

"Oh Annie, you make me feel so ashamed. You're right. I guess we never stop growing. I'll write him back tomorrow and make arrangements for all of us to meet somewhere but not here. This is our life and I'm not sure if I am ready to let him all the way in. Would that be OK?" asked Katy.

"Alright Mama, but I have something to talk to you about. Uncle J and I are going to start our search tomorrow within the prisons to see if we can locate

Nicholas' father. That little one really tugs at my heart and I just pray we can have a happy ending for him this week," said Annie

"Of course you should. I wouldn't expect any less from you. The only thing I ask is to please be careful." Katy pleaded. She knew there would be no reasoning with her daughter about how dangerous this could be. This would be no different than her determination that day to go out into city to find her daddy. And for that cause, the effect was much greater than they could have ever imagined. Katy could hardly wait to see what this new adventure would bring into their lives.

They started with the Fourth Street Prison and in fact not only did the Captain's uniform get them in right away, it also got them a guarded guided tour by the warden himself. It has continually amazed Annie how people survived. With every whiff of near death there had always been sheer resolution to survive in the human race. She saw it in Highland Way, The Weatherly House, Dublin, on The Rosewood, the orphaned children on the streets of New York and now here at the Fourth Street Prison.

The men were sectioned off into large cells holding twenty to twenty five each with not a single personal item or memento of their life before. The only thing that separated one from another was a number that had been sewn onto their shirts. The smell was repulsive. This was a place that had no wind, no rain, no sunshine and no hope. There was nothing to cleanse the smell of rotting flesh and impending death. The cells were so small with so many of them crowded together that it made them look like pigs in a stall. Some of the men behaved like wild animals, screaming out words that she had never heard before. And some of the other poor souls reached their filthy boney hands out through the bars begging her for mercy, as though she was somebody that could change their circumstances. Did it matter why these men were here? No matter what horrible crimes they may have committed, did people deserve this kind of existence? Unfortunately, this was one battle that would have to wait. They were here for one reason and one reason only, to find someone named Nick Smith.

Nicholas didn't seem rattled or shaken during the viewing of the groups of jailed men rather he seemed reluctant to even gaze in their direction. Annie had trouble making eye contact as well and understood, or at least thought, he was perhaps just disgusted and maybe ashamed that he had ever even mentioned that his father was in prison. They went on that day to a prison located on the Hudson and another way beyond the warehouse district, where unfortunately they only saw more of the same.

The following day there was a terrible thunderstorm that literally flooded the streets. Annie saw the rain as God's way of cleaning the waste and filth that littered the streets and wondered how much longer he was going to allow so much indifference and lawlessness. She had listened that day as Lily read the story of Noah's Ark and remembered how horrified she was as a child that God would fill the world with water and allow only a select few to survive on the Ark. But, now she was beginning to understand just how disappointed he had become with his creation. In her first day of prison visits, she felt so much disappointment and pain for the human race that surrounded her that she felt it would take several lifetimes to root out the evil in this city alone. Annie was glad that they would get a break from the darkness of the prisons and welcomed the warmth and hope of the children back at Matthew's House.

After the Captain relieved Annie for the night shift, the girls gathered upstairs for a rare evening alone. It seemed as though recently someone or something had pulled them apart for the last few months. Annie was either on one of her day shifts with the children, the Captain was having dinner with them or they were across the hall with the Claytons. Annie glanced over at Lily during supper and her eyes filled with tears at what she saw. Where was she when this happened? Lily was growing up. She spoke with such confidence over dinner about her vision for Matthew's house and the role that she wanted to play there one day as the leader in charge.

The sun broke the next morning as the Captain and Nicholas arrived for Annie. Today they would visit the Amsterdam Street Prison and Annie promised herself that today she wouldn't be such a coward. Today she would not turn her head, but look at each man as a man and not the animals that life had turned them into. Surely, at the very least they deserved human eye contact.

Rats ran across in front of the first section of jail cells and quickly piled into a corner bouncing on top of each other. Their guard and guide swung his baton and beat at the wall, until they scattered in every direction. They walked up to the second floor as she kept her eyes fixed into the souls of the skeletons while nudging Nicholas along. She knew that he had become quite content and attached to her back at the house, but she couldn't understand why he wasn't more enthused with even the mere thought of finding at least one parent. Even under the circumstances that they lived with at that run down awful place in Highland Way, she still clung to the idea that her mama would be there waiting for them when they got home. And all of a sudden she had a horrible thought. That after all this, maybe Nick was not like her daddy. Maybe he was more like Lord McLaughton. She wondered, in an instant, if perhaps he had beaten poor Nicholas and thrown him out to fend for himself. What was she thinking? She couldn't give him back over to some heavy handed abusive father. In her haste to do what she thought was right, she forgot that all fathers were not the same.

And then it was as though the iron gates of hell opened right in front of her. All the life, hope and love she had ever known poured out of her soul. She felt as though it was her body that had been cocooned in her mama's blanket as she saw it floating in the ocean. Only there was no moonlight, no prayer being recited, just darkness everywhere. Was it her turn now? Had someone locked her away in this madness?

Because right in front of her through those iron bars, she saw those eyes, those dark brown eyes that she had looked into a thousand times before. The body didn't match and his eyes were sunk into his head, but she had no doubt. Prisoner number 1225 was her daddy.

CHAPTER 14

The Reunion

"DADDY, DADDY, DADDY, that's my daddy. There, right there!" Annie shouted between her gasps for breath.

Poor little Nicholas didn't understand who Annie saw or what was happening. He stood there along with the Captain at Annie's near collapse. The guard thought she had taken ill when she nearly fainted as both men caught her.

This hapless creature was lying on the floor up against the iron bars almost comatose staring up at the ceiling. His glazed and fixed eyes gave every indication that he had no knowledge of his whereabouts. And Annie's first glance horrified her that death had arrived or would within a matter of minutes and the only thing left was for someone to pull a sheet over his emaciated body.

"Get him out, right now, please, he doesn't belong in here!" Annie screamed hysterically.

The guard quickly obliged, scrambling to get his keys out and unlocking the door. The other prisoners moved out of the way while the Captain and the guard grabbed each end of his broken down body. Annie had to make herself hold back as she was almost afraid to touch him for fear she would finish him off.

"Oh Daddy, what have they done to you, why is he here? You have nearly killed him! I'm here now. Daddy, this is Annie. Everything is going to be fine now, I promise. We're getting you out of here right now," Annie railed. The reunion she had prayed for was finally here and his breaths were barely there. This was the last place she ever expected to find her daddy who had always followed the letter of the law. What a cruel and desolate existence for such a kind and generous man. Would they ever again have their long walks and talks and would she ever again be able to look into his eyes for the earthly wisdom that she had grown so accustomed to depend on? For nearly a year and a half now she had been running almost on empty, just waiting for her heart to be filled up with the love, wisdom and protection of her daddy and now he probably had no idea who she was. Her mama had waited years for her mother's love only to find her mind empty and now the same fate was rearing its ugly head at her. Her head was screaming at God for allowing such a good man to have wasted away in this dungeon. He had given so much to his family and all he wanted was to be a good son, husband, father and friend. It just didn't make any measurable sense to her why God would allow the likes of Lord McLaughton to have so many years to torment and torture the people in his life that just needed his love as a father and husband and take her daddy from her in this way. The warden and guards scurried around like the rats one of them had earlier tried to beat to death getting Jonathan out of the prison.

Nicholas tried his best to comfort her as Jonathan's body was being carried to their carriage, "Annie, your daddy's gonna be fine. I'll help take care of him. Don't be afraid. Maybe he just needs some food and a bath like you gave all of us?" Then he turned to the Captain and said, "Are we gonna stop looking for the day. I mean, we need to take care of Annie's daddy. We don't have to do this anymore if it's too much trouble."

The Captain quickly assured him they would not give up on their original search. However, his whole world and reason for being had come to an unexpected halt. He knew this day had to come and being reunited again was the best thing that could happen for his girls, but how would he fit in now and where would his place be? Selfish thoughts swirled around his mind and heart but he quickly pushed them aside as they rushed Jonathan Ewing to Mercy Hospital.

Annie's first glance of the hospital gave her some hope and assurance as they made a pass around the front entrance toward the direction of the rear emergency entrance. Waiting for them in front of

Mercy Hospital was a life sized statute with the same outstretched arms she had looked up and prayed to back home. Had they come full circle? It suddenly seemed like only yesterday when she sat with Lily in the Highland Way Presbyterian Church and looked upwards toward those same arms of Christ and prayed that they would all be together again as a family.

The minute they pulled up the Captain began throwing orders around as though he was at the helm of a sinking ship. He wasn't going to allow Annie to lose one precious minute with her daddy if he had anything to do with it. "Get this man inside right now and I want the best doctor you have. And send someone over to The Irish Settlers News building to pick up Katy Ewing. Tell her that we've found her husband and she needs to get here right away!"

When Annie and the Captain were finally allowed in they found Jonathan lying on a bed with two nurses at his bed doing what they could to make him comfortable. He had been washed and cleaned and had on a fresh set of pajamas that at least made his appearance seem less fatal. She hoped that her mama and Lily would be there soon. She just knew that if he could hear and see them all together that would be enough for him to hang on just a little longer or maybe God would answer her prayer and let him live. She couldn't remember ever seeing anyone worse off but then again she had to believe that as long as his frail body had breath there was still some glimmer of hope.

Annie softly held and kissed his hand as he drifted in and out of consciousness, "Daddy, it's me, Annie. Please wake up Daddy. Don't leave us now. Mama is on her way and Lily, too. We came all the way over here to find you and now you must, you have to hold on and get better. You wouldn't believe how much Mama has changed and how much she misses you. Almost as much as I do, I bet. And little Lily is so grown up now. Did you know that she can play the piano and sing? And we found Grandma Lizzie and Jeremiah, too. And the Captain here has helped us so much Daddy. It's as if you sent him to look after us all the way here. You'd like him a lot. You two could be good friends just like you and Pastor Wynne, remember?" Annie continued recalling bits and pieces of their long journey as Katy and Lily ran into the room.

Katy fell to her knees and weaved her fingers into his and for a moment he was awake and aware of his long lost bride by his bedside. Jonathan opened his eyes for just a moment and whispered "Oh my dear sweet Katy, I've dreamed of seeing your beautiful face, where have you been? I thought I would never see you again," Then he appeared to lose consciousness again.

"Oh, Jonathan, I'm so sorry for not being the wife you deserved, but, I've changed so much and I'm here for you now. The only thing you need to think about is getting better. It's my turn to take care of you. We're going to be a family now, a real family, I promise." Katy assured him while Lily just stood and stared. This was not the daddy she remembered. The last time she saw him he had his white shirt sleeves rolled up in his suspendered, dark brown pants. Not this skin and bone creature that looked like it had crawled up out of a shallow grave. She knew that they had travelled here and there and spent days, weeks and months for this very moment but this was not the happy ending she was promised would take place. Somebody lied to her and she was mad and she just needed Uncle J to tell her everything would be fine. He was her rock now. It was his eyes of wisdom that she had grown to trust. In the back of her mind she had come to believe that Uncle J had been sent by God to take her daddy's place and she had become quite comfortable with just the way things were. She didn't like this scene at all. Her mama and Annie were both crying and this room was full of hopelessness and she wanted out right now. But, instead she just stood there rubbing her mama and sister's back trying to give them some kind of comfort and support.

The doctor was not optimistic that he would live through the night much less through the week. "You're lucky you found him when you did. Otherwise, he'd been thrown into a pauper's grave just like all the others. At least now, you can give him a proper Christian burial."

"Lucky? You call this lucky? I found my daddy half dead, locked away in a prison for God only knows what! Don't talk to me about luck right now! I need you to help him and I don't care what it costs. You're a doctor, not a fortune teller! I'll decide when to give up, not you!" screamed Annie.

Annie ran out of the room and found a small waiting area where she knew she needed to collect her thoughts and prayed. "Oh God, Father in heaven, please have mercy on my daddy. Please heal him and make him whole. He has so much left to give and I cry out that he would live to be given to. Don't you think he deserves it? He's always lived a just and honorable life. I now know how you have covered and protected us along the way with your mighty outstretched arms. You delivered us through this wilderness. And even though this doesn't look or feel like the land of promise, it will be one day for us a family if you just let him live. Please God, hear my plea." And with tears streaming down her face Annie looked up and saw the warden.

"I came to check on your daddy and to tell you that I pulled what few details we had on his arrest. It seems that he was picked up well over a year ago with another man who had started a brawl in one of the nearby taverns. There were so many fists flying that the whole bunch of them were just handcuffed and hauled away. I'm really sorry." Annie's blood started to boil. Poor Jonathan had just been in the wrong place at the wrong time and this American justice system was terribly flawed. With no one here looking for him he had just basically surrendered to the constant beatings that he probably knew would kill him one day. Not only had an innocent man been torn away from his family, but an honorable man had been removed from the world. All the good he would do had vanished. This was all old man Beaker's fault. He probably never had any intention of going back home for his family. This was his way of going off and doing whatever he wanted. She remembered him being hot tempered and wondered why her daddy ever gave him the time of day. Because of this man, her daddy was just barely hanging on to the most incredible life in this world worth living. He had given so much. He promised that if you give what you need it would always come back. This come back was all wrong. It was neither fair nor justified. She needed him to be her guiding light. He had to at least live long enough for her mama to make things right and Lily deserved to get to know the daddy that she had so little time with.

The Captain took Lily home for the night while Annie and Katy stayed by his bedside. Annie apologized later that evening to the doctor that was short of having a good bedside manner and Dr. Long agreed with Annie to speak more hopeful when he was in her daddy's presence. Annie had dozed off during the early morning hours and woke up to see her mama staring at her daddy with so much love it made her feel as though God had heard her prayer. Dr. Long came back in for his early morning visit and once again bent down and listened carefully to his breathing. This time he motioned for Katy and Annie to move out into the hallway. "I know I promised not to say anything in front of your daddy, but I have to be honest and tell the both of you that even though he looks a little bit better than yesterday his prognosis is still not good. I hear a lot of fluid in his lungs and I'm certain its pneumonia. And even the healthiest folks have a hard time recovering. There's no telling how long he's been like this. All we can really do is try to keep him as comfortable as possible. I'm really sorry for all of you. I wish there was more that I could do." Katy and Annie kept a constant vigil by his side night and day for the next three days.

On Wednesday, May 12, 1852 without ever really knowing how much he had a part of making the world a better place, Jonathan Robert Ewing passed away.

He had given for thirty seven years. But, what Annie didn't know and couldn't feel at that moment was how truly blessed those thirty seven years had been for him.

The news of Jonathan's death spread quickly due in part to the article that Mr. Clayton had so kindly and thoughtfully written. He had never had the pleasure or honor of meeting the man that he had grown to respect through the words of his dear friends and family. They were strangers in this new country, and had carved out such incredible lives with such generous hearts and hands and it was all because of this man. What an honor it would have been to have known him, to shake his hand. So Mr. Clayton began....

Dear people of New York City, I write this open letter to you today to express my personal profound loss that I hope all of you will share with your family, friends, coworkers, and even the strangers you pass on the street. Life is all too short when you leave behind people that will miss you. And today the flame of a bright light was extinguish all too soon. But his death didn't leave the room dark. Jonathan Robert Ewing had in his short thirty seven years made it his mission in life to teach other people that pure faith was seeing what you believe not believing what you see. Because life here as it is everywhere looks ugly and rude and empty, he saw only goodness, purpose and meaning. The lives he left behind will miss him but their lights are brighter than any star in the sky. His wife, Katy, has shared her countless words of wisdom and encouragement to thousands throughout the city. These were her storehouse full of memories from Jonathan. It was his oldest daughter, Annie, who helped in the founding of Matthew's House that has saved the lives of so many children that would

have surely perished living on the streets. And his living legacy continues with his youngest, Lily, who taught these very children, who had their bellies full and a bed to sleep in but were still ignorant, how to read and write. This is our future. These children will one day be contributors to our great America. They my dear people will live, love, work and worship God because of Jonathan's short life. Yes, he will be missed but no, not ever forgotten. And for that I hope and pray that all our lives will be short.

Please join the family to pay your respects at the First Presbyterian Church at 5:00 p.m. on Saturday, May 15th. In lieu of flowers, donations can be made to Matthew's House.

Saturday was the day that Katy was to meet Samuel and start their lives together. Instead, he held her as hundreds gathered together for Jonathan's final farewell.

And as the Captain sat there in his fine white tailored uniform with his arms encased around Annie and Lily on each side, he could only hope and pray that he would one day be able to fill that farmer's big shoes.

CHAPTER 15

The Secret

WEEKS HAD PASSED AND Annie had yet to begin to feel anything except when she visited her daddy's grave. In her heart she thought her good works here at Matthew's House would be rewarded with him being returned to their family fold and they would certainly all return back to their homeland one day. But, in addition to this personal deep loss she was not at all settled that her daddy's final resting place was here on foreign soil. But, death was about as final as things could be so her loss was encompassing everything that had been part of who she was. Although she knew it was misdirected, there were days when she didn't want to be in the same room with either Lily or her mama so she found herself spending much of her time just going through the motions at Matthew's House. They had cried and mourned over their loss of a husband and father but somehow their worlds had not shattered to pieces as hers seemed to. They didn't know him as she did and she felt all alone in her grief. Nicholas was there at every turn trying to rescue her from falling completely apart but Annie even distanced herself from him. Strangely enough, she felt a tinge of jealousy that his father was still out there. It didn't matter whether he was in prison or not, he still had hope and hers was buried six feet under on the grounds of the First Presbyterian Church.

The Captain had no idea what emotional and mental costs he would suffer when he abandoned his ship for his new dream. There had been some days since Jonathan's passing that he wished he was back on the ocean where he knew there was at least a beginning and end to each voyage. And even though he needed to be needed, if he chose to stay, this was a cross that he would bear for a lifetime and the weight was at times too much. Even in death the Captain surprised himself by thinking what a lucky man Jonathan was. He was dead and yet he still seemed to be sewn so deep into the fabric of the girls that he once claimed, if only for a short while, were his. He wanted the same life but he knew he lacked the maturity for deep relationships and had no experience to draw from to offer any words of comfort and was helpless to know what to do to fix things. He had very little connection to the men working on the ship and rarely spoke to, much less got involved in, the lives of his passengers. He may as well have been the rudder on the ship for all the difference that he made in this world before he met Jonathan. And now he felt his new found usefulness and self-worth disappearing. He wondered had he been sailing along all this time on the back of Jonathan? However, he didn't miss a beat when he drew water from that well of deception from his old way of life as he knew all too well how to hide the truth when he told Annie, "There's no need to look for Nick for a while, just give yourself some time. I'm sure the last thing you want to do for a while is to go back into the prisons. I'll take the boy when you and your mama can spare me."

What Nicholas confessed to the Captain and probably never would to Annie, was that they were never going to find Nick, because there was no Nick to find. Nicholas had made it all up. He told the story so many times that he almost began to believe it himself. He had no idea how old he was and had no memory of a proper bed, home or parents. He picked up his name from a little boy whose mother handed him a bright shiny apple one day at the market he normally stole from. As he was about to slip in for his take of the day, a dark haired young woman reached in her basket and handed him an apple, then turned to her little boy and said, "Nicholas we need to remember to pray for him. I'm sure he's one of those poor little prison orphans." So, he took on the name of Nicholas and made up the story of Nick as his way of self-protection on the streets, from the gangs of bullies that confronted him every day. He figured that if he told the other street boys that his father was in prison and they would have to deal with him when he got out, they would leave him alone and it worked. He wasn't a fighter at all and was actually scared witless most of the time and had become very quick on his feet. That's how he was just a blur of blonde hair when Annie first spotted him. For a brief moment that day he actually thought that Annie was this same kind woman and his hope was that she was there to give him another hand out of food. He had grown accustom to running to, away and from whatever he needed to survive for the moment.

The Captain's presence was pretty much still on course with Lily as her memories of Jonathan were the faintest while Katy just poured herself into her work at the newspaper. The tone in her writings had turned from words of hope and encouragement to words of truth and courage. Katy knew that she had loved Jonathan all along but was afraid to let go and give, not because he wasn't worthy but because she felt so worthless. Her fear was that if he ever really knew her he would reject her and she would never hold back her true self again. She was an immigrant in a strange land but she would not be a stranger in this new world. She had things to offer and come hell or high water she intended to be the voice that Lizzie had so boldly predicted. It would be her mission to see to it that Jonathan's death would not be in vain. She had given Annie plenty of room and time to grieve and now she knew she needed to step in and pick her daughter up. So that evening when Annie got home Katy was waiting.

"Annie, I know how much you miss your daddy

and I'm not saying that you're not entitled to your grief. But, do you think that he would want you to stop living? You've pulled too many young lives from the brink of certain death with your work at Matthew's House. Remember the little boy that the orphanage is named after. Look at how short his young life was cut and where he ended up. And his poor parents who will never see their little boy grow up. Whether you know it or have forgotten it, you made Matthew's life go on and matter. It's time you start celebrating your daddy's life instead of grieving his loss. Visit his grave every day if that's what you need, but you're not going to bring him back. If you want to honor him, then you can start by opening your eyes to all the goodness around you. Those children would all be dead or on their way if you had not been out looking for him that day. Don't you see that this was all part of your courageous journey that brought us here? I know it's not all adding up in your head right now but sometimes God's hand moves in directions that we just don't understand. We just have to trust that as long as we are alive there is hope for new beginnings. If you will just have the courage to let go and move on you'll see that you're not forgetting your daddy but honoring him. And I have no doubt he would be so proud of you."

Annie just stood with her arms crossed as though she was being lectured by a stranger, when she suddenly felt all the ebbs and flows of her slighted life empty her body. She was, in fact, becoming the woman that her mama once was. How ironic that her mama was now the one holding things together. She had prayed for this day. The day her mama would be whole and well and strong but this was not at all the ending she wanted to accept. In that moment even though she couldn't look into his eyes, she suddenly heard his voice in her head, "Always try to give what you need and it will somehow come back to you." Annie didn't know if she would ever be a real mother, but her daddy had taught her how to give and giving these children a healthy and happy home would be her calling.

Annie uncrossed her arms and wrapped them around her new found tower of strength and cried, "I love you, Mama."

The Captain was still trying to find his way through his own maze of loss and grief not knowing where he would fit or even if there was a place left for him. Samuel's presence had added an even greater interruption to their once familiar routine. They were all blood related and he wasn't. In a weird way he felt a little resentful and left out, in spite of the reason, they were all together upstairs. He felt a pull of nostalgia about his own roots and many times had wondered which of those that he left behind that day had really been his family after all. As a child of gypsies they would often times travel in their caravans picking up one stranger after another. This one was his Aunt Ruby and that one was his Uncle Henry but he was never sure if they were the real deal. He couldn't remember ever being tucked in bed at night, patted on the head or one single warm loving embrace. Matter of fact, sitting there on the side of his bed, he couldn't remember ever hearing the words, "I love you" from anyone, but that was a room that he had shut the door on a long time ago. He had wanted to say it a thousand times to Katy but knew that was not a chance he was willing to take right now. When he packed up his belongings from the ship he had thrown most of his things in the corner of his small room only taking time to hang his clothes. He thought he had a small box somewhere that held a few of his childhood possessions and suddenly felt a need for some small glimpse of his past. His search was fruitless for his keepsake box but, he did find a knapsack that for a moment he couldn't remember owning or why he would have packed it up and brought it with his things, but once opened he remembered why. It was Jonathan's. One of his deck hands had turned it over to him when he didn't return and he had it the whole time. He dumped the contents on his bed and there before him was all that mattered to Jonathan. There was a jar of dirt labeled in hand written letters "Irish Gold", his wedding photo, a picture of him holding Lily with Annie by his side in front of their farm house and his worn, leather bound Bible. Inside the Bible he had made some hand written notes as well as pages where he had underlined what he assumed were verses that had special meaning to Jonathan. He had it dogged eared in the book of Isaiah and there was a hand written note placed between the pages that read,

"Dear Lord, if it's your will that I never return to the family and land that I love, please help Katy, Annie and Lily along the way. May they understand that by waiting on you that their hope is in you, and the unseen wind that steers the eagles wings is the very same sweet breath guiding them through your carefully laid out plans for their precious time here on this magnificent and bountiful land that you created. May they learn to

rest in your arms of comfort and lean on your wisdom for understanding.
Your Faithful Son I will remain, Jonathan."

***

The Captain knocked softly on their door, handed Jonathan's belongings to Annie and left. He had a piece of Jonathan with him the whole time. How many times could and would have Katy, Annie and Lily needed them. He felt horrible but would beg for forgiveness later.

***

Annie was exhausted. She was glad her Uncle Samuel was there for her mama, but he was a funny little man that she thought was weak and lost and wondered who would be supporting who before long. Her mama had started over and she certainly didn't want any additional, unnecessary weight or hindrance in their lives. Samuel had spent his entire life scrapping and bowing to her awful grandfather and now she just wanted to put all that behind her. The loss of her daddy still took her breath away at times. But, she was finally reaching the point to at least be thankful that they found him. If it wasn't for Nicholas he would have died all alone buried in a pauper's grave with no acknowledgement or celebration of the life he lived. They were all given one small final window to hold his hand and talk to him even though the doctor wasn't sure how much he heard them, they talked anyway. However, Annie was certain that he had somehow heard and seen every minute from the time he left them in the flat in Highland Way until he closed his eyes for the last time at Mercy Hospital. And he would no doubt be her guiding angel here on earth. Things had been such a blur to her during the funeral she was only beginning to process the memory of that day. There had been such a huge turnout that there were moments that she just wanted to clear the room for her final moments with her daddy. On one hand she didn't want to share this time with anyone and on the other hand she felt like the world should stop turning, if only for a moment, for his proper and due respect. She remembered that there had been people from every part of society, with every child from Matthew's House, the Mayor, the Prison Warden, employees from the Grand Hotel, and hundreds of readers of her mama's newspaper column. Then Annie felt a sudden surge of pride that she hadn't acknowledged until today. Everyone felt they had a reason to be there, some kind of connection to this unknown, yet victorious soldier of humanity.

Now she was holding her daddy's belongings. Things he had treasured. Things he had touched. Oh how well he had planned it all. The verse that was the very last one he would read to her, she had already figured out long ago and in that moment knew their hearts had the same beat. She would always be Annie Ewing, even if she married and had ten children. She would never forget from where she came. A farm girl from Ireland, the richest place on Earth, and she was holding the jar of dirt in her hands now to prove it.

CHAPTER 16

Birthdays and Commitments

ANNIE WAS THERE WHEN Samuel gave her mama a check for one hundred thousand dollars. After months of negotiations, back and forth, the sale of North Highland Estates had finally gone through. Samuel had sold the entire landholding to a banker from Dublin who wanted to move his wife and two daughters to the country. She wondered if it was Jarvis Williams and his family but the thought quickly escaped her because she no longer cared. Her life was here now and she knew she could never leave the city that in principal not only killed her daddy but had honored and mourned him in the end. Just like the proceeds in the sale of her grandma's jewelry, she was astonished that kind of money was in anybody's hands but she was sure her mama would put it to good use. Over three years had passed since her days on the farm and it had been more than two years since Jonathan's death and she had gotten use to the Captain's quiet presence. She thought he would try to move in quickly to take her daddy's place as her mama's new husband and their father, but he never made the first assuming move. He spent his days at Matthew's House as a manager of sorts, in charge of everything from fixing the roof to wiping noses and breaking up fights. And every night he would retire quietly to the room below theirs at the newspaper unless he was invited to dinner.

Annie had turned eighteen somewhere in the mix but Katy didn't forget this birthday nor had she forgotten another since her fifteenth. They celebrated as Annie wanted at Matthew's House with all the children singing Happy Birthday. Her gifts were all handmade except the one she opened from her mama and the Captain. It was a gold locket on a chain that opened to a picture of her on one side and her daddy on the other. Katy had taken Jonathan's treasured photographs to a photographer that used his skills to photograph her keepsake pictures and set them in the locket.

"Oh, Mama, Uncle J, thank you so much. I don't know what to say. It's just absolutely beautiful." Annie gushed as she knew it would suitably always be near her heart. Other than her Grandma Lizzie's pieces, she had never owned a piece of jewelry before as she always felt there were more useful things to spend her money on, but this would become one of the most cherished possessions aside from her daddy's belongings from the ship. However, her curious nature caused her to wonder why her mama and the Captain presented it to her together. Certainly they could have chosen separate gifts on their own. Maybe they were spending more time alone together than Annie had originally thought.

"Mama, do you like Uncle J?" Annie asked.

"Of course I do, don't you," answered Katy.

"No, Mama, that's not what I meant. I mean, do you really like, you know, love him? You know it's ok if you do. I know he's crazy about you. I mean, what man in his right mind would be content to live as he does if there wasn't good reason." Annie assured her.

"Yes, I do love him, darling. But, so much has happened. I know you still miss your daddy so much and I miss him too. I think he's such a wonderful and kind man and I'm certain that your daddy would approve. Don't you think?" Katy asked.

"Yes Mama, you have my blessing and I'm sure if Daddy had to pick someone, it would no doubt be Uncle J. As a matter of fact, I'm thinking that he probably did pick him out a long time ago in his room that night when he wrote his letter to God asking him to take care of us. Like you said to me that day, this had to be all part of God's perfect plan." Annie answered with a smile.

"Well since we're on the subject of blessings, there are a couple of things I'd like to talk to you about. Julius has asked me to marry him and I was just waiting for the right time to bring it up. We were thinking about having a small ceremony with just you, Lily, Nicholas and Samuel at the Clayton's. And then I would like all of us to make a trip back home. I've been writing to Mother and Jeremiah and she really wants to meet him and Jeremiah is just so thankful that the man he met that day before we left has been taking care of us all this time. They are both so eager to see you and Lily again and Samuel has been beside himself wanting to see Mother. I clearly explained that not only was she blind but she had no memory of our life together, but he insists that his mere presence could perhaps change things," replied Katie.

"Yes, yes, of course, a small ceremony, large ceremony, any ceremony that you would like!" Annie shrieked and hugged Katy.

"But Mama, can the visit to Grandma Lizzie and Jeremiah wait, please. Now just isn't a good time. It has taken me a while to get a handful of lawyers to agree to hear me out on my new plan. You know not too many were interested in representing the prisoners much less working for free. So, I have a few meetings coming up and it's just real important that I keep trying. I think if Daddy could've had at least a few minutes to speak before a judge there's no doubt he would have been released. You know how well he spoke on behalf of the tenant farmers back home. Given a chance, anyone would have seen that he was no trouble maker at all and well you know he would be alive today." Annie said.

Katy was amazed that Annie's mind was in constant motion not for herself but for the lives of total strangers. She felt so small at times just writing her column at the newspaper as Annie seemed to completely devote her time to such bigger causes. She was certain that Annie had inherited her tenacity and grit from the Ewing side of the family. And she found herself being more satisfied and grateful for that than for the money Samuel had given her. When he placed that check in her hand she thought of all the times she had wished for a way out of her existence as it were working at the stables and then living as a tenant farmer's wife at North Highlands. Now she had more money than she thought she could spend in a lifetime and all that mattered to her now was the happiness of her two daughters and perhaps one day given another chance as the Captain's wife. She had learned so much about herself over the last few years and found strengths that she wouldn't otherwise have discovered without being tested as they all had. She knew it had never been Jonathan's fault for her being the way she was. He tried to get her to open up about her past hurts and nightmares but she was such a tormented soul that even a thoughtful, patient man such as Jonathan couldn't break through. It had taken her as much time to forgive herself as it had for Annie to pass though her grief and she was not ever going to look over her shoulder again. She would keep her precious memories intact but would never again allow her regrets to hold her back. What would be the point? She may not have the good Ewing blood in her but she had Lizzie's and that was enough of a legacy for her to continue the good fight. She would return home to see Jeremiah and Lizzie one day, but that one day would have to wait just a little bit longer.

Meanwhile, Lily and Nicholas had become

inseparable as they waited for Annie and Katy to heal and rebound. Nicholas didn't understand loss as he never had anything to lose. All he had been experiencing was one new good day after another. Even with all the bad days he watched Annie go through, he was still thankful that he had a safe place to live, food to eat, a warm bed to sleep in and the bonus was that he had more than one someone that cared whether he was alive or not. The fact that Annie ignored him for a while was just a small price to pay for what he'd experienced before she rescued him. When Lily wasn't around he spent hours sharing his dreams with his old four legged friend Daisy, just as Katy had shared hers with her beloved horses. Looking forward to tomorrow and having dreams was a new experience for Nicholas as his only reference of time before was where he was going to sleep or who he was going to steal his next meal from. Thinking about next week, next month or even next year was something that Lily had only recently introduced him to.

***

"What do you want to be when you grow up?" Lily asked.

"What do you mean?" asked Nicholas.

"I mean do you want to be a farmer like my daddy, or a captain like Uncle J, or a doctor or whatever you want one day," answered Lily.

"I don't know, a farmer like your daddy sounds good. I guess I never thought about it much. All I just really ever wanted was a family," Nicholas responded.

"Well you have that now. We're your family now. I

know, how about you be my brother? Want to shake on it?" asked Lily.

"Ok, but the only way that's going to happen is if I'm your big brother," answered Nicholas.

"You have to be older you know," said Lily.

"Fine then, I'll just make myself older, how old are you?" Nicholas asked.

"I'll soon be nine and a half," answered Lily.

"Good then I'll be ten and a half, how's that?" Nicholas answered.

"You're sure little to be ten and a half," Lily said.

"Oh be quiet, squirt, I'm still growing," Nicholas replied.

And they were off just like any other typical brother and sister and his only dream for now was making Annie, Katy and the Captain proud and protecting his little sister.

Lily continued to make her presence known albeit in a much more animated position. She had become not only a teacher of letters, words and numbers but of music as well. When donations poured in after Jonathan's death Lily begged her mama for a piano. "Mama, can we please have a piano? I haven't been able to play since, well since we left Grandma Lizzie's first house. It's what I always wanted. We can put it at Matthew's House and I can teach the children how to play," pleaded Lily.

Within days the Captain found, bought and delivered Lily's piano where she not only taught but entertained the children and guests every chance she got.

Late one evening, while Annie was finishing her dreaded paperwork for the week, the sound of Lily's hands on the piano keys pulled her back to their stay at North Highlands. Annie realized just how little attention her sister had required over the last couple years and it almost made her sad that Lily didn't need her as much anymore.

Who would have thought that this thumb sucking, skirt hanger on would have molded and developed into such a strong, confident and talented young lady and there was no stopping her. Annie leaned back and smiled to herself because she knew that it had to be God's sweet breath underneath Lily's wings.

On Saturday, September 10, 1854, Katy Ewing and Captain Julius married in a quite ceremony in Mr. and Mrs. Clayton's living room in front of the Justice of the Peace, Samuel, Annie, Lily and Nicholas. And as they shared their "I do's", Katy once again experienced a loving and devoted man pull out two gold rings that he had been carrying in his pocket for months.

PART THREE

CHAPTER 17

Fame and Misfortune

SHE WAS TIRED OF velvet. Red velvet, blue velvet, green velvet, she had seen it all. She had seen it at North Highlands, Jarvis' house and in her hotel suite at The Grand Hotel. And now she had to look at the silky backside of it before and after every performance. The curtains opened and somewhere beyond the blinding lights she knew she had an audience waiting. They were waiting on her to walk out on stage and entertain them. No matter how she felt, Lily had to plaster a smile on her face and sing her heart out. All of this money, fame, and the sea of velvet everywhere had come to represent to her an opulent yet forbidden life that she wasn't at all prepared for.

***

Matthew's House had built out over a full city block taking in and housing full time nearly a hundred orphans. The Captain had built Annie and Lily a small but comfortable apartment on the first floor and Lily had taken on more and more responsibilities. This was where she had been building not only her character but her memories. She had very few of North Highlands and even fewer of her daddy. In a small way, she felt she had a connection with the children that Annie didn't. She had started out in all this being closer to the floor with the children and they often told her things that Annie or the Captain never heard or knew. Her best recollection was that she was around seven or eight years old when they began feeding the lost children and she had basically grown up with a host of adopted brothers and sisters. But, Annie was the one that everyone looked up to and she wanted to be that same kind of mainstay to the new children coming through their doors on a weekly basis. She wanted to be their mentor and big sister and maybe help them knit their lives back together like she had witnessed so many times since Matthew's House opened. Lily loved to sing and play the piano but she struggled to teach the children something that just came to her naturally. But, as she listened to the voices over and over from others and her family she had come to accept that what she had was a gift from God and it was her obligation in life to pass it on. It wasn't at all that she didn't want to contribute. It's that she was growing impatient with other people telling her how to do it. She had her own idea of the way she wanted to be looked up to and the height difference between the children and her was not one of them. Something had slowly taken over Lily's once pure and innocent heart. And unfortunately the thing that came calling and she willingly answered to, had a name, pride.

Lily was only sixteen years old when Reginald Wolfe first heard her angelic voice. He was the Chairman of the Board of the New York City Opera House and it had become expected of the social elites to not only contribute financially but to occasionally make an appearance at Matthew's House. His heart wasn't in it but even so it would make for much needed publicity for the opera house. The audience of the once packed performances was beginning to spend their time at the live playhouses that were springing up everywhere and he needed to somehow turn things around.

Reginald had just finished having his photograph taken with Annie and a small group of children downstairs when Lily's voice called to him as she was leading the children's choir practice. They had become the talk of the town performing at the Mayor's reelection inauguration, charity events, and the latest was the grand opening of Taylor's Department Store. As Annie instructed she rarely took center stage because it was the children that needed the exposure. They needed homes. Public opinion had to be changed and it was Annie's idea to take their little show on the road. If the public could just see how well behaved and talented the children were there was little doubt they would be adopted. And it worked. Many of the younger girls and boys were adopted within days of some of the events and even the hardest to adopt older ones were taken in as nannies or hired help. So as dozens upon dozens of the previously unwanted were moved out, that many more moved in. The work was hard but it was rewarding for Annie, but Lily's enthusiasm was beginning to wane. She wanted more and Reginald offered her a chance to be more on that ill-fated day.

"Who does that incredible voice belong to?" questioned Reginald at what would be the first of his many visits.

"That's my sister, Lily. She's the one who adds the real flavor around here. The Captain and I have done our best to pull these children from the streets but it's really Lily that makes them want to stay. She really just gives them something to look forward to everyday with her love of music. Not only can she sing but she plays the piano as naturally as we all breathe. I remember the day when she sat in front of a piano and played for the first time. It's almost like God planted a special seed in her the day she was born and it just keeps growing stronger every day. Would you like to meet her?" Annie asked.

"I certainly would," Reginald answered with delight that he had found the answer to his problem.

Even though she had talent, Reginald thought it was raw and so were some of Lily's social skills. Reginald needed Lily to fit a proper mold and there was no way she would ever sit in front of a piano. He was only interested in her youth, natural beauty and voice.

In a matter of months from their first meeting Reginald set his plan in motion. He knew Lily was still too young yet for the stage and he needed time to convince her family that he could be trusted. So, he cleverly designed his visits on a regular basis trying to talk his way into the family fold all the while seducing Lily with plans for his future star. "You know you don't belong here. The kind of talent you have needs to be on a real stage. These children don't appreciate your talent the way the audiences at the opera house will one day. And how much do they pay you, anyway? You can make more money than you ever dreamed of. In a matter of just a year or two I can make you a star. But it'll take some convincing on your part. You have to want it. You have to want it bad enough to give up all this. I can set you up at the Grand Hotel and arrange for the finest voice instructors in New York City to work with you."

And after every visit Lily's desire to be on the stage became stronger and stronger as the love she once had for the children at Matthew's House began to slowly fade away. And before she knew what was happening and how she got there The Grand Hotel became her home for the second time. Reginald carefully invested in her over the next year paying for private voice and etiquette lessons while patiently earning everyone's trust, everyone's that is, except Nicholas. And Lily finally learned which fork to use and which glass was proper.

***

She had just celebrated her eighteenth birthday and the spotlight was all on her. At first it felt like a dream come true to stand on the stage and sing at the New York City Opera House. Not only was this new kind of limelight contributing to her sense of self-worth she was finally contributing financially. Every week Reginald paid her and in turn, she made generous contributions to Matthew's House. It meant something to her, too. She was, after all, there that cold night when Matthew's final resting place became the Atlantic Ocean. Now she wasn't just a child helping other children learn how to sing and play the piano, she was finally now doing it her way. She was a young woman making the world a better place with a little taste of fame on top. She admitted only to herself that she enjoyed the fame and all the perks that came along with it. Like her Uncle J and his fine tailored white uniform that got them into The Grand Hotel that night, it was her famous voice that got her and her guests the finest table at the finest restaurant and people applauded her every night she performed.

But most of all, it was the recognition. Everyone knew Annie and Katy and now everyone would know her. She would no longer be Annie's little sister. She would no longer be the silent partner.

Katy was also proud to write of her performances and Annie was thankful for the extra money that poured in every week. However, as time went on Lily's special influence on the children's futures were sorely missed. Adoption rates were down since she left and some of the children were beginning to age out on their own but Annie wouldn't dare tell Lily of their struggles.

She and the Captain would just have to work harder to make their cause known. Annie thought that not only had Lily earned the time to follow her dream but she deserved it. She had not once complained about their never ending work and Annie felt that Lily had somehow lost her own childhood in their endeavor to save so many others.

Meanwhile, the audiences at the opera house had swelled to Reginald's delight and most nights boasted a capacity crowd, but slowly Lily's cut of the profit was steadily beginning to dwindle. When she questioned Reginald, as though she knew or suspected he was manipulating the numbers, he would blow her off, claiming that the overhead was to blame. Lily's mere question as to where her fair share of the front office take was going would result in the same defense he used every week "You don't trust me, after everything I have given up for you!"

He had, in fact, given up nothing. Lily had given up everything. She missed Annie, Nicholas, the children, the apartment, her Mama and Uncle J. She now understood Annie's long ago dream to want things to be as they once were. All she wanted now was to have her old life back at Matthew's House teaching the children their school and music lessons with Annie in charge and her brother by her side. But things changed quickly. Her united home front had disappeared like Annie's once did.

When Katy was sure her girls were settled building their own lives she and the Captain finally left for that long awaited return visit back home with Samuel in tow. Katy was eager for her mother and Jeremiah to get to know her new husband and reconnect with her long lost brother. She had written about Jonathan's rescue from the prison and his subsequent death but had shared only a few awkward lines about Samuel. They promised to return in a few months as Katy thought Lily was in good hands with Reginald. He was, after all, old enough to be her father and had earned their trust so much they felt he had become part of their family.

But in Lily's hidden reality she was finally beginning to see the remnants of her Grandma Lizzie's old life. Within a matter of days after her mama and the Captain left, Reginald resigned his position at the opera house, appointed himself as Lily's manager and took her on the road. And manage her he did. He told her when to go to bed, when to get up, when she could eat, what to wear, who she could talk to and he had all the money. She was so ashamed that she had allowed this man to take over her life. How could she have missed all the signs? She had argued relentlessly to both her mama and Annie to let her go find her way that day when Reginald offered her the golden opportunity to be the star performer at the New York City Opera House. She had grown, she thought, to be not only the real talent of this operation but had the surpassed beauty of any stage performer she had seen. She just wanted her chance to be seen and heard by a real audience. Her pride and vanity had become front and center and in her mind she felt this would be her shot at stardom. She knew Annie's notion that she shouldn't overshadow the children had merit, but after all it was her God given talent, so why shouldn't she get to ride a little higher. Now after three long, lonely months on the road, she just went along with

Reginald doing what he told her. As they traveled, the only connection she had with her family would be the hand written assurances she would send Annie in the postcards she mailed along the way.

Dear Annie-

I'm delighted to write and tell you that we just arrived in Toronto. I'm having a splendid time touring the city. We will be here for two weeks and then on to Ottawa. Reginald has been such a dear tending to my every need. Give my love to Nicholas and the children.

Love, Lily

Every single word was a lie and it was slowly sinking in that she had somehow brought all this on herself. What makes a person become so prideful that they become blind to their own self-inflicted wounds?

It had taken her some time to accept that things were not going to get any better for her. Reginald was an opportunist whose only talent was using people, then discarding them and moving on to his next victim. That's what Nicholas called him when they argued so badly the night she moved her things out. But it was beginning to be more frightening than that. She knew Reginald was in love with her and it was his jealously that kept her under his control. He had made an advance toward her while he was drunk one night that she rejected outright by slapping him across the face and that's when his abuse began. She often thought of her Grandma Lizzie and how her grandfather had beaten her half to death and then tried to blame it on her. She wasn't going to have her memory taken away from her like her grandfather had taken away Lizzie's.

How would she ever tell Annie or Nicholas how foolishly she had allowed Reginald to take over her life and now how physically abusive he had become? Countless times he would grab her arms and push her up against the walls going so far on one occasion throwing her across the room. She had been able to hide the bruises but it was getting harder and harder for her to hide the shame. And not ever knowing what would set him off made her feel more afraid that if she didn't do something soon she would never see her family again. He told her he wasn't going to force himself on her. That he wanted her to want him and he thought if he beat her down long enough she would come around to see things his way. However, Lily knew that was never going to happen. When his whiskey breath got within feet of her it made her stomach turn and her skin crawl and she thought she would rather die first. She found herself feeling abandoned at times and wondered why Nicholas was the only one that saw right through him when nobody else did? She supposed it was his lingering street smarts and survival skills that smelled the bad blood. How could she have been so dense about it all?

Reginald had long ago stopped giving her any of the money she earned outright. "It's in the bank, there for you when you need it" he would say. But, when she asked for it, he would just tell her that it was up to him when and if she needed it. She just wanted to go home. All she needed was enough for a one way ticket back to New York City. The place that overwhelmed her the first day she set foot was the very place she was heartsick for.

He had booked weeks of shows throughout Canada. Her last performance out of the country had finally finished in Quebec and then it was on to Albany. From there he said the tour would take them to Pittsburg, then over to Chicago. She couldn't bear the thought of another day with this horrible man. So, during their ride from Quebec she waited till he dozed off in their shared train car, slipped her hand in his vest pocket and took out twenty dollars.

Tonight would be her last night. She would be performing at the Albany Center for Performing Arts. As soon as she finished her last song, she would take her final bow, retire to her room as expected by Reginald, but in the morning she would be long gone. She would no longer be his prisoner.

In the early morning hours, while Reginald was sleeping off his usual night of whiskey and women, she packed one small suitcase and slipped out the lobby into a carriage that the desk attendant had so kindly arranged for her. She poured her soul out to this young desk attendant much in the same way Annie had to the young steward on The Rosewood. She shared the abuse she had experienced and that she just wanted to go home. He promised he would do whatever he could to keep Reginald in the dark of her whereabouts and wished her a safe trip back home. Her train was not scheduled to depart until five o'clock p.m. and with all its stops and starts wouldn't arrive until nine that night. Her insides were in knots and she was sure at any minute Reginald would find her. She paced and prayed and paced and sat and once again thought of her sister and all the times she had been alone with her with no one to lean on. She owed her so much. She had been such an ungrateful little sister and as soon as she saw Annie again she would tell her just how much she meant to her. Then finally she heard the steam from the engine and within minutes boarded the southbound train. The landscape flickering through her window was as warm and welcoming as was the handsome young man sitting across from her. She felt life coming back into her veins.

"Allow me to introduce myself, I'm Francis O'Neal," as he stretched his hand across the car.

"Very nice to meet you, my name is Lily Ewing, I'm very sorry for staring, but you remind me of someone," replied Lily. She felt it in the car and she saw it in his eyes. Had he somehow come back to life to help her get back home? She was admittedly alone and afraid. She thought at any moment she would look out the window and see Reginald running alongside the train shaking his fist and screaming at her. Reginald was right in that it was because of him she had become so famous but, she didn't want fame anymore. This was not the life she wanted or the one he promised. Annie had worked so hard to build Matthew's House. Her mama had her voice in print that reached thousands every day. Her need to be heard, noticed and to be part of something bigger than teaching the children how to read, write and sing had almost ruined her life. She had taken her God given gift in the wrong direction for all the wrong reasons and now all she wanted was to walk through the door of Matthew's House and hope they would want her back.

“So, Miss Ewing just out of curiosity, who do I remind you of?” Francis asked.

“Oh, just someone who was real good at helping people find their way,” Lily answered.

***

It made Annie uncomfortable when the Captain first put the gun beneath the seat of their carriage during their first ride into the city. She didn’t like guns even though she knew there was a need for them in society. Wars were fought and won with them, hunters brought food home to their hungry families using them and on occasion she had witnessed the police firing a warning shot in the air to stop a common thief or pick pocket in his tracks. But she thought she would almost rather die herself than take someone’s life even in self-defense. It wasn’t his life he was concerned with defending on the streets long ago, it was hers. And now she understood so she kept it in the apartment in her desk drawer just in case she needed it to protect her children. She placed Lily’s telegram in that same drawer and waited with anticipation for her little sister that she hadn’t seen in months.

Dear Annie. Stop. I’m coming home. Stop. Train will arrive at 9. Stop. Please have Nicholas pick me up. Stop. Miss all of you so much. Stop.

She knew Lily was all grown up and had become successful in her own right with her fame and fortune but it just hasn’t been the same since she left and she hoped that she could convince her to stay. She needed her. She didn’t like it one bit when Lily went on the road as soon as her mama and the Captain left to go back home. Annie missed her mama’s support and the Captain’s help around Matthew’s House, but it whad been Lily that made her feel whole in a way she hadn't wanted to admit. She had been the one her daddy had relied on when he left. It was her responsibility to keep them together and even though she resented it for years she had finally realized that this had been his gift to her and not the burden she fought to free herself from. Lily was more than her sister, she was her best friend.

Annie made her regular final pass upstairs. On the right side of the building were the girls that were governed by Miss Walters and on the left side the boys were guarded by Mr. Rutherford. Last count there were forty three girls and fifty seven boys but Mr. Rutherford had been a 1st Lieutenant in the war before he was injured and the boys were sure they didn't want to cross him even though he only had one arm left.

Annie decided she would tidy up the apartment a bit before Lily arrived because she knew Lily needed order. As she was putting the last dish away, out of the corner of her eye she saw the face of a man she had never forgotten, with a gun raised and pointed at her head.

"I've waited a long time for this day. You took my boy and now I'm going to take you and one of yours. How dare you use his name? Nobody asked me or his mama what we thought. You, your mama and the Captain were all a part of it. You could have saved him and got him out of that hell hole, now where's your mama and that old man? I want them to watch. I want them to suffer just like I did," Roy said with his hand shaking and his finger on the trigger.

In an instant this man had invaded their safe

sanctuary. And she was looking straight into the likeness of old Pastor Feil with all his spit hurling in her direction along with his vicious rant of hatred. The old pastor had never preached about mercy, love or forgiveness, but instead an eye for an eye and this man was on a mission for revenge. It had been well over thirteen years since Matthew had died. The new sign over the front door was clear to everyone who walked through.

MATTHEW'S HOUSE
FOR ALL THE CHILDREN WHO'VE BEEN LOST AND FORLORN
MAY THIS HOUSE KEEP YOU SAFE AND WARM
IN MEMORY OF MATTHEW O'CONNOR
5-17-1848 9-05-1851

"Mr. O'Conner, please don't do this. Please, why don't you just sit down? I'm sure you're just tired and hungry. I'll fix you some dinner," Annie pleaded.

"Lady, you have no idea how tired I am. I saw you that day. You came right up to me and didn't even notice me or the others. That day you got your daddy out of jail, you and the Captain and that kid. If I had known that was your daddy, I'd killed him with my bare hands. I almost rotted in that hell hole all because the likes of you. And my Emily, she died not two weeks after we got here. All I did was have too much drink one night and got thrown in that place and only got out 'cause some lawyer finally showed up to help some of us out. Then I seen this place. You think you some kind of do-gooder? You think this house and all the little rats you take in are gonna keep you from burning in hell for killing my boy?" Roy raged.

"Roy, I didn't kill Matthew and neither did my mama. She did all she could do to try to help him and your wife. They were both real sick when you boarded. And the Captain had no idea. He didn't own that ship or make the rules. We just thought this place would honor his memory. I think about him every day. I've prayed for you and Emily that God would give you rest and peace," Annie pleaded.

Annie was shaking all over. Not out of fear for herself or the children for the moment, but for Lily and Nicholas. She knew they would be walking through the door at any minute right into this.

Click, "Put it down old man. Don't make me kill you," Nicholas had the Captain's gun in his hand pointed to the back of Roy's head.

Roy fired, then dropped to the floor and so did Annie.

"No! No, please no, Annie," cried Lily.

CHAPTER 18

Life, Death, and Politics

THE WHOLE WORLD WAS going to hell just like old Pastor Feil had said it would. There was just not enough true repentance and they were all paying for it. Lily had played her role in it too. What was she thinking? Why couldn't she just be satisfied with her life as it was instead of following some stupid halfhearted dream that was all wrong for her? She knew there was nothing wrong with dreams, but in the end it was more about her running from something that she had begun to think she was too good for. She was certain she deserved it. But Annie did not.

Lily couldn't believe the country that was supposed to offer so much promise had taken so many. It certainly wasn't up to her to decide whose time here was more valuable than someone else's but that didn't mean she couldn't have her own personal opinion as long as she kept those thoughts to herself. The children had little time to do any harm to humanity, yet she saw firsthand how they were abandoned into the streets and alleys like useless pieces of refuge. Thankfully she wasn't part of the prison adventure with Annie, Nicholas and her Uncle J, but from what she heard countless lives were lost over minor infractions that wouldn't have been taken so seriously back home. There were just too many people trying to live in too little space here and the fight was more over who was right or wrong than what was right or wrong and good common sense had somehow been lost in the battle. From all the bits and pieces of Jonathan's legacy, she was sure that given the chance, her daddy could have turned things around here.

She saw the flashes and still couldn't say who fired first, it just all happened so fast. Roy was dead and she was sorry he died with so much hate in his heart. He couldn't see or didn't want to see that Matthew's short life mattered and it was his death that brought about this house of hope. And for the first time and all the wrong reasons she was there at the helm running things the way that she knew Annie would want her to. She admired her sister even more now for she had no idea just how much work was involved in keeping Matthew's House afloat. The food costs alone were enormous, donations were dwindling again and it bothered her that they had no room to take in more children.

***

His familiar face was a relief and a testament to her growing sixth sense when Lily and Nicholas brought Annie's limp and near lifeless body to the same hospital that her daddy died in years ago. She was covered in blood and barely breathing. But when she saw the man in the white coat was the kind stranger from the train, Dr. Francis O'Neal, Lily knew Annie would be in the most perfect healing hands. The bullet had just missed her heart, but she would need several weeks to rest and heal. She would never forget that day. For at almost the exact day and time that Roy tried to kill her sister, a man by the name of John Wilkes Booth aimed a gun and shot President Abraham Lincoln in the head. Her sister had lived but he had not. They both lived to bring about justice to those that had been treated so unjustly. The country was still in mourning and she wondered more than she had ever before, where was God in all of this? She was more determined than ever to find her place, her position, her calling.

***

Annie was tired of looking up at the ceiling. Complete bed rest was ordered and she didn't realize just how tired she was but each day brought the discomfort of more and more bed sores. She had dedicated every single minute of her life taking care of other people and having someone take care of her was so foreign that she struggled with the idea of being a burden. Her legs were weak and she felt winded and wobbly just walking to the window in her room. So, it was the morning and afternoon visits by Dr. Francis O'Neal that Annie had begun to look forward to and count on when he would roll her out into the fresh air of the courtyard in her wheelchair where they would sit and talk until he was called back to his duties as a doctor. He was charming, witty and the only man she had ever thought about since she flirted with Daniel on the deck of The Rosewood. She had no idea how to react to her feelings for this man. Her daddy had taught her that part of being a godly woman was in knowing when to lead and when to follow. She didn't know if she was just tired of leading and was now ready to let someone else take over or if he was, in fact, the one.

She had wanted to be up and well enough to travel to see the train that would be carrying President Lincoln across the country from Washington, D.C. to his final resting place in Illinois, but instead she would have to read about it in the paper. She wondered why she lived that day and this great man died. She remembered reading the Emancipation Proclamation the day it was published in The Irish Settlers News and didn't get a full understanding of just how important that day would be for so many. The soldiers that would give their lives for the freedom of the slaves and the slaves that would be granted their God given freedom. She never understood how so many people of a country that represented freedom could own another person. The City of New York was far removed from the war that was going on in the states south of them and she hoped it would all end soon. And now, this same kind of vengeful hatred that killed President Lincoln had almost killed her but why did God spare her? And then her thoughts shifted to the only future she was certain of and that was her work at Matthew's House. She had no idea if Dr. Francis O'Neal had the same feelings for her but what if he did? And if she chose to go back to Matthew's House and continue to make it her life's work would he follow her or would she have to give it all up to be a doctor's wife?

***

Lily and Nicholas had visited every day, but it was Dr. Francis O'Neal that insisted on bringing Annie home. He knew he had fallen deeply in love with his patient but had resisted any temptation to show or mention his feelings while she was under his care. She had chattered nonstop about Matthew's House and he not only wanted, but needed to see for himself what his competition for her time would be.

Not one word of the shootings at Matthew's House or Reginald's indecent and criminal behavior was sent to Katy as they had all agreed the bad news would be unnecessary since the girls were now both safe and sound. They would be home in a few days and Annie would be almost completely healed by then and Lily thought there was no need to worry her mama. She found herself finding comfort in visiting her daddy's grave regularly while Annie was gone where she quietly prayed and thanked him and God for watching over them while her mama and Uncle J were away.

Since the Captain left, Nicholas had become the man of the house. Lieutenant Rutherford made his way quickly downstairs that night after both guns had fired but by then it was all over. It was the Lieutenant that pulled the revolver from Nicholas' hand and said, "Son, you did what you had to do, now don't let it sit on you too long."

Nicholas had wanted to join and go fight with the Union Army but Annie and Lily wouldn't hear of it and for the first time he was glad he had listened. Had he gone and fought, who would have been there to save Annie. He had never fired a gun but in that moment his survival skills had once again kicked in. He had been tossed into the streets by parents he couldn't remember and it was all because of Annie that he was here. So much had been taken away but so much had been given. He heard Annie say on many occasions about giving what you need and it will come back to you. He had done what he could to help out at the house but he wondered where would he go from here? He knew he wanted a wife, a family, a real house and a farm. He was tired of the city, the crime, noise and the polluted sky. He wanted to live in the wide open.

The Rosewood should arrive on Tuesday. Stop. Miss you. Stop. Have so much to tell you. Stop. Love Mama. Stop.

Annie and Lily decided when Katy got home they would let her go first. No one would say a word about the shootings or bad turn of events in Lily's life. They would just let their mama and Uncle J do all the talking.

As expected it had been Mr. Jarvis Williams that had bought North Highlands and moved his family there. Katy had written of her father's death knowing how badly Jeremiah wanted to marry her mother. However, Jeremiah already knew because he had been the one discarding Samuel's letters all through the years. He had decided that leaving things the way they were would probably be best for Lizzie. And they were both very happy and content growing old together as Mr. and Miss Fletcher. He was certain he had the intimacy of his best friend by his side all these years and didn't want to do anything to disrupt the most meaningful relationship he ever had. Samuel, on the other hand, used the entire visit in a futile attempt to reignite his mother's love. In the final days however he relented as Katy had that just knowing her would have to be enough. Mrs. Molly was alone now but was still in charge of the yearly gatherings of the old patients.

What was not expected was the news that the Captain had been telegraphed and asked to run for a city council seat in their district. Elections were still foreign to immigrants. No one from their background had ever considered that they would one day have an opportunity to serve in public office. Only the powerful and wealthy land owners had that privilege in Ireland. Mr. Clayton had kept Katy, the Captain and Samuel informed of the goings on in the city and particularly their district. And it was Mr. Clayton that put the Captain's name up for consideration. He said they needed someone that had a genuine vein to help the people and he felt that the Captain should be the one. Mr. Clayton felt that the Captain had the leadership experience along with more integrity in his little finger than all of the council members combined.

The news of President Lincoln's assassination

stunned the people of Ireland as it did Katy and the Captain. And he thought what a privilege it would be to help his people, the Irish community, have a voice for the city they had worked so hard to build.

It was not at all unusual that the many immigrants coming into the city had their last name either replaced or shortened. If the name was too long, had too many vowels or consonants it was changed either by the immigration officials or the families themselves just to fit in. Poor Nicholas had basically named himself after a well to do child and seemed content all these years to carry it. However, the Captain was a grown married man now with possibly a future in politics and his integrity would be first and foremost in his campaign. If there were any skeletons in his past he needed to uncover them and fast.

All he ever knew for sure was Julius. As a gypsy he had no real given last name and it gnawed at him more every day. He knew he traveled with the Kinney clan and he had assumed that name on the ship and on his marriage license to Katy. That would be Katy's new last name that she would bear for the rest of her natural life and he wanted to be sure of that as well.

He knew all about the girls visit with Mr. and Mrs. Toudle and how they had just happened upon an abandoned gypsy camp and decided to settle on it. And he was also very familiar with the area between Highland Way and Dublin as he remembered travelling that area often as a child. So with little else to go on he wanted to make sure before they left to find the Toudles and the old campground. If anything had been left behind hopefully he could begin to piece together his real family roots.

Katy had completion on her family tree and it made her sad for her husband that he was grasping at straws just for his last name. Even though she wasn't proud of her father and all his depravity and wickedness she was thankful to have found the truths in her life and wanted to be there for her husband's reckoning with his own. No matter how painful or ugly it might be. She knew, if nothing else, his past had to be settled before they could really start building their future together.

Mr. and Mrs. Toudle were delighted with their surprise visitors and the stories of how far they traveled and the roads they took. Mr. Toudle was certain he had heard of the Kinney Clan while he worked his trade in the early days but, unfortunately he thought most of them had either died during the famine or left for settlements elsewhere. There were no photographs of any kind left at the campsite but there was one crate full of junk that Mr. Toudle pulled out for inspection.

Katy had vague memories of her childhood at North Highlands and she prayed that the same thing would surface for him. Inside the trunk was a clear round bottom glass bowl, a fiddle with broken strings, a red scarf full of moth holes and a few books on magic and illusions. It was all useless junk and as the disheartened Captain threw the books back into the crate one small brown folded piece of paper fell out. He reached in, opened and read, "King of Kings, Lord of Lords, the Kinney Clan just added another one. On this day, October 10, 1815, Roman and Ruth brought into this world, Julius Markus Kinney. May he lead with the same affection and respect as his fore bearers have done." He just stood there in complete disbelief.

In his hand was his truth and it had a ring of honor to it. It was no longer important, who or where he came from. The only thing that mattered to him now was he had roots no matter how many times they were pulled up. And now he was certain once he got home that Nicholas would become part of his new family. That little boy that darted out in front of their carriage so many years ago would become his son and carry the Kinney name and Katy was thrilled with the idea.

Katy wasn't sure she was ready for a life in politics but as his wife she would follow. She would make him proud, she would make Annie and Lily proud and she would make Jonathan proud and when their ship arrived they all hit the ground running.

Dr. Francis O'Neal's introduction into Annie's life had to be explained one day but she wasn't sure how, where or when to bring it up. And Lily was certain that her mama and Uncle J would want to hear about her singing career in more depth. All of that would come later. For now they had an election to win.

CHAPTER 19

The Dances in Life

IT WAS OFFICIAL, JULIUS Markus Kinney was on the ballot for the much sought after council seat for the 8th District of the City of New York. Katy and the Captain quickly moved out of the newspaper building and in with Samuel on 42nd Street turning the old apartment into their campaign headquarters. Mr. Clayton made signs that he posted on every street corner while Mrs. Clayton scheduled meetings all throughout the district and kept his calendar. Katy spent much of her time writing his speeches while Annie and Lily knocked on doors. Anytime he wasn't needed at Matthew's House, Nicholas became his daddy's right hand man staying at the Captain's side. He was after all a Kinney, too. The adoption became legal soon after they returned and he finally had not only a legitimate family but a real last name. It didn't matter that he was a young man now, he just couldn't stop saying Nicholas Kinney, Nicholas Kinney, over and over again, like he had been reborn. There had already been a few instances when the Captain introduced Nicholas as his son that people remarked at how much they looked alike. Maybe they were just making small polite talk but Nicholas didn't care, hearing that just made him feel an even more integral part of his new family. He was more grateful than ever before that he had been there that night to save Annie and he would make sure that Reginald Wolfe would never hurt Lily again.

There was a big debate scheduled Friday night at City Park and Nicholas was on hand to help settle the crowd and protect his daddy in case things got too rough which they usually did during these types of events. He would be debating the current Councilman Henry Collins who had the backing of the police department and the current sitting city council. That alone made the crowd angry that Henry was in their back pocket and shouldn't be trusted to ever serve the public again. Councilman Collins accomplishments paled in comparison to the list of the Captain's in his few short years in the city and the crowd shouted his name over and over again.

"Captain, Captain, We want Captain Kinney!"

"Thank you very much. I promise to serve this city with the highest standards. Many of us here today are from the same blood, Irish Blood. And we came to this country with the dream of a better life for our families. I was the Captain for many years on The Rosewood that has sailed to and from the shores of America bringing some of you here. So you should already feel safe and secure that our first voyage together was a success. Then I found a higher calling over the last several years helping to build and run Matthew's House which has successfully housed and fed hundreds of our youngest and most vulnerable citizens. These children are our future and we must continue to lay a firm foundation for all walks of life, young and old, rich and poor, men and women. But, let me say that I haven't done this alone. It has been with the partnership and commitment of my wonderful family that made all this possible. Without them by my side none of this would be possible. Furthermore, I intend to make sure that not only will I make it my job to represent this district I plan to clean up the corruption that has permeated the very offices and departments that should be on hand to protect and serve each and every one of you. So, I ask you today, to please give me your vote!"

Nicholas lingered on the stage for an extra few minutes keeping a careful eye back and forth into the sea of constituents for any sign of trouble before his family immersed themselves into the crowd. His face was burned in his mind. He knew it was Reginald Wolfe but in an instant he had disappeared into the crowd. Nicholas held Lily back with the excuse that they needed to wait a bit to let the rowdy bunch thin out.

On November 7nd, 1865, Julius Markus Kinney won the election in a landslide. The people had spoken loud and clear. Nicholas couldn't believe that he was suddenly not only someone's valued son, but the son of the city's first elected Irish councilman. To be pulled out of the gutter of despair into this wide open sea of endless dreams and possibilities was at times more than he could wrap his head around. Why was he chosen that day? Was he just in the right place at the right time or was this, in fact, his destiny from the beginning? From this day forward he would carry the Kinney name with pride. He would never forget the women that saved him in the beginning. He wanted to make his daddy proud and that meant he would always have to live within the letter of the law. The revenge that he had let boil in his blood toward Reginald Wolfe would have to be settled in another way. But it would be settled.

***

It would take some time for Councilman Kinney to adjust to his new life as a paid public servant. He knew the salary wouldn't be much, yet he thought if it was nothing that would be fine with him. Clearing out the people that had corrupted and contaminated the public office he and his family had worked all these months to win would be rewarding in itself. After all, he had never received a penny for his work at Matthew's House. His savings from his years as the Captain of The Rosewood had sustained what personal needs he had. He had earned his keep at the newspaper fixing and repairing the building and equipment and for that was given free room and board. Then once he married Katy, the roof over their heads was provided for by her which still made him feel a little uncomfortable. Now, at least, he would be able to contribute towards their household expenses. Not seeing Katy and the girls during the day would be something he would have to get used to. But, the long hours waiting for him at city hall would be something he already knew how to do. The only difference here was this time he had someone waiting for him when he got home.

As Katy sat in front of her small dressing table she thought of all the transformations that had taken place in her life. She was born a McLaughton and tossed out, raised as a Fletcher by a horse trainer, placed under the care of Pastor Wynne as an orphan, became a Ewing and the wife of a farmer, crossed the ocean in the underbelly of The Rosewood as a second class citizen and now she was sitting here looking at the reflection of a woman married to a councilman and would be for the first time formally introduced tonight as Mrs. Julius Kinney. What a journey and incredible life and none of it would have been possible had it not been for Jonathan pulling her out of that fire long ago. She had been rude and ugly and mean to him from the first time they met on the edge of the estate when she fell from her horse. He picked her up then and carried her every single day until she felt him release her into the safe and comforting hands of Julius Kinney the day they married. She would honor his memory and love him until the day she died. Not in the way she had grown to love Julius. She was glad she had finally learned the true meaning of unconditional love and was sorry that the man that had shown her so much was now gone. If only she had the insight then that she had now that love wasn't always about feelings.

It was an action word.

It was Jonathan moving towards that burning stable house not caring or thinking about his own personal safety or wellbeing. Her scar had long ago become as much a part of her face as her nose was and she rarely noticed it anymore. And what people thought or said had long ago become of no moment to her. She actually saw it as her crown of glory instead of her crown of thorns.

She dressed, pulled her hair up, and was eager to see her girls. They would all be attending the victory party at The Grand Hotel and she would be glad when it was all over. She had a lot of catching up to do with Annie and Lily. It seemed that since the moment they arrived back home they had been either busy moving, tending to the adoption of Nicholas or the campaign. Katy felt like something was different with both of her daughters but she couldn't quite put her finger on it. She was dying to hear about Annie's new beau and how they met and was worried that Lily had shown little interest in her singing career that she was so immersed in when they left. She also was curious as to why Reginald Wolfe had been out of town for so long. That's all Lily would say was that he was out of town on business. Katy couldn't imagine that there would be any business more important than her daughter's.

"Can I have everyone's attention here for a moment please? It is with great honor and my pleasure to introduce the man we have all hoped and prayed so long for, Councilman Julius Kinney and his beautiful wife who has inspired so many of us, Mrs. Julius Kinney!" announced Mr. Clayton.

Where he was once known as Captain and Uncle J in his fine tailored white uniform, he was now Councilman Kinney in his black tuxedo and top hat that night holding on to the arm of their mama. They only had a small gathering in Mr. and Mrs. Clayton's living room when they married and this felt more like the reception Annie thought they should have had. Katy's long pale blue dress was as simple as she was, yet her classic head held high movements caused every women in the room to want to be her. What a transformation from the days when women pointed and stared at her in complete disgust back in Highland Way.

Annie and Lily argued as to which costume and name they preferred for the man of the hour and had finally agreed that were all exceptional in their eyes. However, Annie would have given a million dollars and trade it all, if she could see, if only for a moment, her daddy, standing there in his white shirt with the sleeves rolled up and suspendered dark brown pants covered in Irish Gold. She would take his arm and dance the night away. Just as her eyes swelled with tears, Dr. Francis O'Neal walked her out on the dance floor, held her close and whispered in her ear his promise that he would never leave her.

Lily and Nicholas were as close as a brother and sister could be. He was certain that it was Reginald Wolfe that he saw during his daddy's debate that day and he would not let Lily out of his sight tonight. He would make sure that she would never again fall victim to another predator and not a single available man asked her to dance and she didn't care. That part of her life was over.

CHAPTER 20

Her Brother's Keeper

KATY KNEW SAMUEL was a weak and broken man and nothing Lizzie said or did during their visit changed him or could help him reconcile his past. Lord McLaughton had broken everything that was good in him after years of mental and emotional abuse and Katy took pity on him when nobody else did. Admittedly, she couldn't understand why he couldn't seem to start over or move on. His lifelong tormentor was gone and everyone in his extended family had assured him that he would always have a place at their table. She found it odd that he had been the one to reach out to her not once, but twice with his letters of reconciliation and now it's as though every time she tried to get close he pushed her further away. He had his health, plenty of money to live on or even start his own business and he had the kind of family that he always wanted, but Samuel was the sort that seemed to be always waiting for the next bad turn of events. He was petty and peculiar about the most insignificant things such as having to eat at a certain time three times a day and insisting that the maid never clean his room. Katy and Julius tried to meet his structured meal demands as often as they could but the campaign in the end had made it virtually impossible. She didn't understand why he kept his door closed and locked all the time other than his need for privacy. In any event, she did put her best foot forward to include and engage her brother in their family functions and was determined not to give up on him. After all, where would she be had Jonathan given up on her?

"Why do you treat him like he's a child?" asked Annie.

"That's not at all what I trying to do. It's just that he's been bullied his whole life and I'm just trying to take a different approach," answered Katy.

"Mama, really, look at what happened to you, to me, Lily, Nicholas and we didn't turn into negative or demanding people. How do you talk someone down from the same tree every single day!" exclaimed Annie as she went on. "He didn't lift one finger of support to help with Uncle J's campaign and I haven't been able to get him to come visit here once. You know we can always use an extra set of hands. And why did he write to you in the first place if he didn't want to get to know you, or us? It just seems as though he's consumed with some demon of his own making," Annie declared.

"Did something happen while we were gone that I need to know about? What happened to you Annie? You've seemed distant and a lot less compassionate that you use to be. I know we've been busy with the campaign and election for months now but I feel like you're hiding something. So what is it?" Katy insisted.

Annie held her tongue for a few minutes staring out across her apartment to the exact spot that Roy died and he tried to kill her. She could still see Roy's gun pointed at her head while Nicholas' hand held the Captain's revolver at Roy's. She was as certain now as she was then that both men must have fired at the exact same time because she could only remember hearing one shot. Then there was this awful smell, she felt her flesh tear and finally the last thing she remembered was hearing Lily scream her name. Days later in the hospital while retelling the sequence of events to a more cleared headed patient, Nicholas was fixed more on the carnage of Roy's brain matter and blood splattered everywhere that he had to clean up while Lily simply described the new chair and rug she had waiting for her to come home to. "Ok, something did happen while you were gone and I guess it did change me a little bit, but I don't think it was for the worse. I just think that we can make excuses for people for just so long before it begins to hurt them more than it helps them. Roy showed up here and well, he was so crazy angry at me, at us, he tried to kill me, but before he could, Nicholas shot and killed him, right here, almost right where you're standing."

Katy's knees buckled as she fell into Annie's new chair. "Are you, did you get hurt?"

"Yes, he shot me Mama, luckily the bullet just missed my heart. Nicholas and Lily got me to the hospital quickly and it was Dr. Francis O'Neal that operated on me that day and now you know the rest of the story of how we really met. Mama, I saw the hate in Roy's eyes. It was real. He didn't want to see that this place was started all because of his son Matthew. I really think it just pushed him over the edge. And he told me that he had been there that day when we found Daddy. He said he was in the very same jail cell and had he known he would have killed Daddy with his bare hands. Why would he say such a mean and horrible thing? I know how much it hurts to lose somebody you love and care about and I know I was angry for a while but, I have never wanted to march over to that prison where Daddy almost died and kill anyone. It was a terrible thing that should have never happened. That's why it was important to me to make sure the people that are sitting in there have their day in court and for that Roy got the help he needed to get out. Can you believe? So, I'm not saying that Samuel isn't entitled to his sadness for what happened with his father, I just think he should at least try to find a way through it just like I had to, that's all," Annie said.

Once again, Katy knew Annie was right. She always seemed to know how to untangle the cobwebs, knock off the dust and move forward. She probably had been more of a crutch than a motivator and whether he was just being childish and stubborn or he just had no idea where or how to begin. Katy would sit down with him today and help him map out some sort of fresh start. She knew she had been the lucky one even in her darkest days. But, in some ways she thought she knew how Samuel felt inside, like he didn't belong anywhere and she had to admit that he was hard to be around. He rarely left his room and when he did he complained about one ailment or another, none of which could be substantiated by Dr. Francis O'Neal. She acknowledged on many occasions that their father had taken his mother away too. And even though he lived a life among the wealthiest, there had never been any real substance in his life while she had Jeremiah, Pastor Wynne, Jonathan and her children. They had sustained her. Jonathan loved her unconditionally and Annie pushed her. Her little girl had been the one that helped her break down all the walls that she had built to keep the world at bay. And that's what she would have to do for Samuel. As soon as she could, she would talk to her husband about some kind of new job, new position that Samuel could work at. She thought he just needed to get out of the house, a purpose. He just needed a real hard push.

"I'm so glad you're fine now. And I'm incredibly thankful that Nicholas was here to save you. Please do me a favor and don't ever keep anything like that from me again. I'm your mama and I want to be there for you and Lily no matter, well no matter how old or far apart we are. You don't ever have to protect me in that way. Promise me?" Katy pleaded.

Annie followed reluctantly with, "So, I guess I need to tell you about Reginald Wolfe then."

"What about him? And by the way, where has he

been? Did he and Lily have some kind of falling out?" Katy asked.

"Well, it's worse than that. Lily kind of did the same thing to me that I did to you. She never said a word about what was going on and how he was treating her until she came home. Mama, he not only kept all the money she made for him, but he beat her and tried to force himself on her. He wanted her, Mama. And I guess he thought he could break her down and eventually she would give in and give herself over to him one day. She actually ran away from him and had just walked through the door with Nicholas for the first time only minutes after Roy walked in on me. The timing of all this was unbelievable. It was really hard for her to admit that she had misjudged him but I think she was more ashamed that she let it go on for so long. He was real abusive and controlling with her, Mama. She didn't give many details other than he wasn't at all who he pretended to be. Please don't say anything to Uncle J right now. I'm not asking you to keep this from him forever, but with the election and all, can we just let things calm down for a bit? She just wants to put it all behind her. I think she's fine now anyway. It was a bad experience for her but she said it really gave her the insight she needed," Annie said.

"I just don't know what to say. I would have never thought he was that kind of person. We all really trusted him. Maybe I wasn't paying attention like I should have. I feel like I should talk to her about it. But, if you think she's alright now, maybe I'll just let her bring it up on her own," Katy answered.

When Katy got home she had her thoughts all lined

up in her head what she was going to say to Samuel. It was time for him to join the human race and get involved in something productive. She would insist that he come to work with her every day and maybe teach him the newspaper business until her husband could find him something more suitable. She knew he had never worked a day in his life but there was plenty more work for men than women and all the women in her family had carved out their niche and there was no reason why he couldn't do the same. She opened the front door, headed upstairs to his room and knocked on his locked door.

"Samuel, please open up, we need to talk. Samuel, I know you're in there, open the door, it's important," Katy insisted. She heard her husband's voice calling her from downstairs. It was straight up noon and he promised to be home for their scheduled lunch with her brother.

"Julius, please come up here, I think something's wrong. He won't open the door," Katy's voice was shaking and her worse fear rose up. Again she felt like another door was nailed shut and she desperately needed to get in. Julius doubled up the stairs after his wife's plea for help. He pushed all his weight against the door several times while Katy screamed, "Samuel, please let us in, please I'm here for you, we're here for you, please!" Then Julius pushed his shoulder with one more thrust almost falling on top of him. There was blood splattered everywhere and evidence of only one assailant. Samuel, in fact, had been his own worst enemy all along. The gun he used was lying next to his head in the middle of the floor.

"Oh my God, no, no, Samuel what have you done!"

screamed Katy as she stood over the only person she had left that remembered the innocent life they use to share. She didn't believe in bad luck, curses or even being in the wrong place at the wrong time. Katy knew this was all about a man that had simply given up.

"Katy, you need to get out now and let me handle this. There's nothing more that you can do for him, honey, I'm sorry," Julius said. The newly elected councilman had a full schedule for the day, but everything would have to be cancelled. As she looked at that same wedding photograph of her parents on his dresser she saw a handwritten note that she quickly picked up and read once she was out of her husband's sight.

Dearest Katy,

I cannot go on any longer. I don't deserve the happiness you have and I don't want to become the burden to you that our father was to me. I'm an evil and terrible man. It was me that set the stable on fire that night. Pastor Wynne came by and told father he had found our mother. That's when he told me what I had to do. He wanted the whole place burned down and if I didn't he would throw me out and disown me. He wanted to be rid of Jeremiah and everything that reminded him of her. I had nowhere else to go Katy and I was sure that you at least would escape without harm. It has haunted me every day since and I'm certain if I'm not there yet, I will one day go completely mad. Please forgive me.

I will be your loving brother forever, Samuel

What an awful and strange twist in that Samuel had followed the same path as his own father had. He had allowed his guilt to turn him into a tormented recluse with imaginary ailments. Katy knew it would be wrong to keep this from her husband and she also knew this would be another thing she would have to tell him one day. But, she would never tell her children. There was no reason to. She had not only survived the fire that was meant to finish her off but she had thrived. If he had just asked, if he had just told her, he would have known that he was forgiven and that the only thing left was for Samuel to forgive himself.

CHAPTER 21

The Wolfe's Last Prowl

ONE OF THE FIRST of Councilman Kinney's accomplishments was to make sure Matthew's House had a secure and steady flow of money to keep it going. He introduced and with the support of the majority of his constituents passed the first sin tax on liquor and that money was used to house and support the orphans as well as appoint free legal aid to the indigent prisoners. His approach for the new tax was based on good old common sense. Why not tax the very thing that was probably causing the children to be homeless in the first place? And then most of the prisoners were there for either some drunken brawl or petty crime to get the money to buy more whiskey. Most of all, he did not want another Jonathan Ewing to waste away just because he had no one to represent him.

In that vein not only did Annie create and serve on the board of The Children's Welfare Society but The Prisoners Reform Board as well. Where there were once only the voices of her small circle of family, friends and church volunteers, suddenly it became the thing to do among the rich bored housewives and their husbands. They were more interested in trying to one up each other in their fancy suits and gowns they wore to the fundraising galas but Annie didn't care. She was just happy to see more money and attention being paid to her just causes.

Katy buried herself in her writing for the paper where she left off trying to erase that awful image of her brother's self-inflicted wound. She did, however, take the time to write a much long overdue letter to Jeremiah and her mother about the election, Annie's handsome new boyfriend and Samuel's unexpected death and how much he meant to all of them. It took her months for the finality of it all to sink in and she was surprised at how badly Annie took it. She was almost inconsolable in that she had spoken so badly about him only hours before. Only, Katy was certain she would never expose her brother's violent act against her and Jeremiah. For all she knew he had taken leave of his senses long ago. She knew she almost lost her daughter by the hand of a man that couldn't work through his grief either and the picture of Annie's body lying limp and covered in blood was a vision she was thankful that she didn't see in real time. She remembers now feeling some tension between Jeremiah and Samuel during their entire visit but all this time she thought it was reluctance on Jeremiah's part. She knew how Jeremiah thought Samuel was a weakling as a young man and for her to allow him back in her life was something that even he had trouble with. And now she understood it was either Samuel's guilt or fear or maybe both that Jeremiah somehow knew. If he did, she was sure that he would never confess to her that her father and brother were to blame for what was supposed to be their last day alive at North Highlands. So many secrets were tucked away now. But, she was beginning to believe much like Jonathan and Lizzie did for her sake that sometimes some things were best left unsaid if saying them would change nothing.

This time in her column she decided she would encourage her readers to write about any concerns they had for improvements or changes in the city. In this way she could be the eyes and ears for her husband and all the work that needed to be done. It didn't take long before hundreds of complaints poured in, from closing the taverns at a decent time to too many loose animals running through the streets and her favorite was a heartwarming handwritten thank you note from a little girl whose father had been released from prison. It seems his fate would have been much the same as the father of her children had Annie not gotten involved. One of the most alarming concerns had become the welfare and safety for the women that were forced to walk alone at night. Several women had recently been brutally attacked and left for dead while leaving work from some of the many work houses in the garment district. The streets were poorly lit and the police gave little or no protection at all in these areas. It was their opinion that their time would be better spent in the more affluent areas where they had little to do but stand on the street corners and flirt with the pretty ladies.

Councilman Kinney made countless visits to the Mayor's Office where he reminded him just how easily he could be replaced if he didn't immediately call for additional new hires. They served the same people and it was imperative that these women were given protection no matter what their social standing was and he demanded foot patrol in the garment district from dusk till dawn. There had already been dozens of terminations that he had a hand in from the police force once he was elected. It had become clear there would no longer be a blind eye turned from the corruption that had infiltrated City Hall and those that were either elected or hired to protect the citizens of New York City would do their job.

Nicholas Kinney held his hand high during his swearing in as one of the newest and finest protectors in his dark blue uniform and bobby hat. This had been his long awaited moment in time. He had grown up at Matthew's House never once wanting to be adopted by the strangers that came by for a look. He wasn't one of them in that way. And it was no coincidence that Annie and the Captain always had something for him to do when some interested good Christian couples showed up wanting to adopt a young boy. She didn't for one second claim ownership of her favorite little boy it's just she wanted him to one day be part of their family just as the Captain had. But someone had to present themselves as a couple in the eyes of the law in order to do that. So, Annie just held out hope that couple would one day be in her family and she wasn't at all surprised that he became her adopted brother that day.

"What a fine looking young man you are. We are so very proud of you, Nicholas," Katy said in between her sniffing and quiet motherly sobs.

"Yes, son, this is probably one of the proudest moments of my life," agreed Julius.

Nicholas was proud too. He was proud and thankful to not only belong to the Kinney family but to have been a beneficiary of Jonathan Ewing's legacy. At times he felt guilty that he made it and so many others didn't. He had only known life on the streets before Annie spotted him that day running from one alley to another much like the street rats that old man Roy had called them. He knew all the stealing he did back then was wrong but it was about survival and he wasn't the least bit remorseful. And now he would be ever so careful to build trust with the children that needed help out of their life on the streets and protect the women that needed protection from the predators stalking about at night. He would be a protector of women and children. And if anyone got in his way he already knew what to do.

He was immediately assigned to walk the streets every night from eight to six the next morning and he knew every square inch and every nook and cranny that a mugger or thief could hide. His "just in case" weapon stayed strapped to his waist where he hoped it would stay. He had been able to not let the shooting of Roy sit on him for too long because he knew it was his only option and he hoped just firing his weapon in the air first would be enough at least in the beginning here on his new foot patrol route. He knew how devastating it was for his mama and then his daddy when they were finally told about the Roy encounter at Matthew's House. They were both grateful that he saved Annie but still grieve to this day that Roy, Emily and Matthew were all gone. They had boarded the same ship with the same hopes and dreams as the Ewing girls and the entire O'Conner family was gone. It didn't seem fair to any of them that life handed them such a raw deal. But then again Nicholas knew that it was Roy that chose hate and revenge that night.

Lily was spending more and more time volunteering in the children's ward at Mercy Hospital. The looks on their faces had haunted her during her visits to see Annie. It was bad enough they were sick, but they were lonely, afraid of the unknown and stuck in bed in a cold empty room. She had shared her concerns that the children needed more attention with Dr. Francis O'Neal but the hospital was barely surviving financially with the staff they had.

Katy had been very generous with her inheritance from Samuel years ago contributing more to the causes around her than anything for herself. She had consistently funneled money every month to Matthew's House as well as buying Mr. and Mrs. Clayton a state of the art printing press for the newspaper. So when Lily approached her mama about buying a few toys, books and extra blankets for the sick and bedridden children she didn't hesitate, even adding a brand new piano. It had bothered Katy a great deal that her daughter had all but walked away from her God given gift and while she had yet to bring up the reason for it Katy knew she needed to rekindle it. And without any words being spoken the day the piano was delivered Katy was on hand for her daughter's first public recital in years. Lily played for her captive audience a couple of her long ago favorite hymns that seem to breathe fresh warm air into the cold and sterile children's ward while her mama stood over her.

"Thanks, Mama. I didn't realize just how much I missed my music," Lily said.

"You're welcome, honey. And I'm glad you're back. I really missed you," and that was all that was said.

The children that could get out of bed swelled around her much in that same circle that she garnered years ago, while the bedridden boys and girls still had the flow of music to cradle them in their beds. Lily would soon find her way to add her voice back into the mix and would continue this routine every afternoon until their bedtime.

Lily would be done at Mercy Hospital soon and it had been from day one his first order of business every night to escort his sister back to Matthew's House. Tonight was a full moon and the light broke through the overcast haze in the city and they would walk and catch up on each other's news in their young adult lives.

She appeared on the steps that night like the angel he had always seen her as, dressed head to toe in all white. The only thing missing was her halo and in Nicholas' mind she had one. Lily was exhausted physically from her double duty at Matthew's House and Mercy Hospital but her unwavering spirit was boundless. The children meant so much to her. Annie had told her the story of her start in life and how small and sickly she was and yet somehow she had survived with the heartfelt prayers of everyone around her. Being a child of hope meant so much to her. Giving the children hope meant the most to her. Annie had given her one of the most precious possessions she had that was carried with him from Ireland. She kept it close and read from it nightly out loud while her audience was spellbound. This was the stage that she belonged on. For when she pulled out her daddy's leather bound Bible and read and sang to the children the applause was real, genuine and purposeful. She had finally used her wings to move in the right direction.

As they walked Nicholas was mindful of the surroundings much like he had been when he kept watch over the crowds during his daddy's debates. There were so many dark alleys that at any moment some thug could spring from. And on this night from behind him he heard the voice he had long waited to silence.

"So, you're Sister Lily now, what a joke!" laughed Reginald with his whiskey breath. "I bet if I tell them what you're really like they would lock you up. You a thief, a liar and you owe me. And who's your funny looking boyfriend? Oh, is he here to protect you. What a laugh that is. Now stop all that pretend like, make believe, I'm going to make this world "a better place" garbage and come back with me so we can finish what we started. We had a contract. Tell your little boy here you've got some real work to do."

Reginald reached to grab Lily by the arm, and Nicholas again did what he had to do and in an instant, the world did become a better place, a safer place. Reginald Wolfe was dead. And he did it within the letter of the law. He did it to protect his sister and all the women of the world from this predator. Perhaps he was the one who had been attacking the women on the streets of the city. They will never know for sure but there were no more attacks after that night.

CHAPTER 22

Wide Open Virginia

NICHOLAS HAD ONLY FIRED his weapon three times in the two years he had been on foot patrol, once in the chest of Reginald Wolfe and twice into the air as warning shots. He didn't blink that night. The reaction was the same as it was when Roy held his gun pointed in the direction of Annie's head. It was about good versus evil and Reginald Wolfe had handed out enough evil. He saw it in his eyes and heard it in his voice the first time he met him. He would never lay another violent hand on his little sister much less another woman.

When word got around of how he had killed the man who had been terrorizing the city at night he quickly garnered respect from the good citizens and fear from the criminals. He had on more than one occasion been offered a promotion but moving up the ranks of the police department was not his passion. That passion he found during his nightly walks when he stopped at The Diner and Norah Dodson would hand him a fresh cup of thick black coffee. His daddy told him that when he met the right one he would know it. And every time he saw her his nerves got the best of him so he was certain she had to be the one.

"Son, when I met your mama long ago down below in the steerage section of The Rosewood, I knew something was about to change in my life, I just didn't know exactly what. And then when she put her arm in mine that night in the lobby of The Grand Hotel I instantly knew. But, back then she belonged to someone else and I thought Jonathan Ewing was the luckiest man alive. I don't know what I did to deserve her but I'm just glad she found me worthy. So, when you find her, just be patient. Don't push yourself on a lady. You'll know when the time is right and how she really feels about you."

And it was true. Julius Markus Kinney had waited and waited until he knew Katy had worked through her grief and Annie was ready to accept him. He had walked through the door of the newspaper late one morning after his nightshift at Matthew's House and Katy was sitting at her desk with a troubling look on her face and suddenly went off, "Why are you so late today? I thought something had happened to you.

You're never this late. Where have you been? I've been worried sick!"

That's when he knew that Katy was not only mindful of his presence in her life, but she counted on it.

Nicholas made sure he stopped by The Diner every night at the same time and sat in the same chair. He was certain she was a southern girl with her long drawn out words and funny phrases but she had the most perfect smile and charmed every man that walked in. She kept her head full of dark brown curls pulled back and tied up with the same pink ribbon that matched her heavily starched uniform. Her big, beautiful, green eyes made him want to pistol whip every man in the room that gave her a second look. He didn't like it one bit the way they looked at her and he certainly didn't like it when they flirted with her. She smiled at him and was always attentive but he got plenty of smiles and flirts from women and he knew it was mainly the uniform. His sisters were always telling him how handsome he was but that was a given coming from them. He had grown to almost six feet tall and at what he guessed was somewhere around his real twenty second or third birthday. And Annie said with his blonde hair she could pick him out of any crowd in a second. He didn't want Norah to just like him because he had on a uniform. He wanted her to love him on the days when he was in his old work clothes with dirt under his nails on their farm. That was still his dream and one mention of moving out of the city was all he needed. She said she would go wherever he went. That she would be glad to get out of the city, the crowded tenement apartment and the long hours on her feet at The Diner and live in the country with him wherever that might be.

So he saved every penny for that dream, their dream. Land was plentiful and he had two good hands and a strong back to build their house and work their land. Could they really live off the land? He'd lived in the city his whole life and the only thing he had ever grown was a small garden in the backyard of Matthew's House. And the only animal he had ever cared for was his dog Daisy that he buried in the same backyard. He and his mentor back then had their man to boy talks about hard work and giving God the glory for all things good while cultivating that garden back in the beginning. He hoped he had learned and applied all those things well. He hoped that just good old common sense and his physical fitness would carry him and Norah well out of the only life he ever knew.

He had seen the looks on the faces of the country folks when they would come to the city and how awestruck they seemed to be with all the buildings, lights everywhere, the live play houses and restaurants on every corner. But after a few days he always heard the same talk when they were ready to head back out to the peace and quiet of the country life. His Norah, that is his bride to be, had told him much the same story when he first met her. She had made the long trip with her aunt and uncle from Virginia to pick up some relatives that had come across the Atlantic as his adopted family had. The busy street vendors selling their wares and the fancy dresses on the women tugged at her desire to live a better life than she thought would be possible back home and now she wanted nothing more than go back to the simple life she once had. Would he be in the beginning that awe struck to? Would the peace and quiet and simple life become dull and dreary? He just couldn't imagine it would. Everyday more and more immigrants were filling every square inch of available space and it felt like the city would burst at its seams any minute. He wasn't at all resentful of their new presence he just wished they could figure out that there were roads that led out of the city and there was plenty more room somewhere else. And somewhere out there was a little farm in Virginia that had his name on it.

Shortly after Samuel killed himself, his room was packed up, cleaned, painted and refurnished for Nicholas. His parents insisted he move in and admittedly he had grown tired of living at Matthew's House. He not only wanted, but needed more privacy, if for no other reason but to get a little uninterrupted sleep after his night shift. So when Katy offered he was elated. For the first time in his life he would actually live in a house and have his very own room. It couldn't get any better than that except for the day when he had enough money to marry and move to the country with Norah.

Nicholas walked in the front door after his night shift and like usual his mama was waiting with a big hearty breakfast. His daddy was usually gone off to his job at City Hall by the time he got there so that gave him time to share his dreams alone with her. He valued his daddy's opinion but Nicholas needed his mama's approval.

And this morning he got it. "Nicholas, there's a place for sale right where you said you wanted to be, down in a place called Little Creek, Virginia. Here read it for yourself, fresh off the press.

LOCATED IN LITTLE CREEK VIRGINIA 200 ACRES WITH SMALL FARM HOUSE IN GOOD CONDITION LAND GOOD FOR COTTON WHEAT PEANUTS AND CORN MUST SELL AS SOON AS POSSIBLE $500.00 OWNER DIED CONTACT MR. DEAN SANDERS AT DEAN'S DRYGOODS STORE

"Mama, I only have a hundred and fifty dollars saved up and it's taken me over a year to do that", Nicholas answered as though his dream would never come true. Even though he had been given so much by his new family, he still felt at times behind all the other young men his age that had not grown up as orphans. He didn't have one resentful bone in his body for what life handed him at such an early age and he didn't want to be a burden on anyone and earning his way was what he thought all grown men should do. So his frustration wasn't at his family but at himself. Both of his sisters had done well for themselves. Lily had secured a staff position at Mercy Hospital as head of the children's ward and Annie was engaged to a successful doctor and had not lost who she was or her philanthropic work along the way. And now it was his turn to move on.

"Well maybe I can help," said Katy, and she went on. "Why don't you let me give you the rest of the money? It'll be your inheritance. And the best part is I'll still be here to see you enjoy it."

"No, Mama, thanks, I just can't. It just wouldn't be right. Besides you have given me so much already."

Nicholas had been praying for a way sooner than later out of the city and on with his life with Norah. Maybe this was his answer just not in the way he expected. "What if you loaned me the money? We could sit down and draw up a contract for payment and I would send you a set amount every month just like they do at the bank," Nicholas answered.

"Good doing business with you," answered Katy while throwing the newspaper in the air and shouting, "Sold!"

The following Saturday morning, Nicholas and Norah took their seats in the southbound train to Virginia. He had never seen the inside of a train but clearly remembers picking Lily up that day at the train station when she ran away from Reginald Wolfe. His heart was suddenly torn. Who would take care of Lily when he was no longer around to defend her? Annie had Dr. Francis O'Neal and his parents had each other, but who would look after his little sister?

Nicholas also had never been out of the city and the flashing landscapes through the windows had him almost ready to give up his seat and run along the side of the train just so he could be in the middle of it all firsthand. Within hours he saw not only the brightest, bluest sky he had ever seen but the greenest grass and the trees appeared to be the most magnificent of all of God's creations he had ever dreamed they would be. He thought he finally knew what heaven looked like. And suddenly he just knew that this was without a doubt where he belonged.

When the train pulled into the station they continued their journey in a borrowed wagon until he saw the sign that read,

**WELCOME TO LITTLE CREEK VIRGINIA
YOU MAY LEAVE THIS LITTLE TOWN
BUT IT WILL NEVER LEAVE YOU**

Everything he was seeing and experiencing made him sad for all the people like Lizzie that would never see all the beauty that was as far as the eye could see. He had been blind his whole life and for the first time saw what Jonathan Ewing fought so hard to keep for his family. He stopped their horse drawn wagon in its tracks, helped Norah out and got down on one knee and in proper fashion, asked her to be his wife.

When they found Dean's Dry Goods Store, Lawyer, Justice of the Peace sign all in one Nicholas knew he wasn't going to waste another minute. Mr. Dean brought them out to the farm that would be their pocket in this heaven, and then Nicholas paid the five hundred dollars in cash. And before they left Little Creek, Virginia, he wanted to have one more thing to celebrate with his family. So he decided to take the pages from a story his mama told him a long time ago. Nicholas pulled out two simple gold bands he had been carrying for months and he and Norah exchanged their lifelong vows of commitment before Mr. Dean, who was also the Justice of the Peace and two witnesses they borrowed from the store.

The work was back breaking hard from sun up to sun down. He hurt in places he didn't know he had but he wasn't alone. His daddy, mama, Lily and her new guard dog, Big Man came and helped as often as they could. And when Annie and Dr. Francis O'Neal could get away they would join in the effort. It was after all a family celebration.

Nicholas and Norah would not only succeed in

the wide open, but they would grow and prosper. For within one year after they married the world gave back what it had taken years ago.

Nicholas and Norah welcomed their new son, JONATHAN EWING KINNEY.

CHAPTER 23

Passengers

SHE HAD NEVER DREAMED of getting married, having children and living happily ever after. Those dreams had always been for her mama and daddy. She just wanted all four of them to grow old together on the farm and for her mama to be happy.

That was then and this is now and her mama was immeasurably happy. Rather more at peace and content with her life not only as Mrs. Julius Kinney but also as Katy Ewing, the pen name she still wrote under every day at the newspaper. That's exactly what Annie wanted. She wanted to be the Mrs. in Dr. and Mrs. Francis O'Neal but she didn't want to lose herself in her husband's world. She had one too and it was important, fulfilling and the core of whom she had become. There were three generations of good, strong healthy women still living in her family and she wanted to add to their family just as her brother Nicholas had. Her love for the children that she took in had been the forefront of her life for so long and she often wondered if she would ever know that perfect bond between mother and child. When Annie looked back in the early years when her best friend was born and her mama's inability to bond, she knew it had to be something more than just not being happy with her life on the farm or the circumstances that brought her there. That was the one thing that she had the most trouble moving on from. Why did her mama reject her sister at birth? And then one day, Dr. Francis O'Neal, opened her eyes to this newly discovered condition that they were finding more and more women suffering from shortly after giving birth. There was no name as of yet, only that it seemed to set in motion a long term down cast in the way these new mothers suddenly felt and saw things. At last, she finally had some answer that her mother had in fact loved both her and Lily from the very beginning and the thing that got in her way when Lily was born was something that neither she or her daddy could have ever done anything to repair. She just hoped and prayed that she would never fall victim to the same.

Annie and Dr. Francis O'Neal had taken their time courting. She knew there was no one else to be sure and he would often lovingly tease her that she was his most beautiful and favorite patient ever. However, they both had come from homes with parents that had been torn apart. Mr. and Mrs. Frederick O'Neal had parted ways not for survival sake as Jonathan had to do. But, for selfish reasons as Mr. Frederick O'Neal became too fond of his young son's nanny. As a boy, Francis was quite fond of Laura too and it was several years before he understood why his father and Laura left at the same time. After his mother remarried she struggled with so many insecurities that she would submit herself to whatever mistreatment his stepfather dished out including his own beatings. Finally, when Francis could no longer tolerate his abuse and his mother had dismissed him completely, he left when he was sixteen and never returned.

It was a life of struggle for a man that had in his early years been raised in a life of privilege. After Frederick moved out with Laura she quickly spent most of the money he had inherited from his father and soon left him almost penniless. Francis found his father in Albany and spent the next several years being the loyal son to a broken man. When Francis first found him he was living in a boarding house barely earning enough money as a bartender to pay his rent. But, his father had one dream left and that was for his son to be a doctor.

"Son, I know what I did to you and your mother was wrong and selfish. But, I was just an old man who couldn't see the fool I was being played for. That Laura was good at weaving herself in our house and our lives. I didn't think much when she came to work for us as your nanny but she was a smooth talker. I just was too blind and stupid to see it coming. The next thing I knew, she had me convinced that she was in love with me and well, you know, it didn't end well. I'm sorry things went sour for you and your mother but I'm really glad you found me. I've all but ruined my life but whatever I have to do, you're going to make it," Frederick said.

And he did make it. Frederick dug in and worked two jobs as a cook during the day and a bartender at night while Francis went to school. And when he wasn't in school or studying Francis would wash dishes, bus tables or sweep floors right alongside his father. Whatever money they earned would be pooled together for rent, food and tuition for Francis. After several years Francis graduated from the University of Albany Medical School. He then got his first job as the resident doctor tending to elderly folks that had been living together in one large boarding house. This was the last place his father lived before he passed away. And it would be his ride on the train car from Albany to New York City that day when the next chapter of his life would begin.

So they both shared different losses, but pain was pain. Francis had many years to reconcile with the father that abandoned him but Annie had only a few days to hold her daddy's hand. He would never see his mother again because she died a violent death at the hands of her abusive husband but Annie was able to save hers. They had spent entire evenings talking through to the morning hours of where they came from and what their lives meant to them now and more importantly where their dreams connected. And they loved each other too much not to be mindful of their losses while giving each other time for their wounds to heal. And after over four years they were ready as was everyone else.

She could think of no one else but Mrs. Molly to make her wedding gown. And as much as she had grown to love and respect the Captain, Uncle J, Councilman Julius Markus Kinney, she wanted the only man alive that had given it all, to give her away. Jeremiah, Lizzie and Mrs. Molly would arrive six weeks before the wedding which would be plenty of time ahead for fitting and dressmaking.

It would be an event like the City of New York had never seen. The Ewing women as well as Councilman Kinney were so well respected they had almost become unwitting celebrities of sort by the hands of Mr. and Mrs. Clayton. Their dear friends at the newspaper couldn't help but to print on a regular basis all the great accomplishments of each and every one of them. There was either an article about Lily's involvement with the children at Mercy Hospital, Annie's continuous work at Matthew's House or reworking the prison system or Councilman Kinney's planned vision for modernization in the area of public health. He led the movement for improvements in the water and sewer system that had alleviated many of the health problems that so many had suffered from. And while Katy had her column and worked there she never knew until the paper went to press what the head writer, Mrs. Clayton, would print. So, needless to say, her objections of her constant praise were always voiced too late. However, Annie insisted that they include her in on the announcement so their wedding wouldn't turn into the event of the year.

"Mrs. Clayton, can we just run the announcement

just like everyone else? I don't want you to go overboard here. I know how you can get carried away sometimes," Annie said.

"My dear child, I have no idea what you're talking about," answered Mrs. Clayton.

"Ok, let me put it to you this way. Under no circumstances will our engagement announcement be front page news. Promise me, that you will place it in the society section along with everyone else," Annie said.

"But, it is front page news. I remember the day you, Lily and your mama walked through the door just like yesterday. You were real serious about finding your daddy and determined, too. Mr. Clayton and I knew then there was something really special and unique about all of you and well, I just feel like we've been so blessed to be a part of your lives. We just love you all so much," Mrs. Clayton said as she patted her eyes.

"Yes ma'am, you mean a lot to us, too. You took us in and gave us hope. I know you didn't think we would ever find my daddy, but you always gave us another day to try. And for that we will always be grateful," Annie said as she hugged Mrs. Clayton's neck.

Annie and Lily were thrilled when they saw their Grandma Lizzie being escorted off The Rosewood by the man she had chosen to give her away. Mrs. Molly was at first sight right behind her lifelong companions but somehow managed to pass Lizzie and Jeremiah for the first hug.

"Oh, for goodness sake alive, you're a princess if I ever saw one, Miss Annie. And look at you Miss Lily, if you're not the spitting image of your grandma. Miss Lizzie I just wish you could see your granddaughters.

They are the loveliest creatures that God ever put on his good earth. I can certainly tell they were born and bred on The Emerald Isle," Mrs. Molly went on.

"Grandma Lizzie, Jeremiah, it's been too long. I'm so happy to finally see both of you again. I'm sure you're really tired and want to get settled. Everybody is back at the house waiting for us," Annie said leading them into the carriage.

"That's right, I've heard all about Nicholas. I can't wait to meet this young man and his new family. Julius talked about him quite a bit when they visited," said Jeremiah.

Lizzie remained quiet but alert on their ride to her daughter's house. Then as the carriage pulled to a stop she remarked "there are just so many different and unusual sounds here. And I'm having a little trouble making out some of the smells, too. But, don't worry about me I'll soon get a fix on things, right Jeremiah?"

"Absolutely you will. Matter of fact, I'm pretty sure that you can already smell what we're having for dinner tonight," Jeremiah said with a grin.

They were all there at the dinner table for their second family reunion and as Annie looked around at Francis, Lily, Nicholas, Norah, baby Jonathan, her mama, Uncle J, Mrs. Molly, Lizzie and Jeremiah, she no longer saw an empty seat. She reflected on her mama's last special journal entry from their voyage on The Rosewood and the final Bible verse that her daddy left her with. In her mind now, her daddy had been the driver and they had all been his first special passengers with all their unexpected stops and starts along the way. And unbeknownst to them they had helped each other find their wings and which flight to take. All that he loved and those they would come to love had finally all arrived safely at their destination and he had moved on to his next assignment in heaven.

Jeremiah would never be held or touched by the woman he had been so devoted to for almost fifty years, yet none of that mattered to him today. He had missed out on nothing. As he stood by her side Jeremiah was full to the brim with honor, joy and boundless pride. Annie had chosen him to give her hand in marriage over to Dr. Francis O'Neal.

Her dress had been made by the other kind protector of her Grandma Lizzie and it was as breath taking as the young woman that had grown into it. She knew she had the right man escorting her down the aisle just like she knew she had the right man waiting for her at the end. It had taken her all her life up until now to arrive at this point and she was absolutely sure she would do it all over again if she had to.

It was 6:00 o'clock on August 7, 1869 in front of a packed crowd at the First Presbyterian Church. And the minister was nothing like old Pastor Feil. For his words were not of hellfire and brimstone, but were full of love.

"It is a choice....so choose well.....let all you do be done in love. May I introduce to you, for the first time, Dr. and Mrs. Francis O'Neal. Let us pray that from this day forward their courageous wings of flight will forever be together as husband and wife."

THE END

Passengers

by ELIZABETH COLLUMS

About the Author

- About the Author
- In her own words

Interviews

- The Writer's Life
- Questions with Katelynn

Reading Groups

- Author's top five
- Reading Group Questions

About the Author

Ann C. Purvis chose to publish her first novel under her birth name, Elizabeth Collums; this is her true roots and where she has drawn from many of the experiences she wrote about. She retired from the USPS and lives in Denham Springs, Louisiana. She enjoys decorating and DIY projects. She has two daughters, a step daughter, son-in-law, two amazing granddaughters, and her dog Daisy.

In her Own Words

AS FEATURED ON THE BOOK CONNECTION, STOREY-BOOK, AND MYTHICAL BOOKS

What I wanted to be when I grew up was never addressed in my house. My Dad was gone a lot as a truck driver trying to scratch out a living for us so my mom was my only companion. I called myself an unaccompanied minor long before that phrase was popular. Because, you see, physically she was in the house, but mentally she was in her own world. Maybe she still had an emotional hangover from The Great Depression that she often dwelled on or it could have been the dark cloud of the Vietnam War that overshadowed any thought of dreams or celebrations in our home. My mom worried for years that my brother would be drafted and then she stayed in a deep depression when he was and then she didn't want to let him go when he came home alive and well. She was so consumed with bitterness of the past and worry of the future she didn't make room for living her life much less mine.

So, I made every feeble attempt behind my closed bedroom door to reach for my own stars with my dog, Pete, and every stuffed or plastic creature I owned. Public speaking? No problem. I had spent countless hours practicing my very own interview with Johnny Carson in front of my dresser mirror. Sewing? No problem. I taught myself how to sew by making clothes for my dolls. Writing? Again no problem. Whatever the teachers assigned, I did double what they asked for. My room was my sanctuary. However, nothing my parents did or didn't do could keep me from putting my best foot forward to get out and on my way.

I think so often how sad for my mom that she spent most of her life looking down and missed out on the journey. That's what life is. One event after another. I've had more than my share of making stupid decisions, as well as experiencing personal triumphs. I've been married, had children, grandchildren, widowed and emptied nested. I've worked at jobs ranging from cleaning houses to postal work. And it's been the most colorful, aggravating, heartbreaking, joyous, challenging, earth shaking, blessed life I could've ever imagined. And I have never been alone. God always sent the right person at the right time, as long as I was looking up.

My bucket list is long. Publish my book, travel to Ireland, United Kingdom, see penguins and pandas up close and personal, learn how to ride a horse, master a pottery wheel.....and the list goes on and on. I don't ever want to forget to dream, learn, explore and yes, I still play make believe. Every time I look in the mirror, I still see that little girl from the reflection of this sixty-one year old, young woman.

Interviews

The Writer's Life

FEATURED ON THEWRITERSLIFE.BLOGSPOT.COM

Q: Welcome to The Writer's Life! Now that your book has been published, we'd love to find out more about the process. Can we begin by having you take us at the beginning? When did you come up with the idea to write your book?

A: It was in my late twenties. I was given some ancestry info that showed that my great, great Grandpa William Ewing was born in 1820 in Londonderry, Ireland and immigrated to America during the potato famine. I clearly remember going to the library and checking out books about Ireland, particularly this time period. Reading those books started the process in my mind.

Q: How hard was it to write a book like this and do you have any tips that you could pass on which would make the journey easier for other writers?

A: This one wasn't hard for me. As a matter of fact, it was very therapeutic. Through this writing process I was able to create the kind of courage and integrity in some of my characters that I had longed for in my life. Writing Passengers simply flowed out once I started.

I'd thought so much about it over the years that I was just ready. My advice is that it has to be something that you're passionate about.

Q: Is there anything that surprised you about getting your first book published?

A: I didn't expect to be as excited about publishing Passengers as I was. I am also surprised at how fulfilling this process has been from start to finish. And the finish part is having someone tell me how much it touched them on a personal level in a positive way.

Q: What other books are you working on and when will they be published?

A: I have a few other books in my mind. I'm trying to decide which one to go with next.

Q: What's one fact about your book that would surprise people?

A: That I actually had that much to say. I'm typically very reserved and a bit of a loner. My comfort zone usually encompasses small intimate gatherings.

Q: Finally, what message are you trying to get across with your book?

A: Those awful moments in your life don't' have to be the end of the story; the second half is in what you do with them.

Q: Thank you again for this interview! Do you have any final words?

A: Sometimes you have to be the root, be buried in the ground and let others be the fruit. Give what you didn't get and nourish others. In one way or another you always get it back. My comeback was the joy in writing this book and sharing it with my family and friends.

With Katelynn

When did you know you wanted to be a writer?

It was in my late twenties when I knew I wanted to be a writer but really had no idea how to get started and the life I needed to take care of really didn't leave time for my dream.

What made you decide to write historical fiction, particularly about this event/time period?

I've always been drawn to documentaries and didn't begin to realize how important history was until a relative gave me some ancestry info about my mother's side of the family. This is when I discovered they immigrated from Ireland during the potato famine.

Are any of the characters in your novel inspired by people from your own life or from history?

I entwinned many of the weaknesses and strengths in the characters that I witnessed from three generations in my family.

Are you a plotter, or do you just write as it comes to you?

With this being my first novel, I had ideas and writings that I kept. Matter of fact the first paragraph of the book had been stashed away in my nightstand for years. Once I started with that as my opening, the rest just flowed like the dam had finally broke open.

Describe your typical writing routine.

I write at the dining room table with classical music playing and my sweet dog, Daisy, in my lap.

I love to read with a cup of coffee or tea - or a glass of wine. What's your favorite beverage?

Coffee! Caffeinated during the day, decaffeinated at night.

Reading Groups

Author's Top Five

AUTHOR'S TOP FIVE FAVORITE BOOKS TO READ

Orphan Train
by Christina Kline

The Memory Keeper's Daughter
by Kim Edwards

Before We Were Yours
by Lisa Wingate

Where the Crawdad's Sing
by Delia Owens

And her favorite daily devotional:
Streams in the Desert
by L.B. Cowman

Reading Group Questions and Discussion

1. In the opening of the book we learn that Annie believes there are only two ways to live with our memories? Which way would you say you live? Do different memories cause you to feel like you live both? If so, why?

2. Soon we learn that Annie's father fostered Katy's, her mother's, self-imposed isolation from the village. Annie knew he was protecting her from something; however, she was still annoyed by it. Why do you think Annie didn't feel the same protection over her own mother?

3. Annie adores her father and places him on a pedestal. How does that affect the relationship she has with her mother? Do you feel Johnathan deserved it? How do we place people on a pedestal in our own lives? How does that affect other people around us?

4. Annie uses this quote by her father's throughout her life: "Always try to give what you know you need and it will somehow come back to you." Do you think Annie gave what she needed and did it return to her? Did it for Katy? What about for Annie's father? In life, do you feel you give out what you need? Do you also feel it returns to you?

5. Early on we learn that Annie has a strong dislike for her mother. She often describes her as

depressed and unengaged. We also learn that Annie takes care of her younger sister most of the time. When the book starts to unfold Katy's past, do you feel she has reasons for her behavior? Do you think Annie has a right to be upset? What in our lives causes us to neglect others? Do you have people upset with you for not engaging more in a relationship? If so, do you feel they are right to be upset? Or do you think your reasons are enough to warrant your actions?

6. Annie talks about her mother's feelings of entitlement. Once we learn more about Katy's past, do you think somehow deep down, Katy knew? Or do you think Katy was simply a dreamer who became disengaged when she never got what she longed for?

7. Katy felt at one point that because she lost her beauty, she'd never be able to marry Samuel and live on the estate. Why do you think Katy placed such a value on her looks? When she settled for and married Johnathan, how do you think that changed her life? When you settle, how does that affect you?

8. After Annie realized her mother had abandoned them. Why do you think she was so desperate, if her mother had never really taken care of Lily and her?

9. It was apparent that Annie recognized the difference between money and happiness. She said she never really saw any sign of abundant life on the estate like she had on the farm with her daddy. Why do you think Annie always correlated her happiness with her father? How will that affect her later in the

book? What would she have to overcome? Have you ever had to overcome a similar situation?

10. When the hurt Katy feels from being abandoned by all of the men in her life surfaces, do you feel sorry for her? Does it bother you that Katy couldn't see how she also had abandoned the ones she loves? Do you feel any of the men that abandoned her, did so for noble reasons? Has there ever been a situation where you've felt abandoned and later found that you too, had done the same to someone else?

11. When Miracle came along, Annie had already experienced some new moments with her mother, such as giggling and playing. How do you think watching her mother do something that worthwhile for them as a family changed Annie?

12. When Katy fully learns of her past, how do you think Mrs. Toudle's words at the end of the chapter on page 71 helped her throughout the book? How would those same words help you?

13. On page 96, discuss when Katy realizes her truth about the way she treated Johnathan. Again on page 114, when Katy sees another truth about Johnathan and herself. Ponder about something in your life that may reflect the way you've treated others who loved you.

14. Katy changes and starts to understands that we all have stuff to overcome and that hanging onto to what could have been, kept her from being the person

she should have been. Is there something you are holding onto that is stopping you from being who you should be? How hard is it to let go? And why?

15. Matthew's house was created with young Matthew in mind. Discuss your thoughts at how the underprivileged are treated, even today. How can we change our own lives to pay closer attention to those who might slip through the cracks based on their social standing?

16. When Katy became determined to find Johnathan and regretted how she had treated him throughout their marriage, did you feel she was truly repentant? Why now? What caused her transition?

17. Annie spends so much time trying to find her father, and a lot of her future happiness is based on it. Express how you felt when she did find him. How was it different than you expected? Discuss how our expectations of others, or in life, can derail us from living at our fullest.

18. What is the groups thoughts about Captain Julius? Did it seem inappropriate for him to be with the Ewing women? Or was it good that he felt the need to protect them? What of his feelings for Katy?

19. On page 171, Annie talks about her feelings of destiny. Do you believe in Divine intervention and destiny? If so, why? If not, why? Give examples to the group and discuss.

20. When Katy apologizes to Johnathan, do you feel she received closure for all of her years of disinterest? How do you feel, knowing the man Johnathan was, that he felt about her apology?

21. Discuss Lily's situation on being discovered and how often people, especially women, fall into this trap. Have you ever felt you were trapped by circumstances? How did you find your way out?

22. Nicholas finally found a home. How did Nicholas help the family as well? What would've happened had he not been there on several occasions? How did his 'street smarts' help him?

23. Discuss the apple. How many times have we all been the giver? The taker?

24. Ironically, the circumstances of Mr. O'Connor's release was due to Annie. Do you feel just because bad things happen, it means we sometimes shouldn't help others?

25. Discuss Samuel. With all the wealth he had, how was it that he ended up where he did? Why do you think he made the decisions he did? Katy longed for his life for many years; do you think it was a blessing in disguise that she didn't get her wish? Is there a circumstance in your life that is similar?

26. How did each one of the Ewing women fulfill their purpose? How were their lives enriched by others around them? Could they have fulfilled their purposes

without the others? Do you feel you have found your purpose yet?

27. Lastly, of all the ways each women thought their lives would go, and with all the derailments along the way, do you feel they each used their own experiences and talents to find their purpose? Or did their purpose find them? Are you searching for yours born of your own circumstances and talents? Or are you waiting for yours to find you?

ACKNOWLEDGEMENTS

It took some time, over thirty years to be exact, to bring this story to life. It wasn't that I felt the story wasn't ready to be told, it was more about me not being ready to tell it. I had too much yet to learn about where I came from and the passengers in my life. Still insecure that anyone would care to read this story or that it would even be worth reading...

Then along came, Alice Service and Teri Hedgepeth, my two first special readers and friends who encouraged me to continue when I finally had the courage to show my hand.

To Mallory, Amber, Madison, Denny, Michelle and Emerson who kept asking when? Thanks for waiting with me through the process and for all our special family nights.

To my friends at work (Walker Post Office) thanks for all your enthusiasm and support as I move into the next chapter in my life. Tracy, Christie, Andre, Nathan and everyone: what an incredible, blended and harmonious melting pot of personalities we are.

Alexis Jester, Deborah Dawn Hall, Dawn Sowaller and Mallory at Tell It All Editing were all part of the editing process that was so critical to me. Not once did any of them make me feel less than.

To Larry for your incredible art cover. All I can say is "you nailed it!"

And to my new friend and fellow author, Michelle Jester, your wisdom, smile and "you can do this" after a long day at work was the big push I needed to move this story from the bottom of my closet out into the wide open.

Also from Rope Swing Publishing

Inside her father's old weathered barn, Eve and her siblings find an old tarnished tool box that sits waiting for them as their father languishes in the hospital. To most, the items in the box would be considered insignificant junk, but to Eve they held priceless insight into not only the man her father was, but also the woman she was about to become.

From a very delicate relationship with her mom as a teenager, to being forced to live with her father in a town she never felt at home in, Eve learned to grow and live. When adversity hits through both tragedy and disappointment Eve soon finds the strength to push to survive.

With the help of the items in the toolbox, Eve is beset with uncovering the treasures it holds…ones that propel her on a journey of self-discovery and revelations.

Whether your decision was made by you, or made for you, it is within your control to make the right decisions for your children.

Vickie's parents divorced when she was only nine, wedging her in the middle of a dispute many kids face every day. It still remains one of the toughest times of her life. As she shares parts of herself and other people's experiences with you, she hopes you will be better prepared to make good choices for your children.

"Please Don't Divorce Me" is candidly written as a parent's guide from a child's perspective aiming at fostering a healthy transition and minimizing hurt for what is already a difficult time in a child's life.

Divorce is not pretty, but it doesn't have to be ugly either. Choose children, love, and happiness above all else!

Olivia Brooks has been able to keep her life in Sugar Mill, Louisiana held perfectly together, far away from the small town where she grew up. Even though her past still haunts her, she has found a perfect process of surviving, until a string of events brings Luke Plaisance to Sugar Mill and turns her organized life upside down.

While Olivia fights to hold on to the life she's created, unraveling it may be exactly what it takes for her to truly survive. She must accept her past in order to live, or let it threaten the only future she's ever wanted. Because some secrets can't stay buried… and shouldn't.

An inspiring and heartbreaking tale of abandonment, survival, and purpose. A harrowing journey of self-discovery and perseverance.

www.ingramcontent.com/pod-product-compliance
Lightning Source LLC
Chambersburg PA
CBHW051954240626
47153CB00005B/1757
9781954058071